THE 43RD MISTRESS

D1206148

THE 43RD MISTRESS

_____

a sensual odyssey

by Grant Antrews

© 2000 by Grant Antrews

All rights reserved. Except for brief passages quoted in newspaper, magazine, radio, television or Internet reviews, no part of this book may be reproduced in any form or by any means, electronic or mechanical, including photocopying or recording or by information storage or retrieval system, without permission in writing from the Publisher.

Woodcut by Kirsten Francis.

Published in the United States by Greenery Press, 1447 Park Avenue, Emeryville, CA 94608.

www.greenerypress.com

ISBN 1-890159-21-2

Printed in Canada

This book is dedicated to the memory of Mme. Dominique Aury, an accomplished French journalist and writer who passed away in the summer of 1998. Mme. Aury is believed to have been the author of "The Story of O" under the pseudonym Pauline Réage. Her daring thoughts and words had an immense impact, especially upon that most sensitive bit of the human anatomy, our minds. Ms. Aury was always a very private person, and the author hopes she has found peace.

"Who am I really," said Pauline Réage, "if not the long silent part of someone, the secret and nocturnal part which has never betrayed itself in public by any thought, word, or deed, but communicates through subterranean depths of the imaginary with dreams as old as the world itself?" – Pauline Réage, "A Girl in Love," published in RETURN TO THE CHATEAU (New York, Grove Press, 1971)

I find it absolutely fascinating to be in control in situations where lack of conrol might be considered normal, or the easy route. That's what makes it interesting. – Pauline Réage, CONFESSIONS OF O: Conversations with Pauline Réage, by Régine Deforges, Viking/Penguin, 1979

introduction

This is a work of fiction. Any resemblance between the characters in this book and actual characters, either living or dead, is unintentional and coincidental.

That said, I must admit that my inspirations in writing this collection were quite real. I am a masochist, at least in my sexual orientation. I find sexual pleasure in pain and shame. To the best of my memory, I have done fifty-six sessions with forty-two professional dominatrices. Some of those were beautiful events; strenuous, worthwhile, character-building, even spiritual.

The Forty-Third Mistress is heavily influenced by those experiences. *The Forty-Third Mistress* is about S&M, which is also known as sadomasochism, SM, bondage and discipline (B&D), dominance and submission (D&S), or an amalgamation of them all (BDSM). S&M is sexual expression for the Type A personality. Competitive, accomplishment-driven, and measurable, S&M gives the chronic overachiever a quantifiable experience within which he can set goals and measure his own performance. If a man endures twenty-four strokes of the whip today, chances are he'll test himself against thirty or thirty-six strokes next time. What is often overlooked is the fact that an S&M scene is a form of drama, as preposterous as the concept of pleasure from pain. The disquieting truth is that pain *can* ignite pleasure. However, I've never met a masochist who becomes sexually aroused when he hits his thumb with a hammer or slams his finger in the door. The play that links pain to sexual pleasure is fetishistic and theatrical, and incredibly personal. The dominatrix advertises her stock in trade as "role play" or "psychodrama." To the observer, it can seem very bizarre.

S&M is a curious culture, thriving in the world's busiest and "most civilized" countries. Erotic dominance and submission is readily available in America, in Canada and England, Holland, Japan, Scandinavia, Germany, and France, with the emphasis on the submissive *male* humbly kneeling at the feet of his dominatrix, who is most apt to be within range of a local call in most communities, certainly most cities, in America.

In recent years, that odd word "dominatrix" has found wide acceptance in the English language. We read that Gaultier or Versace have designed haute couture dresses with "the dominatrix look," or we see a Vanity Fair photo of Mary Tyler Moore in dominatrix leathers astride a docile Dick Van Dyke, her upraised hand brandishing a riding crop! We find the word used to describe a Madonna video, novels by Anne Rice, Erica Jong, President Reagan's daughter Patti Davis, Stephen King, or Mary Gaitskill. Rosie O'Donnell played a dominatrix in the spoofy film version of Anne Rice's *Exit to Eden*, and Dan Ackroyd the submissive lead role. The *L.A. Law* staff has defended a dominatrix; Susan Sarandon got kinky in the all-American baseball film "Bull Durham," and even kitchen queen Martha Stewart has been described as a "domestic dominatrix" in The New York Times.

Nancy Friday, the wonderful chronicler of modern sexual trends, titled her 1991 update *Women On Top: How Real Life Has Changed Women's Sexual Fantasies*. Real life? Well, yes, for some of us! "Hot Air," the complimentary in-flight magazine found in the seatback pocket on Virgin Airlines flights in early 1995 featured a colorful cover story titled "S&M, Consenting Adults Only." The premise of the article was that S&M has become *almost* mainstream. The August/September 1998 issue of "Bride's" magazine reports that it surveyed 3,000 engaged women about their sexual intentions after marriage, and nearly 53% said they planned to engage in spanking! 50% plan to try bondage! The staid New York Times has recognized the success of "WHAP!" magazine, which is an acronym for Women Who Administer Punishment. In a very cheeky, fun-filled manner, this mag's editors give instruction and encouragement to women who want to spank, tie up, diaper, or cross-dress their husbands. Today the neighborhood lingerie shop offers restraints and riding crops! Have you noticed? Something akin to an earthquake has impacted our society's concept of sexual roles.

What seems significant about this phenomenon is that it's not only the ladies who are the masochists or submissives any more. In a strange twist of reality, it seems *The Story Of O* has become the *Story of Oliver*, with women testing the boundaries of their dominant erotic power and successful, powerful men eagerly yielding themselves to the dominatrix and her curriculum of the most humiliating, painful, and yes, ridiculous ordeals.

The dominatrix exists because she must. In the realm of supply and demand, the dominatrix trade is thriving. The truth is, most men are ashamed of their interest in S&M, and afraid to broach the subject to their wives or lovers. Masculinity has been imbued with a rigid set of prescribed behaviors, and to deviate from that regime is to imply that one is "less than a man." The result is, of course, the professional dominatrix. How many practicing dominatrices are there? I don't know. I became a close friend and confidant of one lady in Manhattan, and I know that her machines averaged fifty to sixty calls per day from men seeking appointments. I estimate that there are 100 professional dominatrices on Manhattan island alone! A recent issue (#30) of DDI, or Domination Directory International magazine, lists approximately 180 dominatrices who have purchased expensive advertisements, many of them full-page and/or four-color. DDI is the most prestigious catalog of its type, and the publisher has seen fit to offer a second, European edition to offer ads from European dominatrices who are eager to attract Americans traveling to the continent for business or pleasure.

S&M is theatre of the absurd on a bold and personal level, and it satisfies. In the latter years of the twentieth century women have ascended to more and greater positions of authority in our society, and seized more and more power. Today's women expect greater opportunities, respect, and accomplishment. Some even seek adventure! And as they redefine their femininity, they have also reallotted their expectations regarding masculinity. Today's woman doesn't suffer fools. No dominatrix, be she professional or a daring suburban housewife wielding a riding crop, ministers to a loser! A modern, '90s woman can order a successful, professional gentleman to go over her knees for a spanking, or to wear her panties under his business suit! She feels free to experience a powerful, exciting sense of accomplishment when he complies. His willingness is an acknowledgment of her, a gift that is far more meaningful than a vase of flowers or a lace nightie. Naked, powerless, today's macho man presents his bottom to the paddle, the leather strap, the whip. He dares to shed tears, to weep and beg his lady for mercy. He dares to feel, to be vulnerable, and to adore his woman. The submissive male S&M enthusiast is very often highly educated, successful in business, and an overachiever. Affluent, intelligent, perhaps slightly jaded, the S&M couple peels away the various trappings and masquerades of modern civilization to arrive at some-thing primitive but honest, which is wonderfully escapist! People do S&M because it feels good, because it is worthwhile, incredibly intimate, and fulfilling.

"Civilization" in the second half of the twentieth century has created an insulated, frightening existence serving a complex variety of hi-tech monsters with voracious appetites and inhuman tastes. Our computers, cellular phones, carpools and cam-corders, voice mail and E-mail, bank card machines and cable

TV shopping networks, Nautilus and ab-trimmer exercise machines have not set us free. Stress and tension are a modern epidemic, and yet to say this, to recognize the folly in our modern corporate or social communities is to invite disaster. Honesty is obsolete, replaced by "word management," icons, purposeful distortion, and ultimately, blatant corporate and governmental corruption. What can you believe? There is no deception when the whip or cane slices your bare behind.

Still, for many outsiders the great mystery remains. Why do powerful, successful gentlemen invite pain, or find their sexual stimulation in bizarre costumes and rituals? What's the point? And what does this phenomenon indicate about changing values and roles in our society? Very little information on the topic is available, especially from the submissive male's point of view. The classic work is *Venus In Furs*, by Chevalier Leopold von Sacher-Masoch, a valid and delightful novel published in 1870, prior to the invention of the automobile, the airplane, or the electric light bulb.

As stated above, my fascination with this subject has extended to numerous actual sessions with dominatrices, and my obsessions have led me to study the subject in considerable detail. S&M dredges up all the very best in me, all that matters, everything that I consider essentially masculine and strong and courageous.

I don't know why I think the thoughts I do. I don't know why I've had the experiences, why Dame Fortune has put such peculiar obstacles and opportunities in my way. My sexual obsessions have brought me much pleasure and adventure, but also heartache, paranoia, and suffering. If there is dichotomy in the pursuit of pleasure from pain, be forewarned that the practice of sadomasochism requires great duality. Yes, it is bizarre, the costumes of black leather or polished latex, the swaggering women laced into Victorian corsets proclaiming their emancipation, the successful, powerful businessmen slipping down their pink lace panties and going over the lady's lap for a sound spanking. I cannot explain it all, and I don't purport to speak for anyone but myself. To those who hear its calling, it is simply necessary.

I think of S&M play as a sport, and I perceive of it as a beneficial and respectable practice. In all my life's experiences, only the terror of combat rivals a whip stroke for intensity. I found war to be obscene and despicable, but it is widely accepted by all human cultures and civilizations as an art form, and worth the risks. Activities related to sex, of course, offend the established authorities. I'm not sure why, unless they resent anything that promises to allow the powerless to glimpse ecstasy. One need only look at a magazine, television, or movie screen to see that sex is universal in its appeal. Still, the hypocrites often cry out for censorship and proclaim their superior "decency" even as they drop explosives or flaming gasoline onto peasant villages. The careful, traditional, consensual suffering I have witnessed in many a professional dominatrix's studio bears no comparison to the atrocities I have seen on the battlefield, or on the evening news!

S&M is about pain and humiliation, but so much more. It is also about trust, communication, escapism, and self-esteem. Done properly, S&M hurts but does not injure. We applaud football players when they overcome pain to accomplish something worthwhile. We applaud marathon runners, boxers, mountain climbers, women who deliver babies via natural childbirth. We recognize the cerebral challenge inherent in those endeavors, the focus, determination, and long hours of training that go into a successful performance. We have all grown up with an all-American sense of adventure, whether from TV westerns or cop shows, the movies, or sports. Television has raised our expectations, the stories and programs that invade our homes are bold, colorful, and exciting. Sadly, especially in this "information age" of computers and faxes, our everyday existence in the job world is often pale by comparison. Adventures exist, but they require generous expenditures of time and money. Frustrated, some of us find intensity and excitement in sexual adventures, and S&M offers the most exquisitely heroic accomplishments, performed under the watchful and admiring eye of a sexy, beautiful member of the opposite sex, that can possibly be crammed into a lunch hour!

This book is more than a little autobiographical. I can trace my attraction to S&M back to the age of five! I first submitted my bare bottom to a lady for discipline in the autumn of 1963! Twenty-eight years later I admitted my obsessions to my wife, and disclosed my experiences with paid professional women, dominatrices. Our marriage barely survived, but I am very pleased to say that today our relationship is the best it has ever been. My wife loves me very much, but she doesn't fully understand me or my obsessions. She has accepted that I am interested in S&M, but she isn't an enthusiast herself. She rarely finds it within her to inflict real pain upon me, no matter how much I beg her to do so. Ahh, but when she does I can honestly say that there is nothing more wonderful or exquisitely rewarding than being disciplined by one's wife and lover.

Properly stimulated, I can find pleasure in pain. I have gone to great extremes in pursuit of that pleasure, but I have never been so satisfied as when I have been disciplined by my wife. She's not the most glamorous or the most skilled, but my wife is the most exciting dominatrix I've ever known. Her efforts to express her love in this way, which is so very unnatural for her, must be acknowledged as the most loving and profound experiences of my life. It is so wonderful to share my excitement with my life's companion, and to truly serve her, and offer her the intimate, profound gifts so key to the submissive's role! Now, I am allowed to fall to my knees and worship her, to kiss her toes or other exciting areas of her anatomy, and to tell her what I am feeling! I no longer have to hide phone numbers or squirrel away money, except for gifts to lavish upon my beautiful Mistress, my lover. I have undergone great hardship and pain to achieve this intimacy, and I regret that I also caused my dear wife considerable pain. But, that is my only regret. I do not regret that I am a sexual submissive, a masochist, a pantywaist cross-dresser, or a whipping boy. I know in my heart that many men play those roles for entertainment and escape. I am a very good submissive. I am proud of my skills, my training. I am especially proud that I have found (at least partial) acceptance and understanding from the woman I love. I have nearly merged the two realities of who I am; I am nearly whole now. I am loved by my dominatrix, I sleep with her and share my most daring thoughts, and sometimes I lower my trousers and go across her lap to be spanked. I love her, and I am incredibly fortunate!

I'm just an average guy, probably not too unlike your next-door neighbor, your brother, or your husband. To be honest, I've had a few more successes than the average guy. I'm a husband, a daddy, a businessman, a member of the hometown community, and a friend to many people. The stories in *The 43rd Mistress* will only be valuable if they can be told honestly. Still, I cannot jeopardize myself, my family, or my friends. Events, names, times, locations, and physical descriptions have been disguised, hopefully without distorting the feelings or meanings of any incident. My purpose is to explain, to seek understanding and acceptance for the sport of S&M. If there has been a recurrent theme to all my books, it is that S&M can enhance everyday lives. I believe that! I hope this collection might give a husband the courage to broach the subject to his wife, or allow a wife to accept her own husband's kinks. Repressed sexual urges are more painful and destructive than *anything* I have described in these pages. Believe me, I know from experience!

Part One

1

When capitalism is introduced, it becomes obvious that male workers are frequently placed in a position more comparable to masochism than sadism. – Lynn S.Chancer, SADOMASOCHISM IN EVERYDAY LIFE, Rutgers University Press, 1992

I am very busy, very stressed. E-mails and voice mails, faxes, monthly and quarterly reports. My staff are far afield, generating expenses far in excess of their sales. Memos and position papers, legal reviews, bold marketing strategies, itineraries for upcoming trips, and the ubiquitous mountain of month-end computer reports clutter my office. I keep a small clear space at the center of my desk, but the accumulated chaos has overwhelmed the credenza, the round meeting table, and five of the seven chairs. There's a picture of my family on the wall, and a faded poster of the Golden Pavilion in Kyoto. And, the charts. Sales are on the incline but gross profits are lagging. My phone rings constantly. John Tesh and Yanni scant melodies discourage aggression via Muzak while scientifically encouraging urgency. I was a Rolling Stones fan! Has it come to this?

It is a Wednesday, late morning. Mid-month, and it's really going to take a push to make our monthly sales objective. The boss calls. He is an Executive Vice President; I am only a VP. He has noticed that the Frederick account is stagnant. What am I doing about it? I begin to explain that Jacobson was just there Monday. They have been moving into a new facility, and a larger warehouse promises improving sales. This is just a transition period. The green letters abruptly disappear from my computer screen. A voice outside loudly reports "System's down!"

Wilkinson sticks his curly head in my door. "Lunch?"

"Can't today," I say. "Sorry. I'll have to get a sandwich from the deli in the lobby."

"You can't live on that crap." He makes a comical face.

"Duty calls. Tomorrow?"

Wilkinson nods and disappears. The phone jangles again. The Elliott account is a hundred and twenty days in arrears. I'll call them. They should go on C.O.D. That would only drive them to buy from Rogers. We need to see some money before Friday. I'll call them. Can Schmidt go by there today and pick up a check? Schmidt is in Niagara Falls working on the Pro-Gro account. Yes, I'll let you know what they tell me. Yes, certainly put them on C.O.D.

The phone jangles again, fraying my nerves. It is Jacobson, another Executive Vice President. It has become necessary to reschedule two deadlines. Sales are disappointing. I try to be positive and optimistic. Each month is a lifetime, and to make one thirty-day sales objective buys only the opportunity to try again for another thirty days. Family, mortgage, financial obligations mean nothing. One must "crack the nut." There is no other reality.

Smitty, my secretary, brings me the mail. She's looking very cute today in a mint green knit dress that hugs her slender frame. She is a pixie, ruddy freckles splayed across her nose and cheeks, dark bangs, a youthful body. Smitty overflows with cheer, and she is the most efficient secretary in the building. She's not a drop-dead beauty, and she doesn't flaunt her sexuality. As soon as she learns to do that she'll be taken upstairs and promoted to someone's executive secretary. I can see the bumps from her nipples under her bib, and my groin stirs. Smitty is an exciting woman. She exits quickly because her phone is burbling. Mike Malone is calling from L.A. and his voice is trembling with excitement. "Hey, Boss, great news! I had breakfast with Komoko-san this morning. They're players. I need you to fly out here and make your Vice Presidential commitment to deliveries within three days of order, and they'll sign the contract. Can you get out here next week?"

I fumble through my Frankie. Little League game Monday. Dinner with the Campbells Friday. Something exciting kindles in my stomach and brain simultaneously. Spontaneously! I am quiet for a moment, searching the recesses of my mind for any vague commitments I may have neglected to write down. "How about Wednesday afternoon?" I offer.

"Sure. What time? They're ready."

"Suppose I fly out Tuesday afternoon. I'll meet you for breakfast Wednesday morning, we'll go over all the details and meet them about one. Their office is in Torrance, isn't it?"

"Yeah. You want to stay by the airport? I'll pick you up."

"No, I'll rent a car and stay at the Marriott in Redondo. Maybe I can have dinner with friends Tuesday night, and visit that Malaysian company before I fly Thursday."

"I've got to be in court Thursday morning."

"That's right. No problem. They want to beat us up for a lower price. They think I have the authority to bottom-line the whole thing. That's something else we'll discuss Wednesday, and I won't hurt you. Frankly, I'm not inclined to go any lower with them."

Malone seems to swallow hard. "Seven-fifty," he says. "I think we can go to seven-fifty. I've spent days with those guys, Bob. We need to get an order just to pay for my time."

"Yeah, but it won't pay you to give the stuff away."

"We'll talk about it Wednesday."

"Yeah, I've got another call. I'll make all the arrangements and call you to confirm."

My mind takes a short vacation, shifts into that special secret space where it can be so free, so stimulated. My thoughts crackle with urgency and sensual anticipation.

I check my Palm Pilot, jot down a phone number and tuck the slip of paper into my pocket where it can hide amongst the quarters and nickels and dimes. I am prickling with excitement.

"Smitty, I need you for a few minutes."

She is standing in front of my desk before I can replace the receiver onto its plastic multi-button base. "Mike's got the Nippon deal ready to finalize. I want to fly to L.A. next Tuesday, to arrive about three or four in the afternoon. I'll need a room at the usual Marriott in Redondo, to check out Thursday morning. A car. See if you can get me a convertible." I wink.

"A Corvette?" Her eyes play with me.

"Yeah, I wish! I need to get home by six o'clock Thursday."

"Shouldn't be a problem. I'll get on it."

I try to be casual. "I think I'm going out to get a sandwich. I'll be back in a few minutes."

I'm bubbling inside. It's a little after nine o'clock on the west coast. Will I be able to reach her? I'm so anxious I have to pee.

Out the mirrored-glass revolving door and into the parking lot my clothes absorb the humidity and shrink-wrap themselves to my ribs. My car is an oven. I crack all the windows and turn the air conditioner on full. k.d. lang is singing something sultry. I rush to the convenience store on Maple Avenue, where no one from work ever goes. My secret place, a private little island I sometimes visit to escape the cruel corporate seas. A phone card worth twenty bucks, two hot dogs with onions and ketchup, a Coke and a York peppermint patty. I drive to the pay phone in the park. It is a shady, relaxing place, another of my secret sanctuaries, almost private. It's getting cooler in the car. I retrieve the little slip of notepaper from my pocket, spread it open atop the console, lower the window, punch the buttons on the phone. The 800 number, my card's pin number, her number. I raise the window, kill the CD player, and close my eyes. Second ring, third, I imagine her, the classy patrician looks, the elegant clothes. Fourth ring, she's not...

"Hello."

"Mistress Mary?"

"Who's calling?"

"Jeremiah from Philly, Mistress."

"Oh, hi!"

The complexion of her voice changes. "I haven't heard from you in a long time. Coming my way?"

"Yes, next Tuesday, Mistress. Can I make an appointment for Tuesday evening? Please say yes."

There is a long pause. "What time?"

"Whatever pleases you, Mistress. Six? Seven?"

"How long has it been since you've done a session, Jeremiah?"

"About five months, Mistress."

"Who did you see?"

"Mistress Amanda in Milwaukee, Mistress."

"She's supposed to be very good."

"Yes, Mistress. She has a medical facility. Lots of discipline, but she took my head into a whole new space. She put me up on an examining table, it was very embarrassing and exciting."

"Five months ago?"

"Yes, Mistress."

"What kind of session do you hope to experience next Tuesday?"

"Very formal discipline, Mistress. Flagellation, reprimands, humiliation. I'd like you to make me cry, Mistress. Allow me to get it out, you know what I mean."

Another pause. "Suppose you arrive at six. We'll do two hours in the schoolroom. Your curriculum will consist of the hardwood paddle, the tawse, the cane, and then I'll put you across my knee and fill in the pale spaces with the hairbrush. Two hours for the price of one, Jeremiah, because I enjoy working with you. When we finish you can take me to dinner. Consider it a field trip, naughty boy! I'll require you to perform in public. You like humiliation."

"Yes, Mistress." I feel a cold chill of fear, but there is no time to wallow in my self-serving emotions.

"You will arrive precisely at six, Jeremiah. Under your business clothes I'll expect to find a very lovely pair of panties chosen especially for this occasion. Briefs, something snow white and frilly, silk I think, or satin. If there's a ribbon or bow at the waistline I'll use my hand instead of the hairbrush when you're over my knee. If there's a red or pink rosebud, you know, a little flower made of material, I don't mean anything printed on the fabric, I'll excuse you from your appointment with the cane. I'll expect you to wear them all day, Jeremiah, and they'd best be immaculate."

"Yes, Mistress."

"And pettipants over your panties, Jeremiah. You'll be attentive to your behind all day, I'm sure. A lady is familiar with layers of slippery lingerie moving against each other under her bottom as she is seated. You'll find it an exquisite sensation, dearest, especially on the plane. How many hours is your flight?"

"Six hours, Mistress."

"Splendid. Think of me during those hours, Jeremiah. I'll be preparing for you. But be careful, my dear. You have a tendency to ooze when you think. If I find stains or wetness on your panties I shall be personally offended, Jeremiah, and I shall make my displeasure known. Am I clear?"

"Very clear, Mistress."

"Yes. I know you'll strive to please me."

"Yes, Mistress."

"Are you aware that I moved into a new studio?" I say I'm not, and she gives directions. It is actually only about two blocks from her old location, but she has more rooms and a far nicer decor. I ask her current rate, and it has not increased from before. She asks me to call from the airport when I arrive, just leave a message on her answering machine to confirm. I promise I will. "Till Tuesday, then. I'll enjoy seeing you again, Jeremiah. Goodbye."

I hear her phone impact its cradle, and then stillness. I sit for a few moments, unmoving, trying to absorb all I have heard. This is unbelievable, but so clever! I will have to get to a store, buy some things. Embarrassing things. Pettipants! Where the hell do you get pettipants? And, how will the sales girls view a man who purchases only white briefs and pettipants, after searching the racks feverishly looking for ribbons or rosebuds on the waistband? The Mistress is diabolical!

And, then on the plane... I feel the heat of a blush suffusing my cheeks and ears.

2

Indeed, we sadomasochists have found something that makes us feel wonderful, yet there are few with whom we can fully share our happiness. Had we taken up painting or sculpture or writing or athletics as a recreational activity, there would be no reason to hide it. – Charles Moser, Ph.D., M.D., and JJ Madeson, BOUND TO BE FREE: The SM Experience, Continuum Publishing Co., 1996

Assume that you are not "deviant." Be honest from the start with your intended love partner. Take it as a life principle always to communicate with those closest to you. Without this communicative bridge you are likely to remain locked in a separate world. – Gerald and Caroline Greene, S-M: THE LAST TABOO, Grove Press, 1973

Driving to work the next morning, I must focus my thoughts. I consider and prioritize the business aspects of my day and then eagerly begin to consider preparations for my appointment. The weekend is booked, there will be no time to visit a department store and search for rosebud panties and pettipants. I can stop at the mall on the way home tonight, but it would be risky to buy such things locally. If a neighbor or friend, or even a co-worker should stumble upon me as I am shopping for lingerie it could be a disaster. However, Barney Williams will be visiting Laurel today, and I need to do his performance review. I can meet him, get the review out of my hair, and then stop by Eastview Mall for lunch and a quick shopping expedition.

I stop at the automatic teller machine to draw out a few bucks. Silk panties ought to cost about twenty dollars, and pettipants a bit more because of the amount of material used. My thoughts dance for a moment. Pettipants were a fad one year when I was in college. All the girls wore them and showed them off, sleek shiny thigh coverings with an outrageous cuff of lace that crept out from under their skirts at any opportunity. The guys noticed! I used to adore

Lori Mattison's pettipants, snow white with emerald green ribbons woven into the lace at her knees. What a sexy, provocative woman Lori had been. Rich and aloof, overpowering, but so beautiful! I had never had guts enough to ask her out. What a shame. Now I was destined to wear pettipants myself, my bottom sentenced to be severely punished by an equally magnificent woman. I feel that odd electricity coursing through me, the faint buzz of anticipation that I always get when I'm waiting to see a dominatrix. Not sexual, really, but something fundamental and vital. I will soon have the opportunity to prove my manhood, my mettle. And I know Mistress Mary will not be lenient. I am going to suffer, and dearly. I have condemned myself. Four days from now. Under one hundred hours. No, in fact it is closer to 125 hours.

The office is in chaos. The computer has hiccuped during the night, our daily sales statistics aren't available. E-mails have been lost. Smitty calls all the field staff and informs them, then brings me a legal pad of estimates and comments. I have been locked in an office with The Boss, explaining that we may still be able to meet our monthly objectives. Are my performance reviews complete? Well, no, I have two to do, but I was hoping to do Barney's today. Good. There is no mention of repairs or upgrades to the computer system so that these crashes might happen less often. Some sacred cows are allowed to graze to their hearts' content.

I escape at 10:45, rushing down the parkway to meet Barney at the Sea Shanty at 11:30. I have rated him "very good" in nearly every category. The company discourages "excellent" ratings as they could create an unpleasant dilemma if a dismissal or other strong disciplinary action ever becomes necessary. My staff understands these limitations, and knows that I will become more aggressive when annual bonuses are determined. Barney has been an employee for seventeen years. We have king crab legs for lunch, and laugh often. He is playing golf with a client this afternoon, teeing off at 1:30. I will cover for him. We shake hands and he says he enjoys working for me.

The mall isn't crowded. A stunning young woman pushing a stroller veers out of Fashion Bug and marches briskly in front of me. She is tall and shapely, with a wonderful cascade of dark brunette curls and a pair of skin tight white shorts that seems to reveal every stitch and detail of her panties. Her white leather sandals have tall cork heels, and her bottom is prominently displayed. She rolls her hips in that exaggerated way some women do, and I watch the rippling of the crescent seam that marks the rear of her panty's crotch panel as I follow. She is wearing a tight pink halter top and her bra straps stick out everywhere, but it is the clearly defined feminine swell of her ass that excites me.

She steers the baby stroller into a shoe store and I go on toward Macy's. I like to shop at Macy's first because the salespeople all have personal business cards. A former Mistress required me to get a business card from the salesgirl whenever I bought panties to wear to a session, and to explain clearly to the clerk that I would be wearing the delicate garment, and why. Mistress would call the girl while I stood before her clad only in the panties, my wrists and ankles fastened to the whipping frame. If the sales clerk did not acknowledge my candor, I would be punished without mercy. If, however, that salesgirl was not on duty, Mistress would keep the card and contact her later, and save my penalty or reward for another occasion. I have developed a habit.

Macy's lingerie department is on the second floor in a broad alcove near women's swimsuits and Misses sportswear. The department is composed of large sections such as robes, nightgowns, bras, shapers, coordinated sets racked by makers such as Maidenform, Olga, Lily of France, Vanity Fair, Bali and Warner's. Behind these I see a broad area of panties, again segregated by name brands, that extends up onto wall displays. Slips and petticoats are to the far right end of this selection, and I guess that I might find pettipants there. I see two saleswomen. To my left, waiting on a buxom customer in the shapers section there is a harsh-appearing fiftyish matron with heavy plastic glasses and a starched white blouse. Her demeanor seems stern and methodical. I am reminded of a high school English teacher, and I doubt that the woman ever smiles. To the right, fixing the stock on a display of Wonderbra satin bras and matching underpants I see a rather plump mid-thirties housewife, an attractive, smiling woman crisply dressed in a pastel yellow suit. She is blonde and vivacious, cheery, and when the time comes I want her to be the one to wait on me.

I plunge into the rows, pass by the many coordinates until I arrive in the panties. Silk will be upscale, so I move toward the designer racks. Calvin Klein, Natori, Ralph Lauren, Yves St. Laurent. Lovely pieces, but I see no silk, and no rosebuds at the waist. Oscar de la Renta. Perla. I am growing frustrated, and I retreat back into the coordinates. I am nearer to the attractive sales clerk when I discover a small selection of classic ivory briefs and bras in heavyweight glossy satin, and the panties have little faux flowerbuds of matching material at the front of their waists! I touch one, feel the slippery smooth, luxurious texture of the fabric against my fingers, and I imagine it encasing my ass. Satin, I know, is often quite rough inside, but these delicious garments are doubled material and so they are as slick and luxurious to the wearer as to the lucky man she will rub them against. The gusset is inset with soft, absorbent white cotton, and it extends well up the backside so that it will expose an unmistakable crescent "panty line" across the wearer's lower posterior. These lovely garments are carefully constructed to provide exquisite sensations of luxury for a lady's sweet sensitive regions, and I feel a stirring in my groin as I contemplate wearing one. The top panty has no price tag, but I search and find a Medium, my size, and a price tag on one of those thin plastic strings dangling down inside the butter-soft depths of the interior. I slip my fingers inside, and it is not unlike slipping into a ready woman's sex. I grip the paper tab between my fingertips and gently withdraw my hand, but the outermost plastic hangered panty leaps off the rack and clatters noisily to the floor. Twenty-seven dollars! I see the price, stoop quickly to retrieve the escaped garment, and a distant womanly voice asks, "May I help you?"

I push the noisy plastic hanger into line with all its brothers... or sisters, considering where I am, but the rack is overfull and it catches precariously. To remove the Medium from the depths of this melee would be to invite an avalanche. I am hurrying, knowing one of the women is approaching. I try to recall my gameplan, the clever things I must say to gently but surely inform the clerk that I am shopping for myself, and secure her acceptance. I glance over my shoulder, and the perky housewife in yellow is stepping sideways between two racks just a few feet from me. She has a broad, pitying smile. She thinks I am a typical husband, completely out-of-place and baffled, a bumbling idiot desperately in need of her assistance. "May I help you?" She is artificially cheerful, and I suspect she is laughing at me. Do I dare?

"Thank you, but I'm really just looking."

She is at my shoulder now, and she is heavily perfumed. "A gift for someone?" she asks, but she whispers, and as she moves adjacent to me her substantial breast brushes my elbow. She is flirting, turning to bat her eyelashes at me. Her blouse is unbuttoned so that I can see a darkly tanned display of decolletage underscored with a hint of lace. I think she is a sensual person; she reaches toward the rack of ivory satin panties and I see a wedding band and a huge diamond. Her stockings are opaque black and she is up on a set of stiletto heels, and I find her curiously sexy.

"Not exactly," I reply, inhaling sharply.

"This is a lovely item," she says, arranging the plastic hangers and their steel hooks into some semblance of order. The outer one attempts to jump again but she is ready for it. "Do you know the size?"

"Medium." I wish I had said something like: "They're for me, of course I know the size." I am determined not to fall into the role of bashful husband. She searches with her right hand, holding the assemblage in place with her left.

"Ahh, here's a Medium." It won't release from the tangle. I put my hands close to hers, spread the intertwined hanger hooks, try to separate the interwoven hangers. They are incredibly tangled, but we work the prize free. Her scent is rich and floral, and it excites me. "It's beautiful," she says, smoothing the luxurious satin, displaying it upon her outstretched left hand.

"Yes. But a little pricey."

"On sale!" Her tone is triumphant, sweet beyond belief. Her eyes are heavily outlined in mascara, but they sparkle. "Everything in the department is twenty-five percent off today." She touches the little satin rosebud, tilts it toward me so that I can fully appreciate the craftsmanship.

"How can I resist?"

She smiles and nods. "And what size bra to match?"

Do I dare? It must happen now! "No bra, ma'am. I'll be visiting a dominatrix, and she has specified that I'm to wear a silk or satin brief with a rosebud at the waist." I pause, dammit, and almost lose momentum. I steal a quick glance at her, and she is positively beaming! Her eyebrows are upraised so drastically her forehead is creased, she is staring at me with huge, dark eyes, and her opulent lips offer a huge, delighted smile.

I see her tongue flick over her lips. "That's marvelous," she whispers breathlessly.

Somewhat softer, looking down at the beautiful ivory satin panty, I admit, "They're for me. To attract my attention all day under my business suit, before she... well, before she applies some other attentions to the same area." I can feel a heavy, hot blush rising up out of my collar and coloring my entire head. My cheeks are prickly.

She bubbles with delight, her eye twitches. I think... she winked at me! "That's terrific!" she exclaims. "I love it!" She looks around nervously, but no one is near to us. Nevertheless, she lowers her voice and I am grateful. "So, are you going to be spanked?" Her carefully shaped eyebrows arch high, her eyes twinkle.

"Honestly?"

She is heaving, bursting with excitement. "Please. It's important to me."

I glance about. We are quite alone. "I'll be whipped. Paddled and strapped. The riding crop. Perhaps the cane. It's going to be a hard session."

She blushes, turning her attention to the luxurious satin panty. "I... I've read stories. Wicked stuff. I have fantasies, but I've never met anyone... Do you want these?" She busies herself folding them. She's a little plump, but quite attractive. She speaks very softly. "Are you..., umm, when. And where?"

"Tuesday evening. Los Angeles."

"California. *That* figures."

"It's not uncommon here."

"Will there be anything else?" Her eyes are searching me now, and I'm afraid I'm making her uncomfortable.

"If I say pettipants, do you know what I mean?"

Her smile actually expands. "I love it! You're going to wear them with these?" She has her fingers on my left arm, and she gestures toward the racks of slips and camisoles. We begin to move that way.

"Mistress wants me to experience the sensation of them sliding against each other under my bottom."

We are working our way through the narrow aisles. This end of the department is utterly deserted. We arrive in the area where pettipants may be found, and she begins to search a round rack of half-slips. "You'll want ivory, to match your panties." It is just a statement of fact. She pauses, turns her eyes to me. Kind of apologetically, with a stifled giggle, she says, "I'm Brenda."

"Hi. I'm Jeremiah. Call me Jerry." It is the name I use when I'm seeing the Mistresses, and it seems very appropriate here.

She's blushing again, her eyes sweeping over this end of the store. Her nipples are very prominent. "Can I ask you a question, Jerry?" She is almost breathless. I nod. She hesitates, paws through the frilly lingerie again. She's looking away from me, and she speaks very quietly. "Are you in panties now?"

"Not now. Only on special occasions."

Her fingers touch my arm, her eyes imploring. I can detect the scent of her perfume, perhaps released by her rising heat. She is flushed, trembling. "It *is* a special occasion, Jeremiah. Mine're soaked." She turns the circular rack, paws the glistening delicacies. "Ahh, here they are. There are different lengths. I think the long ones would give you the most sensation." She withdraws a garment from the crowd, but it is snowy white. She stabs it back into the frothing chaos, tugs out an off-white creation with very opulent lace at the knees. Brenda has been stooping but now she straightens and offers the glamorous underwear for my inspection. "I feel very honored to know your size, Jeremiah." Her voice is low and quivering. I search for the price ticket; it is a beautiful garment. "What time Tuesday?"

"Excuse me?"

"Your appointment. What time Tuesday?"

"Six o'clock L.A. time. That's nine here."

She caresses the doubled satin brief as if it is a puppy. "I'm going to buy one of these, Jeremiah," she whispers, "and wear it Tuesday. I'm going to think about you a lot until then."

I take her hand and she shivers so violently I fear she might fall. "That's very sweet." It is a lame statement, but the lady is losing control. I grab the pettipants. "I'll take these."

"Oh, okay. Can you... explain, you know. Tell me how you... how she... what it's like. Not to pry..." She seems preoccupied, her imagination trying to put some form to an idea that excites her beyond belief. I am entranced just watching her struggle with the concept.

"She admits me to her home, accompanies me down the hall to her studio and accepts her tribute in a plain envelope. She asks me to undress, then stops me when I'm wearing just the panties she has ordered." Brenda's eyes are closed, and her breathing is ragged. No one is near. I move close and whisper into her ear, my arm around her waist. My fingers are spread across her lower belly. "She'll fasten me to the whipping cradle. It's a wonderful antique device, German I believe. Dark old hardwood and leather restraints. I'll be up on tiptoes, up against a bolster at the hips, and drawn far forward and down. She'll buckle my wrists and then caress me a bit, my bottom, maybe pinch my nipples a bit." She gasps, writhing, moaning. "She'll finally break away, arrange her instruments on a table where I can see them, lower the lights, perhaps ignite some incense and start some subtle New Age music. She'll take down my panties, Brenda. These panties." The woman is going to take this all the way. I put my palm upon her rounded buttock. Still no one around. I pat her. She is desperate. "She'll touch me, separate the buttocks, wash me with a hot cloth, then a cold one. Oil me. Finally, she'll take up the crop, put it to my lips so I can kiss it." Brenda is sweating, grinding against my hands. "I'll hear it cut through the air a scant moment before it strikes me, Brenda. It's an explosion, a burning, stinging shock no matter how you've prepared for it."

She growls, deep in her bosom. Her teeth are gritted, her lips drawn back in a mindless sneer. She begins her primitive ceremony, pulsing and jerking madly in this most incredible of locations. I pat her bottom, a bit harder this time. She climaxes, sighing and panting and uttering cramped guttural sounds, dancing insanely within her neat clothes, communing with her most secret fantasies. I hold her left hand in both of mine, accompanying her at a distance, standing watch while she travels to exotic lands. A final cataclysmic series of spasms grips her, wrings her. She shudders, begins to return to the present. Her eyes open slowly, and she blushes deep crimson. "Oh God."

"Are you all right?" I ask.

"Yes, but... I'm embarrassed."

"Don't be. You were beautiful. Do you fantasize about being spanked?"

She is tugging her clothing, regaining control. "No. I always see myself doing it to a man. Someone like you." Her eyes compliment me.

"Are you married, Brenda?"

"Yeah." There is a note of resignation in her voice.

"Does he know your fantasy?" She is beginning to search for my purchases.

"Geez, I'm soaking wet. I've shown him books, a couple of videos I've rented. It's available to him."

"You've got to make it happen, you know."

Miraculously, we are still very much alone. I put an arm around her shoulders, feel her pulsing contortions deep inside, her knees still threatening to buckle. "Spank your lover, Brenda!" I whisper into her ear with some urgency in my voice. "Punish him!" She sobs, shuddering massively. "Put him in a pair of your panties." I am goading her. She drops my beautiful ivory satin briefs. Her eyes are clamped shut. She mews, desperately holding it in, then shudders grandly and opens her eyes.

"I see why women spank you," she says. "You're a naughty, naughty man."

"I've got to get back to work."

"Oh, I'm so sorry. Jeremiah, I'm... ohh... Mmmmmm."

"I will be punished. Brenda, I want one of your business cards. My Mistress will probably call you. Tell her what just happened. Describe it to her."

"But she's in Los Angeles."

"Do you work Wednesday?" I have retrieved the beautiful underclothes I want to purchase and I begin moving slowly toward a distant cash register island. Brenda follows closely, wiping her eyes with a disheveled tissue.

"Yes, but I can't. You see what happens..."

"Do me a favor, Brenda?" I lean close, my breath hot at her ear. She smells great, her scents blending to sweet, sensual compounds. "Sunday. Take him by the ear lobe and tug him to a chair. Undo his belt and push down his trousers, then his underpants, and just put him across your lap. Smack him twice for me, Brenda. I don't think he'll fight you. For me."

"But I couldn't..." It is almost a hushed cough.

"The secret is, Brenda, you can. And the whole truth is, you must. This weekend, next weekend, it has to happen. Doesn't it?" Her eyes are huge, scared. "Take control, Brenda."

She is wrapping my purchases in tissue paper. She wants to say something, but cannot.

"Sunday, Brenda. Promise me you'll try."

"My stockings are soaked to the knees."

"Sunday, Brenda. Promise me."

"I'll try." Her eyes avoid me.

"Promise, Brenda."

"I promise I'll try." She punches buttons on the cash register. I am holding out a slip of bills. She glances at them, massages the buttons again. "Twenty-six eighty." Her eyes flutter to mine, and I think she winks again.

"Can't be."

"Employee discount, Jeremiah. I've been married seventeen years, and you're the only man besides my husband who's ever given me an orgasm. The transaction is in my best friend's name. Please. And thank you."

I hand her the money. She sorts it, pushes a few bills toward me on the slick formica counter, the drawer opens and she makes change. "Brenda, can I get your card? Two of them?"

She finds them on a lower shelf. Her eyes are wet and very expressive. "Tell your Mistress I may not be able to talk."

"She'll know."

I pick up my package. "Jeremiah..." I turn, she comes out from her cubicle. I hug her, feel her breasts and her hair. Her scent makes my groin squirm. I break away. She stretches up close to my ear, kisses me lightly on the cheek. "Good luck Tuesday," she whispers.

"Thanks."

"You're not putting me on?" Her fingers are at her bodice, loosening her clothes to let some cool air into her molten depths. She is really sexy, and I smile broadly.

"You know I'm not. Shall I come by next week and show you the marks?"

"Marks?" She savors the thought a moment, then her vivacious eyes challenge me. "You'd better get on to work."

I turn to leave. "Jeremiah..."

I turn back toward her, but only about halfway. "You be careful. I don't want you to be hurt." I glance around the store. An older woman is looking at bras about thirty feet away, but her back is to us.

I step toward Brenda, plunge to my knees as I have been taught. I kiss her toes. "Thank you Mistress." Then I'm up, and I gather my package and turn and walk away, and I don't look back. I have to get back to work. My underpants are also sopping.

The down escalator dumps me out in the hosiery department, where I pause to purchase three pairs of finest quality seamed black stockings as a gift for Mistress Mary. "Are you sure she wants the ones that fasten to garters?" the sales clerk inquires, wrinkling her nose emphatically. She is an unattractive woman, a drone. I take the stockings to gift wrap where each pair is individually encased in scarlet tissue before they are assembled into a thin goldfoil-wrapped box and tied with a maroon velvet bow. Very classy.

Out in the mall I see a pay phone and call Smitty. "Anything going on?"

"Not a thing."

"Anybody want me?"

"No. Where are you?"

"I'm at Eastview Mall."

"It's late enough. Go on home and try it again tomorrow."

"I shouldn't, but you've talked me into it."

I am swept up in a moment of inspiration. I hurry to the car, open the doors to let the heat escape, pop the trunk. My treasures have to be buried. I lift the plywood trunk floor and tuck them carefully around the spare tire, then smooth the trunk mat and close the lid. Air conditioning on high fan speed, I hurry down to the enormous new bookstore a few blocks from the mall.

The Erotica shelves are abundant with titles. I am searching for classics, *Different Loving* or *Sensuous Magic, or Screw the Roses, Send Me the Thorns.* No luck, but I find a P.N. Dedeaux novel to read on the plane. Then, finally, I discover what I've been seeking. A small hardcover by Claudia Varrin entitled *The Art of Sensual Female Dominance: A Guide for Women.* Perfect!

The checkout girl looks like a college student, and she takes her time inspecting the "guide for women." She arches her right eyebrow and looks at me with some amusement. "Will there be anything else?"

Back to the mall. Before I get out of the car I write a message inside the cover of the hardcover: "Brenda, Try!" I sign it "Jeremiah", open the trunk and hide the Dedeaux book near the spare tire, and I hurry back into the mall.

To giftwrapping, where another young woman waits on me. Another college student. "Did you buy this here?" "No." "I'll have to charge you extra." "Okay." "Interesting title." "It's a classic!"

As soon as she's finished I rush up the escalator to Macy's lingerie department. Brenda's with a gaggle of teenage girls, all giggles and braces and zits. The stern older woman is still at the left end of the department, checking out a pretty young housewife at the other cash register island. I go to her, wait patiently behind the young woman, admiring her tush. Her buttocks are wonderfully rounded and hugely separated. She has decorated them in a pair of faded, worn denim shorts that is adhered to every detail of her bottom. She is purchasing padded bras and matching panties. My loins stir again. Her hand comes back, her fingers delve between those magnificent buttocks and smooth her shorts in a discreet little sweeping motion, then she glances at me. "I'll only be a minute," she says, enormous sexy eyes behind rounded glasses. Her lips are red and sensuous.

"I'm fine."

She hurries away with her package.

"May I help you?" The woman is stern.

"Yes, I hope so. Would you give this to Brenda when she's free? I don't want to interrupt her." I hold out the gaily decorated book.

"Sure." She takes it, slides it down under the counter. Perhaps onto a shelf, perhaps into a trash can; I will never know. "Is there anything else?"

I realize that there is another woman behind me. I hurry away.

It takes about an hour to drive home from the mall. All the way I am rehearsing, preparing for my meeting with the Mistress. She'll take me into one of the rooms, probably the one with the wrought-iron and wood antique school desk and blackboard in the corner. "Tell me," she'll whisper, "what you're thinking. How can I make this special for you?" What will I say?

3

The masochism, then, of the late nineteenth-century male, and his manipulation of the image of woman as an all-destroying, rampaging animal was an expression of his attempt to come to terms with the implications of his own marginalization, his removal from the true seats of power in his society. – Bram Dijkstra, IDOLS OF PERVERSITY, Oxford University Press, 1986

Friday morning is rainy and oppressively humid. My wife's car has a nearly flat tire, and she needs it to take our son to the dentist at ten o'clock. I leave the car on a jack while I rush the tire to a service station. She has run over a nail, they plug the leak and I repair the car. My shirt is dirty, I change quickly and rush away but I arrive at the office more than half an hour late.

There is a message from the boss. "As soon as you get in, come to my office." He has noticed that I am late. The message is intentionally vague to cause me some concern. With a fresh mug of coffee I go directly there, but he is with someone. I wait, idly chatting with his secretary, watching the minutes tick away. The meeting breaks up; he waves me in.

"I looked for you yesterday about four, and again this morning. You aren't moonlighting are you?" He smiles, but it is a very pointed criticism. "The regional steering committee meeting has been moved up due to the Las Vegas trade show. Can you have your presentation in rough form Monday? I want to review it, then you can make any changes and have the finished product by Thursday."

I cannot show my distress. "Sir, I have an appointment in L.A. Wednesday with Mike Malone to meet with the powers at Far East. Komoko-san himself! And Thursday I'm going to see the Malaysian folks, we think we can get an order by month-end. I've got to fly out Tuesday, and I'm not sure what Smitty has arranged for flights. By the way, Delano's coming in this afternoon. His is my last performance review, so I'll have that folder on your desk Monday morning."

He has to be gruff. It's required by his job description. "Just don't shortchange me on this presentation. You may have to catch a late flight Tuesday, tell Smitty to see what's available."

"Sure, but I'd like to get together with you Monday afternoon for a first look at it. Then I can make most of the revisions Monday evening on my PC at home, and we can put it to bed Tuesday morning."

"Can Malone do the meeting with the Malaysians? It would be best if you catch a red-eye Wednesday night and be in here Thursday early in case we have to make any last minute changes to the presentation."

"Malone's got to be in court. I'll leave everything with Smitty. She can fix anything minor."

"Sometimes I think Smitty should be a Vice President. What can't that woman do?"

"She's terrific," I agree enthusiastically. "I'm going to promise the Malays that we'll ship to put goods on their doorstep within three days of order. Malone has cleared it with the freight line; they'll break down a truck and get Malaysia's stuff across town in under six hours guaranteed."

"In writing?"

"In writing."

"What will we make on this deal?"

"Two and a half points on the stock stuff, three and a half on the specials."

"You can't get them to four? We've got to invest in a blister-packing machine."

"That's why I'm trying to sit down with them. I think I can get four across the board. The delivery time is the deal-breaker."

He nods, one big motion of his graying, wrinkled head. "Go to work."

I rush downstairs. I have seven voice mail messages this morning, and three E-mails. "Smitty, what did we come up with for flight times to L.A.?"

She brings them to me. "Your wife called while you were upstairs. Danny has three cavities. Don't forget you're having dinner with your friends tonight. You'll have to pick up Cindy after school, Barb's going to have her hair done. And accounting wants to know what you worked out with the Elliott people. There's a seventeen thousand dollar order on the dock, but it's being held. JoAnne says you're putting them on C.O.D."

4

He talked of "cuts" with a liquorish accent, and gave the technical word "swish" with a twang in which the hissing sound of a falling birch became sharply audible. The boy was immensely proud of his floggings, and relished the subject of flagellation as few men relish rare wine. As for shame, he had never a second thought of it. A flogging was an affair of honour to him; if he came off without tears, although with loss of blood, he regarded the master with chivalrous pity, as a brave enemy worsted. – A.C. Swinburne, LOVE'S CROSS CURRENTS

It is Tuesday, late morning, and I am waiting to board my plane. The past few days have been extremely taxing and I am grateful for this period of relative inactivity. I have called in, a necessary but ridiculous ritual only eighteen minutes after I walked out the office door. I will call in from LAX before I get my luggage. It is amazing how obedient I am in everyday life, and no one notices. Do they recognize their own submissive tendencies? If they knew my secrets, might they envy me that I can take satisfaction and pleasure from the act of being obedient?

I dislike airports, but I enjoy flying. My suitcase has been checked, I have a light briefcase with my book and magazine and a package of mints. The most sensitive parts of my anatomy are acutely aware that they have been encased in layers of rich, luxurious feminine underclothing. Mistress is correct! Two separate, glossy undergarments play against each other in the most remarkable ways when one sits down, and the sensations are especially noteworthy to a male backside which is so unaccustomed.

In the terminal I have noticed a most elegant middle-aged woman, slender but sensual with long and shiny black hair and lips waxed fire-engine red. She seems aloof in some way I cannot define, but also vampish. It's the hair, and her eyes. She is Spanish or Latina, I think, wearing an open suede vest over a crisp, sheer white blouse and a conservative grey pleated skirt that swings freely, expanding outward whenever she swings her well-rounded hips.

She is clearly confident, carrying a polished black leather portfolio in one hand and clutching a cellular phone to her ear with the other. She is not animated in her conversation, and I cannot stare, but I am certain that she is berating a man. Her nostrils flare, her chest heaves with exaggerated deep gulps of air and she seems to stamp her foot at times. I am forty feet away, but I can appreciate her high-heeled black leather shoes, and the tawny dark sheen of her stockings.

We will board in a few minutes. I go to the mens room, into a stall. When in panties I have been trained to urinate in the feminine manner. "B & D" a former Mistress termed it; bare and descend. Trousers down, then the panties, and the feel of my naked bottom against the seat. I sit, eyes lowered, regarding my male organs and the rumpled feminine garments I am wearing at a lady's order. Having finished my business I take a long strip of paper and fold it into a pad and dry myself carefully. Stains upon my panties would be severely punished tonight, a sign of disrespect. I fix my clothing, delight in the slippery texture of the satin as it slips up over my ass. This awareness is exactly what Mistress intends; I am anticipating the impending ordeal, and preparing mentally. The toilet flushes automatically, triggered by my motion.

Returning to the gate area, I see that pre-boarding has begun. I go to the desk, present my frequent flier card and request an upgrade to first class. The young woman has dark red rouge on her cheeks, and thick makeup. She seems sad or tired. Would I mind a window? I prefer an aisle seat. The only thing available is a window. I take it, seat 3D, she modifies my ticket and upgrades the computer, then sends me to board.

The aisle seat is empty, and I am tempted. Behind me I hear a feminine voice say "3C," and so I slide back into my corner... and the beautiful woman with the long hair puts her portfolio beside me! I am acutely aware of my satin panties and the pettipants' lace at my knees. She searches the overhead storage compartment and takes out one of those miniaturized airplane pillows. Taking her seat is a flurry of activity, and I try not to notice. She places everything with deliberate precision, then steps in front of the seat and smooths her skirt under her bottom with both hands as she lowers herself majestically into the seat. Her movements seem exaggerated somehow, but very feminine and sexy. She has, I notice, what seems to be a very shapely bottom. I am enveloped in a cloud of scent, a thick leather smell from her suede vest contrasts with the aroma of perfume which I believe to be Elizabeth Taylor's "Passion." I smile and say "hello," and she nods. Her hair is draped over one eye in a Veronica Lake manner, and I am once again impressed by the lush coloring of her lipstick. She is, by any measure, an exciting woman.

The flight attendant brings my scotch and water. I settle back into the wide leather seat, adjust my seatbelt, kick off my loafers. The fragrance of the scotch overcomes her perfume, and the taste of it seems to give me permission to relax. I have, indeed, escaped the office for a few days. She has settled. "Going home?" I inquire, hoping to break the ice. The scent of scotch is heavy, and I think it provides a masculine boundary. I am quite satisfied for her to inhale the fragrance of my Glenlivet.

"At last." She sighs.

"Business trip?"

"Mmmm, yes, mostly." She sits very proudly, her delicate neck fully extended. I am aware of her breasts, the sheen of her stocking stretched tight over her knee. "And yourself?" She turns her head toward me, pushes back the cascade of shiny hair from her cheek. Her eyes are carefully outlined in black, mascara and eyeliner, and there is a hint of blue shadow on her lids. Her brows are crisply penciled, and her complexion is utterly flawless.

"Well, I have a number of sales presentations and business meetings, and tonight I have an appointment with a ladyfriend."

Her face becomes animated. "An appointment? That's an odd choice of words to describe an evening with a lady. Is she a doctor? A dentist?" The woman seems amused by her own query, but I suspect she is trying to establish dominance from the first.

Very carefully, I lean closer. "She's a dear friend, a very trusted confidante." I pause. The engines have started to whine as they are brought to life. The cabin lights dim for a moment, and the fan slows. My companion retreats slightly, buckles her seatbelt, pushes at her hair again. There is a small lurch as the flying machine becomes active. The engines are winding up now, growing louder. "She is my disciplinarian." My voice is little more than a whisper. The woman shows no sign of having heard me, but I am pleased with myself. I have admitted the great secret of all my life to this magnificent stranger, and successfully. I have told the truth. I am proud of my accomplishment. I settle myself into the wonderful seat, impervious to the pressures of my office for almost the next six hours. A deep, deep breath helps me to relax. I am very conscious of the exotic material on my loins.

We begin to taxi. My companion leans forward and turns her torso toward me, twisting to confront me with a stark outline of the bra cup that cradles her left breast. I can see the pattern of the fabric, the clear silhouette of lace and straps. "Have you ever been to Santa Monica?" Her eyes are lively and challenging. She hopes to enjoy the flight, and a conversation with me. She is exotic, vivacious and attractive. The flight attendant checks our seat belts, tray tables and seatbacks. I guess she didn't hear my confession. The plane is inching forward, turning laboriously. The engines wind up, and we begin to roll toward liftoff.

The wheels leap up from terra firma and are noisily, hydraulically folded away to reduce drag. We are pushed back into the sumptuous leather seats, the nose is up and thousands of horsepower are pushing us into the clouds. I am looking at the airline magazine, thinking of *that* "Hot Air" magazine I once found in the seatback of a Virgin Atlantic flight to England. The cover story was "S & M: Consenting Adults Only," accompanied by a photo of a pensive young beauty wearing a shiny black latex maid's outfit. The photos inside were incredible! Friends in London told me that the head of Virgin Atlantic is a personal friend of Tim Woodward, the publisher of "Skin Two" magazine. Was it really three years ago? I feel her fingers on my left wrist. She is leaning toward me, her wonderful eyes looking enormous.

"You *must* explain," she whispers; her voice, deep and breathy as Kathleen Turner's, is nearly drowned out by the hiss of the engines. Her lips make my groin stir. I think "must" is a very strong word. Few women know how to use it. This one does, and I instinctively yield.

We are accelerating out over the suburbs, circling toward the West. I only want to sink back against the deluxe seat and close my eyes. I must prepare, both mentally and physically. Dream a bit. Intense erotic dreams. Shed my corporate persona and revel in the truth nudity allows, perhaps romp in a broad field of yellow wildflowers with my male appendage flopping merrily against my thighs. No dinner engagements or Little League games, no lawn to mow or cars to wash. I want to laugh, to shout and cry, to breathe clean air and sing a few bars of "Hey Jude," not because it would be my accomplishment. No, that melody once defined our generation, and it hasn't been heard lately. I want to be alone with a woman, both of us nude, and worship her before she grows old and dyes her hair blue in preparation for bingo. I want to swim in a cold stream or lie on a beach and feel the sun begin to shrink the skin across my shoulders. I wriggle to feel the satin under my backside, and I glance at my watch. In about nine hours I will present that flesh for flagellation, and I will perform with polished restraint and dignity.

She touches me again, her fingertips on my left wrist forcing my tired eyes open. I roll my head listlessly onto its cheek. She is lovely, womanly and sexual. "Please." Her right eyebrow, the one nearest to me, is upraised provocatively. It is more order than request.

"Ma'am?"

"Your lady friend. The disciplinarian. You really should explain a comment like that."

A few moments ago I was a bold crusader, recklessly espousing truth. Now I am tired, seeking refuge. I need to be at my best tonight.

"I have a friend," she whispers delicately. "The woman has her own cosmetics business, she's worth millions. She has a yacht, and a husband. She also has a secret. She keeps an apartment in Las Vegas. A secretary. Men make appointments and she drives out there for a day or two, sometimes two or three times in a month. The men are executives, athletes, professional types. Powerful men, rich. Celebrities sometimes. They pay her to spank them. Can you imagine?" She has kept her voice low, respectfully.

I have to answer. "My friend is an interior designer."

"And a disciplinarian."

"Yes."

"There's a word for it. Carmen has told me..."

I lean close to her, inhale deeply as if her perfume is smoke from an illicit cigarette. The leather scent from the vest jerks my gonads awake. I whisper. "A dominatrix..."

"Yes!" She seems to erupt with joy, claps her hands together. She seems childlike, innocent. "Yes, a dominatrix. Do you..., ummm, will you...?" Her eyes are wide and sensual and I feel blood rushing toward my groin.

"Yes, ma'am." I whisper, eyes lowered, being boyish.

"Tell me about it. What it does for you. Will she spank you? Whip you? Will it hurt? Linda spanks men on their bare bottoms. Will you have to take down your trousers? I find that image amusing, but it arouses me."

"I'm sorry." I throw back the last vestiges of my scotch.

Her fingers touch my wrist again.

"No, I'm sorry. I'm sure it's quite personal."

We sit quietly for a long time, eyes closed, absorbed by our thoughts. Secret, individual thoughts despite our proximity, despite the possibility that our imaginations are on some taboo parallel set of tracks. The flight attendant hands out lunch menus and in-flight catalogs. I order another scotch and water, and a red wine for the lady.

Her fingertips are at my wrist again. "I'm sorry. Really." I watch her tongue moisten her lips, and gaze into dark brown eyes that smoulder with intensity and caring.

"Don't be. I said something intending to be bold and outrageous. You're sitting close; you couldn't help but hear. I'm the one who's sorry. I was out of line."

Her touch is insistent against my wrist. "Are you frightened?"

I look at her, and I melt. "Yes, to some extent."

"Can you avoid it?"

"I could, but I won't. It's when I feel most alive. I wait long, long months for these sessions."

She looks down at her lap. "I hope you will pardon me. As a woman, I am amused at the thought of it. I have an image... of you, with your trousers around your ankles and your underpants at your knees, and the lady summoning you to place yourself across her knee. The thought is humorous and also... I'm, well... quite, uhh, stimulated, Mister..." She seems to take a deep breath and looks away. She is blushing.

"Jeremiah. Please, call me Jerry."

She turns back toward me and extends her hand. Her dark eyes are playful and twinkling with amusement. "Maria Helena De Portago." I take her fingers in mine, and find them sweaty, but I lift them to my lips and kiss her knuckles. She is breathless, her hand to her chest. "It is, I think, somewhat selfish of me to enjoy your shame so much, Jerry. But all of this is just a fantasy for me. A flight of imagination. I cannot conceive of why you would do this. Is there not pain?"

"Yes, ma'am. Very much so." The flight attendant interrupts, bringing our drinks. When we are alone and our drinks are ready, we touch the rims of our plastic cups together. She is flustered, perhaps uncomfortable. She adjusts her skirt, tugs it daringly far up her legs. Her face is flushed. Her fingers play at the uppermost button of her blouse, daring it to release. I feel that she wants to ask something, but cannot bring herself to utter the question. Once again, I lean back to relax.

"Jerry!" Her lips are incredibly close; her breath assaults my inner ear. It was a tiny voice, but impatient. "Will she use a whip?"

"Yes."

"Will there be blood?"

"I doubt it. Bruises. Welts. Thin streaks of blue-black agony. Small concentrated kisses that make me scream. Broad swathes of scorching hurt. A mosaic. She will vary the sensations and stimulations to extract the very essence of my endurance."

"Why don't you have dinner with me instead?" Her eyes are enormous, penetrating me. I lift her fingers and kiss them again, and then I turn her hand over and kiss her palm. It is sweaty, salty. I am stunned. I hold my lips to her knuckles for a long, long time.

"I'm sorry."

"She must be a very special woman."

We both sit back and close our eyes. The Captain announces that we are over the Mississippi River.

5

A masochist has a parallel pride: no one can outdo him in the art
and extremity of subjection. No one submits better, sooner; no one
bends to deeper degradation with more finesse, style, and endur-
ance. Masochism is an art of holding oneself in oppositional
extremity. The masochist sees himself living – appears to live – in
extremis, at the very edge of danger, madness, death. A masochist's
pleasure is extremely painful and his pain, extremely pleasurable...
There is a pride in this cliff-hanging extremity, in maintaining these
impossible opposites without plunging over the edge. It is an
extreme pride, a pride of extremity, of going to extremes and
surviving. – Lyn Cowan, Ph.D., MASOCHISM, A
JUNGIAN VIEW, Spring Publications, 1982

"Sir..."

I jolt awake. I have been dozing. The flight attendant has brought lunch.
She touches Maria-Helena, who stirs lazily toward consciousness.

Lunch on an airplane cannot, despite the accessories provided in first-
class, be upgraded to anything more than a necessary act of fueling one's self.
Rubber chicken and limp lettuce, thick brown gravy served artificially
microwave hot over expressionless faux potato mash, and all of life's condiments
presented in those impenetrable little vinyl envelopes. We eat silently, Maria-
Helena and myself, probably equally unsure how to restart our conversation.
Wouldn't it be crude to resume discussions of my aberrant sexuality? But, does
not such a bold pronouncement offer a rare opportunity for the voyeuristic lady
to peep and peer into the shadows of male sexuality? She munches carrot cake
and stirs milk into her coffee as I stir sugar into mine.

And then, suddenly, she touches my left wrist again and says, "Where
were we, Jerry?"

"I don't know. Perhaps we should move on to other topics. What do you
do?"

She seems to recoil slightly. After a sip from her coffee, she whispers, "I'm divorced. I am a marketing and customer relations consultant to a number of west coast fashion houses, and I've begun to accept assignments in the East, and one in Europe."

"What brought you to Baltimore?"

"My sister lives in Annapolis. I was visiting for a few days."

"You have a beautiful tan. Were you out on the bay?" Chesapeake Bay dominates summer activity in the area. I am pleased at my ability to offer a sly compliment.

"Yes. My sister has a sailboat. We sunned ourselves every day! It was wonderful."

"How does Maryland sun compare to the famous Los Angeles variety?"

"Oh, it's much stronger. It penetrates the atmosphere!" We both laugh. The flight attendant is collecting lunch trays, and my companion hurries to drain her coffee. Would she like more? Enthusiastically, yes. My tray is removed, and I also retain my cup. Maria-Helena is a beautiful woman, and if we talk I can steal glances at her. I am to take corrections tonight. How appropriate to indulge myself with this svelte, sophisticated woman as I am preparing for the trial. As if she is psychic she whispers, "What does your wife say about your unusual tastes?"

I hesitate to form my answer carefully. "She does not share my enthusiasm. We rarely discuss it."

Her enormous dark eyes are leveled upon me. "She does not know that you see the..."

"The dominatrices." She has trouble remembering the word. I am obsessed with it, and so her unfamiliarity serves to reconnect me with the usual world. "My wife does not know that I do this, no." I take refuge in my coffee.

"Certainly there will be evidence after?"

"Marks? Yes."

"She does not see them? There can be few explanations."

"I have to be careful. No, she has never discovered the marks."

"Do you feel a sense of accomplishment after?" Her fingers have dropped to the armrest, and are playing upon the back of my hand.

Again, I do not hurry my answer. It is an insightful question. "Yes, I suppose so."

"When will you go home?"

"Thursday."

"Would you hold this, please?" She hands me her coffee cup, and the tiny silver sugar bowl and creamer. Her spoon, and napkin. I settle them all upon my table as she folds hers away into the armrest and leans far forward to retrieve her purse from under the seat immediately ahead. Her blouse is very sheer and I can clearly see the tiny swirls of lace edging on her brassiere, and the silhouettes of the straps and catch. Her hair is luxurious, dark and shiny. She lifts the purse, extracts a pen, a small notebook and a business card. She puts them purposefully onto her lap, settles the pouch beside her left hip, and takes out the tray from the armrest again. After retrieving her coffee, the napkin and silverware and sugar and cream she begins to scribble into the notebook. I know that this activity will somehow be focused on me, but I am helpless to interfere. She flips the page in the spiral-bound notebook and begins to sketch. I shouldn't look, but I do. It is a small map.

She rips the notes free, shedding small bits of paper onto her skirt. She tucks the pen into her purse, then swivels to face me. Adding her business card, she offers the small clutch of papers to me. Her eyes are very expressive, clearly smouldering with desire. "I know I'm out of line," she whispers. "I've never met a man who partakes of the things you have described. I have had fantasies, Jerry." Her eyes fall away now. She is blushing. "I would like to have dinner with you Wednesday evening. After your appointment, before you fly away home. I know you have business. Would you please indulge me this one small pleasure?" She is staring down at the armrest, and her forehead is scarlet.

"I'll have to see what happens. If I can..." I reach out, touch her hands which are twisting in her lap.

"Do you know Santa Monica?"

"I've seen the Santa Monica freeway. It's at the western end, I suppose." She smiles at my humor, but still she looks frightened, reminds me of a kitten. "I have to meet clients in downtown L.A. I'll have my field rep with me all day. At this moment I cannot predict how the day might go."

"I understand." Her eyes rise to search mine. "Please try."

"If I can." I doubt that I would, but I don't want to shatter the lovely woman's fantasy.

"I'm going to make reservations at my favorite restaurant. Would eight o'clock be acceptable? I will pay for everything. I would only..." She pauses, squirms in her seat. She swallows hard, almost chokes, takes up the coffee which must be cold and sips from it with eyes closed. "Pardon me." It is a small, frightened whisper. I reach out again with my left hand, the hand that wears the wedding ring, and I cover her small, delicate fist. Her face is hidden,

I see only the top of her head, the part in her glossy black hair, the tiny channel of her scalp so pink in contrast. I wonder if her pubic bush is so livid. Does it contrast so eloquently with the flesh there? I must not think these thoughts. She struggles to say what's bothering her. "I'd like you..." Her eyes rush up to mine, and away. "I would like to see... the marks... your ass." I can barely hear her, leaning close. "If you could just show me, that's all. Just show me." She raises her head; her lower lip is quivering. "Please."

She is a mature woman, mid-forties, divorced, worldly. A professional success, exquisitely attired, cultured and sophisticated. I recognize her struggle, though God knows I shouldn't. Once again my fingertips touch hers, and she can be felt to yield slightly, relaxing. "Isn't it scary," I whisper, "to tell someone your fantasy?" Her look tells me she has realized exactly what I mean.

"I've told you more than I've ever told Linda."

"Is that a bad thing?" My hand takes hers, squeezes it gently.

"I feel... relieved."

"And I am very honored. I will make every effort to justify the faith you've placed in me. If we cannot get together Wednesday, don't desert yourself. I have obligations, but you have to be free. Of that I'm certain."

"Thank you," she whispers. "Please try." She seems to shudder. "Would you...?" She begins to put her coffee cup and all its accompanying paraphernalia onto my tray again. "I have to go to the ladies..."

I lean back, close my eyes. I am hours away from a hiding. I will bare myself, accept the restraints, and then the fiery, maddening kiss of the instruments. Ultimately, I will survive it and walk away appearing as if nothing happened, the evidence secreted within the impenetrable vault of my underpants. My slippery, satin underpants! My fingers clutch the small bits of paper. And now, the next night I am invited to display my pride, the marks. She will, I suspect, appreciate them. Perhaps touch them, tentatively with her fingertips as she might touch the wings of a butterfly. I suspect she is locked into the tiny confessional booth attending to her needs, caressing the sensitive bud that has roared to life this morning. I know what I *should* do, but I also know all too well what I *must* do.

We land at LAX and taxi interminably. We bump over the pavement, reminding me that we have been riding a vehicle, and the ride is nearing its end. From my window I can see the row of planes parked, the passenger tunnels adhered to their sides like feeding tubes. Am I insane? Will the gentle stranger beside me appreciate what I am considering? Do I dare? The engines' whine dies away, there is a final jolt and the fasten seatbelt light blinks off with a solid ding. All the occupants of the plane erupt into action, retrieving articles from under seatbacks or from overhead bins. Maria-Helena says good-bye. I say I will walk with her.

We bump against the throng, step into the tunnel and emerge into the bright, airy terminal. There are rows of hard steel-and-vinyl seats, a colorful amalgam of travelers, and all in a frantic environment of lighted schedule boards and public-address announcements. We are part of an urgent discharge from the plane, swept along toward the baggage claim area and the resumption of our lives. I tug her aside, out of the rush. We are in a loosely populated seating area. I put down my briefcase and stand to face her, and she seems almost intimidated by my bulk.

"My appointment is at six o'clock this evening," I say, watching her incredible eyes. "It is for two hours. Please think of me about seven o'clock."

"I will. I promise."

"And I will try to see you tomorrow. And if I can, I promise to show you my bottom. Thank you for being so accepting."

She shakes her head softly, bringing her lovely hair to life. "No, no. I thank you."

We must move on. I reach out, take her left hand. Her eyes tell me she is wary, unsure what I may do next. "In ancient Rome, the gladiators entered the arena and acknowledged the emperor saying, 'We who are about to die salute you.' I am just a few hours away from a similar trial, Maria-Helena, when I will surrender myself to the powerful force that is femininity. You are a beautiful, incredible woman. I who am about to suffer salute you." I drop to my knees as I have been taught and lean far forward, and I kiss the toes of her delicate black-leather pumps. Her heels are towering, and her nylon-clad calves are shapely. I pause for effect, kiss her again, then rise. A huge ring of spectators has noticed, and they are staring.

When I am upright Maria-Helena steps close, rises up on tiptoes and kisses my cheek. "Your courage makes my panties wet," she whispers. "Farewell, and I will see you tomorrow night." We gather our things and walk on toward the baggage claim where we become separated. Will I see her tomorrow? I have far greater challenges to overcome first. I dial Mistress Mary's number and confirm my appointment. I must be there in less than three hours.

Despite Smitty's request, the rental car company does not lease convertibles. I throw my things into the trunk of a Ford Taurus. Sliding onto the driver's seat I feel the unmistakable sensation of my layered lingerie sliding against itself under my bottom. In less than two hundred minutes those layers will be ceremoniously removed, and the alert, vital flesh within will be tormented. I begin to earnestly search my soul, to plumb the depths of my heart in preparation.

6

Hope is brightest when it dawns from fears. – Sir Walter Scott,
THE LADY OF THE LAKE

I arrive at the hotel a few minutes after four. Because I have accumulated
a lot of points on my "frequent sleeper" card the attendant assigns me to a
particularly luxurious room overlooking the Pacific. A forest of aluminum
masts stand upright from a fleet of sailboats in the harbor. The palm trees are
like massive umbrellas casting patches of shade onto luxurious beds of
decorative flowers and rich, carefully manicured lawns. I open the sliding door
and step onto the balcony to glory in the ocean breeze and afternoon sun, and
to gaze at the women sunning around the pool. One darkly tanned beauty has
undone her bra strap, and she is lying magnificently in only the narrowest
possible snow white thong. Her buttocks are simply beautiful, firm and round
and deeply divided, and the thong seems to emphasize their beauty in the
loveliest but most exotic manner. In contrast to the buttocks her waist is tiny
and delicate. I imagine that my arse will soon bear some resemblance to this as I
am displayed for the pleasures of the dominatrix. Once again, I ooze into the
satin panties. Mistress Mary will make me pay, and soon!

It is always an adventure to unpack a suitcase, to view the few treasures
of one's life that were deemed necessary to haul across the continent, and also to
discover what has been forgotten and left behind. There is inevitably something I intended to bring that isn't here. I am comforted to see that the
wrapped gift for Mistress Mary has arrived in good shape and I lay it out
alongside my car keys. There is my well-worn map of the Los Angeles area. I
have to go to Downey, and it will be rush hour. I hurry to put everything away.
I have forgotten my travel alarm. I call the front desk and ask for a wake-up call
tomorrow at five-thirty. I know that I will be hopelessly awake at three-thirty,
exactly two hours too soon on this coast. To yawn tomorrow would be
disastrous. I am stalling, allowing inconsequential lethargic thoughts to play
with my mind even as the clock moves toward my appointment. I have to hurry
now. One does not arrive late for a session with the dominatrix.

My expensive European electric foil razor is an indulgence in good grooming. My cheeks and neck are soon smooth and hairless as a baby's bottom. I flick on the TV and watch the national news as I do a few calisthenics to overcome the stiffness from the flight. One last time today I check my messages. Smitty's sexy voice assures me that all is well, and then she adds a sly "Have a very, very special time tonight." Damn! I have to pause, to review everything. There is simply no way she can possibly know about my plans for this evening. All of my calls were from the pay phone at the convenience store. She cannot possibly know... but can she detect my excitement, the rich anticipation coursing through my veins? If so, can my wife?

It is time to call home, to check in and share a moment out of the day. It is already dark on the east coast. Brad was thrown out attempting to steal second base tonight, but he got two singles and a walk. The wife's Acura is due for servicing, and there was nothing in the mail but bills. The cat hasn't been feeling well. I suggest she may have gotten a bad mouse. Is there any such thing as a good mouse? We share I love you's and then she is gone and I have to hurry.

I buzz the electric razor over my chin one more time, and inevitably it finds some small hint of stubble and mows it down. I must be immaculately smooth tonight. I place the tubes of scented Calvin Klein shampoo and shower gel into the tub enclosure, and the small plastic box that contains a bar of matching scented soap. The water is refreshing, its thousands of needles invigorating my skin. I examine each nail for catches or rough spots, and I wash my behind three times with extravagant cauldrons of lather. The towel is thick and luxurious, and I rub myself briskly. The mirror wraps around two sides of the opulent bathroom, and I vainly examine my naked body. All too soon I will be helplessly restrained and this flesh will become the devil's playground. I turn my smooth white buttocks to the mirrored wall and imagine the striations she will place across them. I stand full-front and try to evaluate my maleness as she might. The curls are thick and dark, the penis is shriveled and not remarkable. The aftershave produces its own splash of jolting pleasant pain. The cologne is more subtle. I am very liberal with it tonight, knowing that I will soon be naked and sweating. Tonight my body is something sacred, an offering to the Goddess, and only I can convey its real value. My pride, the way I carry myself, and yes, my grooming all communicate to the Mistress, all speak of the value of the flesh I will place reverently at her feet. She will test my valuations, extract the truth from skin and sinew, and so I wonder if my bathroom attentions have been more for her or myself. I notice that my mind has become introspective, searching for a solid footing before it receives the inevitable screaming sensations.

The ivory satin panties are waiting on the bed, carefully laid out as if by a maid, and the pettipants alongside are certainly complementary. Despite the fact that they have been worn all day, these are rich, luxurious, seductive garments. I step into the briefs, raise them slowly into place. In a short while she will greet me, view me in this humiliating costume, then remove it and...

I slip into khaki Dockers and a pale blue polo shirt, dark socks, Bass Weejun loafers and a thick brown leather belt. My sportcoat is by Hugo Boss, very stylish. The hairdryer blows my tangles into a crazy misshapen mane to be combed and brushed into submission. I like the direction my thoughts are taking, the anxious tactile awareness spreading across the surface of my body. I can feel the satin panties vividly, and the distinctly different pettipants against my thighs. There is something heating in my loins, something insistent becoming ripe with masculine sap, and I must divert my attention.

The keys, gift, map, a small plastic container of breath mints, I am ready. I leave a light on in my room, the TV loud enough to be heard at the door. The elevator smells like raw plastic; the bell captain seems to be watching me with more than usual interest. A lovely young blonde in skin-tight white jeans smiles broadly as we meet at the main door, her eyes seeming to recognize my destination, its significance to herself and all members of her gender. The Taurus starts instantly. I find a soft rock station on the radio, pull the shifter in "drive" and rush out of the parking lot. Ten after five! South on the PCH to Sepulveda, East to the 110, then North. The radio plays Annie Lennox's "Why" and I think it is the most erotic song I've ever heard except that a Mercedes sedan is weaving wildly in and out across lanes and into precariously tight spaces, and fast approaching my left rear fender. She pulls up alongside, a bleached beach goddess holding a small vial and the steering wheel both in her left hand and a tiny silver spoon in her right, and as she accelerates she deftly puts the spoon up under her nose and inhales her own private pathway to ecstasy. The Mercedes rockets on into traffic, slewing and diving in exaggerated response to every perceived opening. The radio sends Donovan's "Catch The Wind" out across all of Southern California. I turn up the air conditioner. There is wetness in the armpits of my shirt. I gnaw breath mints and exit onto the 105 East.

I've got to travel about ten miles on this highway, and then things will get hectic. I must focus myself. It is twenty-five after five. An hour from now I will be in the jaws of my obsession, probably sobbing and struggling to overcome the pain. I am in the center lane, just moving with the traffic. All around me are people rushing to their own appointments, to boring jobs or an exotic rendezvous, to squalling children or loyal, obedient canine companions. To health clubs for exertion or recliners and beer, to personal computers and daring on-line fantasy sites. I have done this so many times, amazed myself and countless women. I perform well under discipline. My thoughts are at their very clearest, and my body can endure a lot. Still, I am acutely aware of the tenuous nature of sanity. Soon there will be no cars moving in orderly rows, no red or amber or green light to forbid or allow progress. No sky. No trees. The chamber where I am to suffer will be dark and lifeless, almost clinical. No comforts, except those I carry in my mind. Funny, I've never realized that before.

My sexual obsession always leads me indoors, into a sanctuary. I have fantasies of the whipping post on the village green, but my struggles must be hidden from the general population. Few understand my cravings, the immense mental challenge I must overcome to survive the whip. The emotional control I must achieve, so like meditation. The intense process of putting my senses into order, subduing all of my "natural" responses until I can safely shed all protection and offer my nerve endings, the tender flesh of my ass for God's sake, willingly, daringly to the torturer. That she is a beautiful woman is significant, but I know it would be the same if I were to be punished by a male and the women only watched. It is fundamental that they witness my agony, the endurance I am able to call up in moments of extreme duress. It is crucial that the Mistress know I perform for her, that this is my equivalent of a mating ritual. I am about to strut my masculinity despite her bonds. Decorated by restraints, adorned in stripes and blemishes and bruises and tears, naked, defenseless, I will display my heart for her. My thoughts seem to burrow into my soul at moments like this one. There is a secret gland somewhere deep within me, a kernel of resolve or courage, the syrup of my mental being. I have known about it a long time. I found it one night long ago, in total blackness, in combat. Look at my right leg, the evidence is physical. The grenade killed Adams, ripped apart my calf. Three shadows pounced, we struggled, I survived. Utterly alone, I heard whispers in their language. The pain in my leg was excruciating, but the fear overcame it. I had to think clearly, had to put the pain aside in order to survive. These moments happen in life, unexpectedly. I know. I prepare myself. It is sexual, sensual, physical and mental. It is simply necessary.

My flesh prickles with anticipation. I can feel each hair, the blood coursing through my wrists at the steering wheel. I am acutely aware of the layers of lingerie under my ass, the sweet fruity scent of my cologne, the cold currents of sweat trickling down over my ribs. I am finding that inner reservoir, coming to grips with the appointment, with myself.

North on the 605 to Firestone. I exit into Californian suburbia, tiny cramped houses and carefully landscaped tropical vegetation, kids on bicycles and adults in Japanese economy sedans, and I take a third left, two blocks and another left and then a quick right and look for a parking space. Number 177 is just another stuccoed tropical two-story surrounded by bougainvillea and thick palm trees. There is a chain-link fence, a small gate. I park the Taurus, retrieve the gift, check my appearance in the rear-view mirror. I am sweating, anxious, frightened. Naturally! I am also ready. I concentrate on my breathing, on slowing my heartrate. Eleven minutes to six. I shake out a half dozen breath mints and sit back until my skull is against the headrest. Closing my eyes, I recall last time, the other location. The rattan cane, the terrible weights she hung from my scrotum. I remember crying, pleading, the pitiless way she looked at me as she input another swipe of flaming red discomfort.

A deep breath. I could easily start the car and drive away, find a terrific restaurant and sip expensive scotch while the chef prepares an abalone souffle. I could catch a movie, or go back to the hotel and swim. All of the above!

Who am I fooling? In exactly six minutes I will knock on that door. I will greet the Mistress, kiss her feet, give her an envelope of cash in tribute to her willingness to torture me. She will smile, watch me get naked. She will see my underpants, and she will discover the wetness that has accumulated there. I will offer my flesh, and she will make me regret every self-indulgent moment I have ever enjoyed. I will, ultimately, scream. My mouth is terribly dry. I toss in another cluster of mints. Four minutes. I think I need to urinate before discipline. I cannot smell my cologne now. Will Mistress smell my perspiration? Will she sense my trepidation? Can she recognize the importance of this for me? These are the moments when I feel most alive. All the other times I am just waiting.

I trip the door latch, take the gift, slide out into the clear California evening air. Funny, you can see the smog hanging overhead but the atmosphere is so crisp and comfortable at ground level. The gate squeaks as I enter, and clangs shut behind me. There is a doorbell button. I watch my expensive Tag-Heuer. Before I left home I set it to WWV, Greenwich time. At precisely ten seconds before six o'clock I push the button. I am trembling, losing control of my body. I nearly panic, but...

7

The masochist trusts that the Superior has the power to elicit his hidden desires, help him express them, and remove the guilt from them: that the Superior accepts, and perhaps even approves of his masochism. Only the true Superior is capable of inspiring this... – Terrence Sellers, THE CORRECT SADIST, Temple Press, 1990

The door opens.

A young lady's face peeks around the edge. "Can I help you?" She is youthful, freckled and ruddy with a pert, upturned nose and high cheekbones, and a tousled shock of rusty brown hair cut short. This is *not* Mistress Mary.

I must be cautious. "Hello. I was hoping to find Mary."

"Your name, please?"

"Jeremiah."

"And the purpose of your call, Jeremiah?" She smiles sweetly.

"We have an appointment."

"You are to be disciplined?" Again her look exudes delight at the discomfort she has caused me.

"Yes." I lower my eyes and immediately affect my role as submissive. She is a woman, and obviously a confidante of the dominatrix.

"You were precisely on time, Jeremiah." She swings the door open. "Won't you please come in?" I enter into a comfortable suburban living room. The door is closed behind me, and I hear a heavy locking bolt slide home. "Did you have any trouble finding us?"

"No, ma'am."

She steps in front of me, and even though my eyes are lowered I am pleasantly shocked. She is dressed in gleaming oxblood leather, head to toe. The bustier is dominated by her bosom, a beautiful pair of youthful rounded swells encased in shining, straining cups. Her tiny midriff is similarly garbed, but crisscrossed with an elaborate pattern of matching nylon laces one might expect to find along the backbone of a Victorian corset. There is a wide belt with a heavy golden buckle, and then her hips and legs are decorated in skin-tight matching trousers that seem to caress every contour. Her hips flare boldly, but her thighs are not heavy. Below her knees I see tall boots with outrageous heels, all in matching oxblood cowhide with duplicate matching laces. There is a tall tongue extended a few inches above the laces, which are identical to the heavy laces across her midriff. She is a lean, athletic woman, probably in her early twenties, and her outfit fits incredibly well. I stand quietly, electric with anticipation and dread. I am surprised at this turn of events.

She circles me, touches my elbow. "Legs apart!" she barks. "Hands flat, fingers extended, one on top of the other in the small of your back." I comply. "My name is Candy," she snarls. "I will be assisting Mistress Mary this evening." She has a clipboard now, and lifts a sheet to view another underneath it. "You've seen the Mistress before. She said some very nice things about you." Her voice has softened slightly. "You'll be entertaining us for approximately two hours tonight, harsh disciplines, bare bottom, and then Mistress Mary is taking you out on a field trip and to dinner." I do not reply. "Don't plan to sit down tomorrow, Mister Jeremiah. You'll embarrass yourself. Any comments before we begin?"

"No, Mistress."

"Do you have Milady's tribute?"

"Yes, Mistress."

"Hand it to me." I break position, take out my wallet, withdraw two hundred dollar bills. She takes them, places them on the coffee table and weights them with a riding crop that is waiting there. I snap back to the required position.

"You smell very nice, Jeremiah. Did you shower before coming here?" She is approaching from my left.

"Yes, Mistress." She stands directly in front of me, still holding the clipboard. "Please lower your trousers, Jeremiah." Her body is magnificent! Eyes perpetually lowered, I tug at my belt to release its catch, unbutton, unzip, and allow my pants to puddle at my ankles. Mistress Candy examines my pettipants, goes behind me and smooths the material over my left buttock and traces the lower edge of the satin panty with a fingernail, from the area of my anus up and across the lower curve of the left buttock to the front of my hip and then down into the recesses of my groin. "You follow instructions very well, Jeremiah." Her finger abandons me; she moves in front again.

"Thank you, Mistress."

"Will you be caned this evening, Jeremiah?" She tugs the waistband of the pettipants far out from my belly and bends to peer inside. With just a fingertip she plays with the little fabric rosebud on the center of my precious satin briefs.

"If Mistress Mary desires it, Mistress."

She lets the elastic snap across my abdomen, stinging me.

"So you don't hope that ridiculous little flower will spare you?"

"I trust Mistress Mary to provide for me as she sees fit, Mistress. I have attempted to comply with her suggestions, but I have no expectations."

"You expect to be disciplined?" Her voice mocks me.

"Yes, Mistress."

"I'll prepare you, Jeremiah. Come with me." She takes my right earlobe between her thumb and index finger and tugs me. My trousers are at my ankles and I have to shuffle awkwardly. My hands are rigid at the small of my back, and my eyes are kept lowered. She opens a door, drags me into a corridor and then into another doorway on my left. It is very dimly lit, and I smell the sweet aroma of scented candles or incense. "Everything off but your feminine things," she whispers. "Fold your clothing neatly and put it on the chair, shoes underneath. Stand in the corner and wait for me, hands at your sides. Your things will be safe here. Are there any questions?"

"May I have permission to use the bathroom, Mistress?"

"No. Be quick about it, Jeremiah. We have a great deal to accomplish tonight. I'll be right back. Don't disappoint me." I hear the door close.

The room is barren, the walls covered in plastic panels that resemble stone walls. It is a very small chamber, the floor is tiled, and I notice a closed door. There is only a straight-back wooden chair and a low spanking bench for amenities. I undress quickly but lay out my clothes with some care, for I must wear these things when I accompany Mistress Mary to dinner later. I must look my best. I am quite fascinated by the bench; I have seen photographs of similar designs but this is a wonderful example, a true piece of flagellatory furniture. At one end the device features a low hardwood crossboard with cutouts hinged to accommodate one's neck and wrists, similar to a colonial pillory. The bench portion angles up toward the other end, and it features a thick leather-covered pad fastened in the antique manner with bronze round-head tacks. The rear legs flare out abruptly and are abundantly braced. A thick leather restraint belt hangs listless from the bench, and there are comparable straps on each of the rear legs.

Will I be fastened down upon this thing for punishment? The idea both thrills and chills me. Time enough for that. I take my place in the corner, toes and shoulders tight against the two converging walls, hands at my side. Deep breaths. Perspiration trickles down under my arms. Soon the need to urinate will become acute. My right ear itches, but I do not dare reach up to scratch it. Alone, dressed in shameful feminine attire, shivering in suspense, I wait, searching within myself for the resolve and courage to withstand the approaching storm. My hearing is acute, I have recognized gentle jazz from somewhere above, Bob James, and then Jeff Golub's Avenue Blue. I hear my heart pumping, a far-distant jet plane. I feel an air current fluffing the curls on my calves, and I note an apple scent from the candles.

I do not hear her footsteps approaching. The door handle creaks, the hinges moan, she is beside me. "How you doing?"

"Fine, Mistress."

She opens the door to my left and snaps on a bright fluorescent light, then comes back behind me and abruptly tugs the pettipants to my knees. "Feet together." I comply, and she pushes the delicate garment to my ankles. "Step out." It is an awkward thing to do with one's shoulders tight into a corner. She removes the wisp of material, bending low behind me. I hear her leather outfit creaking as she squats. "Now these." Her fingers are suddenly at the waistband of my beautiful doubled satin panties, and she tugs them down and off me. "Step out." I stand, utterly naked now. I hear her move to my left, into the brightly lit room, and return. "You've been aroused today, Jeremiah. Mistress Mary will surely punish you for the puddles in your panties." SMACK! Her palm explodes against my left buttock, startling me. I bump my forehead into the corner. It has begun.

"Come here." She is alongside the hardwood spanking bench, holding open the pillory's jaws. "The position is obvious..." I clamor down onto the thing, belly onto the leather pad, my legs askew. I fit my neck and wrists into the lower halves of the cutouts and, without giving me time to settle myself comfortably she lowers the top, snaps the hasp and slides a padlock into place. There is no need to lock it. She is alongside me, bringing the broad leather belt up around my waist. She fits the two ends into each other, tugs it tight, and then she expertly puts her leather-clad knee onto the small of my back and shifts her weight. The breath rushes out of me, she pulls the waiststrap excruciatingly tight and fastens it, and suddenly my upraised ass feels bulbous and very obviously exposed. The rich animal scent from her leather costume assails my nose, and I feel the blood beginning to rush toward my dangling organs. She straps my left thigh immobile, then the right. My knees are spread wide apart, my head is lowered, and my hindquarters are the most prominent aspect of me. I expect to be thrashed, and I am frantic to prepare my mind to deal with the pain... but she leaves me!

I hear water running in the lighted room. The apple scent is thicker down here. My wrists are helpless, and I cannot turn my head. The thick hardwood collar fits tight up under my jawbone. I am utterly defenseless, capable only of waiting, and then enduring. Eyes closed, I search deep inside myself. I hear a k.d. lang tune, and then Jim Chappell. I expect the whip at any moment, and I am anxious for it to begin. She is busy off to my left; I think I hear latex stretching and snapping.

I feel her palm against my left buttock, placed gently. "You washed yourself so nicely, Jeremiah. Mistress appreciates your respect and consideration. Now we'll cleanse you inside, and then prepare the flesh where you'll feel her fury, and then I'll take you to her." With these words I feel her poking at my anus, a cool glob of thick cream, her finger stroking, invading me! She immediately withdraws, and then I feel a colder, harder probe at the same gate.

"Please, no..." I realize what's happening to me.

"Mistress Mary requires it, Jeremiah. Her notes reveal that you broke wind last time she disciplined you, and the scent wasn't agreeable to her. We'll just wash you out a little and avoid that possibility. Deep breath now..." I hear the little metal clamp ping! as she releases it, and the flood begins to invade me. It is hot, and insistent. I wasn't expecting...

SMACK! "Take your medicine, Jeremiah. It's actually good for you, you know. Cleans you out, keeps everything functioning nicely. You should have your wife administer an enema weekly. Come on now, relax. You're about halfway there. I have instructions to empty the full quart into you. Do the Mistress Mary's will, naughty boy. You *don't* want to make her angry, we both know that. You've never experienced my disciplines, but I assure you I can soften your big behind up a little before you go to Mistress Mary. Take your soapsuds like a good boy. That's it. Let it flow."

The flood is diabolical, urgent and angry despite its simplicity. I feel the heavy bloating seeping under the waistbelt, flattening my internal organs out upon the leather pad and the hardwood platform. I am suddenly aware that my erection has become rampant, that my testicles are swollen and hanging like grapes just below the Mistress's gloved fingers. Horribly vulnerable! I am nothing except vulnerable, filled as I am. Now I need a bathroom desperately, so much more than before. "Almost done. Relax, sweetheart." She pats my rump, the sticky latex glove unmistakable against my proffered flesh.

"Okay." She squats behind me, I feel her attentions, a different filling, and I hear the hiss of air pumping. "I'm inflating a device called a Bardex, Jeremiah. A little balloon inside so you can't expel the enema, another outside to hold everything in place. We'll just let the soapsuds scour you for a few minutes, then I'll let you up and train you to evacuate your bowels only when your Mistress gives permission. Have you had the wooden spoon upon your testicles before, Jeremiah?"

I am lost in an intense other world of sensations and shame. Daydreaming, perhaps. Searching my mind for some semblance of self-control. She spanks my scrotum, hard! Fastened as I am, the distress is unimaginable. My belly recoils, slammed hard shut like a steel animal trap. Two different intense discomforts now, so distinct, and yet they somehow complement each other. I struggle, but I am rigidly confined, at her mercy.

"Have you had the wooden spoon upon your testicles before, Jeremiah?" I recall hearing the question before, but I'm not sure when.

"No, Mistress."

I feel her gloved fingers manipulating me now, tugging and stretching and kneading my tender sex glands, weighing them, smoothing the wrinkled sac that contains them. "Well, yours certainly are sensitive, Jeremiah. I'd suggest you focus on obedience when I take you to the toilet, naughty boy, or you'll be in no shape to go out with Mistress Mary later. I'm just a little disappointed that I wasn't invited to go with you, you see, and so I feel some inclination to create some little remembrance that will accompany you all night long. Ahh, but that will be later, darling. Right now you just wait here and feel the cleansing taking place in your bowels. I'll be back when you're done." She turns off the fluorescent light in the other room and quietly exits.

I am alone again, in the near-darkness, on my belly, ass and genitals upraised. The enema is churning inside me, gurgling and bubbling and scorching my tender inside tissues. It is pushing to escape, expanding, magically growing inside me like a living thing clamoring for freedom. I can feel the apparatus at my anus. In fact, I can clearly discern the two parts of it, the inner and the outer. What must it look like? How must I appear?

Only one in a thousand men might understand this moment. Only one in ten thousand would not despise me for undergoing this ritual. And women? I am here to perform some sacred rite, to debase myself in honor of femininity, and still the average woman who might walk in here and see me like this would probably scream and rush away. Why am I here? Why do I bring these storms down upon myself? What am I proving? And to whom? I am frightened. This is just the appetizer; the main course is to be a long and terrible ordeal of merciless flagellation. I will break.

And then I realize that I cannot break. I will not be destroyed by this. I have an opportunity here to see that tiny kernel inside myself, to drink from the cool well that is my essence. I can call up my truth, summon my courage, and I can experience this with dignity. I search the recent past. Things were vivid for a few moments, but I don't think I have disgraced myself. I must access the very best parts of myself, and hurry to do it. Flagellation? I know it well. I have suffered, and I have survived. I have the means. The ability. I cannot help the wretched soaking that is cleansing my intestines. I cannot succumb to the cramps. I can only call upon that sacred guardian something, that precious mysterious mental quality that I sometimes find. I need it now, and soon my need will be even more acute. I close my eyes, accept the music and the scent of the incense and the rubber bubble at my anus and the cauldron bubbling in my gut. I accept that I must obey the Mistress, even upon the toilet. I accept that governments are corrupt, that illnesses infect good people, that evil sometimes wins, that winter inevitably follows summer. I cannot fight inequity or disappointment or pain. I can only accept, and coexist alongside, and find my own internal pleasures to outweigh the bad.

8

Masochism does provide a balance... Masochism is a mode of psychic survival... to feel oneself reduced, exposed, and chained is to accept oneself at the mercy of the gods. This recognition is a necessary precondition for submission to one's fate. – Lyn Cowan, Ph.D., MASOCHISM, A JUNGIAN VIEW, Spring Publications, 1982

"I'm going to let you up," she says, sweeping into the room and interrupting my meditations. I feel her fingers at my restraints. "You will interlock your fingers behind your neck, and you will sit upon the toilet as upright and proud as a king upon his throne, and you will open your knees wide to give me access to your tender little balls, Jeremiah. You will recognize only two words from the entire English language. 'Empty' and 'hold'. Do I need to explain what is required of you when you hear those two simple words, Jeremiah?"

"No, Mistress."

She is loosening the waistbelt. Waves of nausea erupt in my belly. As my body expands it unleashes the fiendish suds to wreak havoc upon new areas of my inner tunnel. I am desperate, frantic for relief. I hear her at the padlock, releasing the hasp. I am afraid I will lose control and utterly despoil the room. "Okay," she whispers. "I know what you're feeling, sweetheart. You *can* do this, Jeremiah. I'm going to release your head and hands. There is no need for you to rush. I understand exactly what's happening inside you, and your need to move carefully. The Bardex will not fall out, and you won't spill. Are you nauseous?"

"Yes, Mistress." I feel weak and powerless and sick inside.

"Good. That's the intent." I feel the heavy wooden yoke lifted off my neck and wrists. "Carefully now." I am jelly inside, shaking and sloshing. I can feel the Bardex now, hanging down against the back of my scrotum. I am on my knees. I focus my thoughts, rise up from the floor. Bent forward at the waist like an old man, I shuffle off toward the fluorescent room. It is a simple bathroom, blinding after my long stint in the darkness, and I see the toilet. The lid is up, seat down awaiting me. Mistress Candy is alongside, her rubber gloves on my arm to steady me.

I turn now, horribly nude in front of her, and carefully take my seat. I guide the plugging device with my hands, then settle over the hole and struggle to straighten up my torso. Hands behind my head, fingers interlocked. Knees open. More. I can feel my testes dangling, fully exposed. My eyes are lowered, but the incredible young woman standing between my knees can be seen to be clutching a wooden spoon in her right hand.

"There are two bulbs to the Bardex, Jeremiah. Bring them up alongside your pathetic little tinkler so I can release the balloons. And Hold. You will not allow a drop to escape until I order you to do so, is that clear?"

The pressure is exploding in my entrails. I am surprised to find that tears are running down my cheeks. "Yes, Mistress." I feel her hands between my legs, against my sensitive parts. The air sizzles out of the outside balloon. I can do nothing. It is a change in feeling, nothing more. And now I hear the inner plug deflating. I feel it! The way is opening, Mistress is withdrawing the device, and it seems to create a suction inside me. I must concentrate, tighten myself... I must! I must! It's out! She brings it up out of the bowl, and I catch a quick glimpse of a very technical-appearing contraption with black hoses and egg-shaped squeeze bulbs decorated with tiny chrome fittings. There must be five thousand gallons of solution inside me, weighing upon my sphincter. I sit upright, hands interlocked behind my neck, knees spread. Mistress puts the Bardex into the tub, then returns.

She caresses my cheek. "You're very well trained, Jeremiah," she whispers. "Now shit for me. Open yourself, let it out. Let it escape, Jeremiah. I know the hurt, the churning. Your intestines become encrusted with a residue of fecal material, Jeremiah, and what you've been feeling is the cleansing of that material. It's free now, churning in the soapsuds. We've done a good thing, darling, but now we must complete the task. Shit, Jeremiah. I order you! Fill the bowl with your offering, and keep those knees far apart so I can witness your shame."

She pauses, touches my cheek again. "You're really very good, you know. Okay, naughty boy. You may *empty*."

I have been squinting my eyes, wrinkling my nose in desperation. I allow the flood to...

"Hold."

I knew it. I clamp my internal muscles, the sphincter. Agony. The room is filled with a contradictory scent, a heavy soap's perfume unsuccessfully attempting to mask the other. I am prickly, sweating, trembling.

"Too slow, Jeremiah. You call that obedience? Two strokes, I'm afraid." I feel her fingertips, still in the rubber gloves, lifting the tip of my penis. Surprisingly, I am able to clearly hear the cupped portion of the spoon each time as it impacts my scrotum. Things seem to happen in slow motion.

"Oooh, ...Nargggh!" I wrench my feet, preparing to rise.

"Position, Jeremiah!" I settle back onto the seat, stretch my knees apart. My gut is a rock-hewn vault of discomfort. She rustles her fingers through my hair. "I know," she whispers. "I know. Empty."

I squeeze. The torrent is abundant, noisy and aromatic. There is a great explosion of air. "Hold!" She slaps the wooden spoon against her left palm. "Now we're getting somewhere. You certainly wouldn't want to do *that* in Mistress Mary's company!" She leaves me, goes to the wash basin and begins to clean equipment. Eyes lowered, I can only listen. I hear a gurgle, and then she goes to the tub and starts a flood of water. She bends forward. I raise my eyes only slightly but I am able to see her sleek, beautiful behind and legs as she bends over the tub. She is lovely, but she is...

She turns, rises, catches me peeking. She has the off-pink rubber bottle refilled, swollen to the brim, the hose in her other hand so it stretches across her. "Empty," she says, smiling at me. "Empty completely, Jeremiah. Then wipe yourself and come into the other room and take your place upon the whipping cradle as before. We won't need restraints this time. The second rinse is so much easier for a trained man to take." She hangs the bulging, foaming sack on a chromium-plated medical stand and wheels it away, and I squeeze hard against my bowels in a frenzied effort to flush them completely. She reappears at the door and smiles at my primitive dilemma. "Please flush, Jeremiah. You stink!"

9

Elsewhere men and women kiss, cuddle, and lie. Here they lash each other and tell the truth. The truth, however horrible, does make you free. – Erica Jong, ANY WOMAN'S BLUES, Harper & Row, 1990

The second enema is more immediate and more violent than the first. This time there is no Bardex, and the soapsuds seem to melt my inner abdomen. The pressure is excruciating, there are hard cramps and my rear portal seems to have been enlarged. I struggle, but I fear I will be unable to hold all of the treatment and I groan an appeal to the Mistress through gritted teeth. "Mistress!"

The metal clamp squeezes off the flow with an audible click. "Too hard, Jeremiah? We know you can hold it, you just did. Gather up your resolve, dear. I'll give you the rest when you ask for it."

"Please, Mistress. I can't."

"Six with the cane."

"Please, Mistress!" I am desperate.

"Six with the cane? Tell me you accept the trade-off, Jeremiah."

My teeth are clamped, and I am afraid to remain here as I am afraid to move toward the toilet. I am at the very ragged edge of control, and about to... "If I must, Mistress. Please!"

"Okay, sweetheart. I won't withdraw the tube. I know what you're going through. I'll let you up, but don't you dare shit on my chamber floor." The crossbar is lifted off my neck and wrists. I am afraid to open my eyes! Gently, ever so carefully, I try to lift my bloated belly up off the bench. It is awash, and the waters slosh inside me. They descend as I raise my torso, and increase the pressure against my stretched and fatigued clenched anus. I am jellied inside, sick and exhausted and quivering, my physical strength depleted. I cannot run! I am hunched, my left hand's fingers clamped tight up against my ass, waddling awkwardly, smartly, the beautiful young dominatrix following closely with the enema bag held high and the damned hose like a leash controlling me as I try to resist this most animalistic of urges. I cannot rush as I want to; I am ashamed and blushing and bitterly aware of my sex organs flopping against my upper thighs, and now there is no hint of an erection, and I turn and lower...

And I stop. "Permission to be seated, Mistress?" It's coming! I am out of control!

"Permission." She is inches away, I can smell her perfume and the scent of her leathers, and her face is childish but also cute, and beautiful, but she is staring at me in a mocking way, and it doesn't matter, I squat down hard upon the plastic seat and expel the tube, the soapsuds, my innards, everything! I am gutted, utterly empty inside, and now the desperate tension has been replaced with a quivering, quaking internal emptiness, a sick shrunken disemboweled feeling and I want to cry, to curl into a fetal ball and hold my aching shaking gut... "Sit up, Jeremiah. Hands interlocked behind your head! You're disobeying!"

"I can't."

Her palm explodes against my cheek, the fluorescent light assails my burst opened eyes, I am goosepimpled head to toe and cold and weak and she is so beautiful I have to try, and I regain something deep inside that is not physical but it allows me to begin to uncoil and stretch, and I groan feebly as I slowly return to almost the position I held before. My lower digestive tract is on fire, revolting, undulating like a beheaded snake on a hot summer blacktop driveway. I may vomit, but no. I open my eyes again, sort out the room, recognize the young woman who has broken me so easily.

"I may have used a little too much soap that time, Jeremiah. Sorry!" There is concern in her expression, but humor in her tone. She breaks into a friendly, co-conspirator's grin. "You okay? You shivered so hard I was afraid you might fall off the commode." Her hand touches my cheek. It is still encased in a latex medical glove, but it helps me to focus. It feels rather nice, and then she slips it under my chin and grasps the point of me there and lifts my head up so she can look at me. "Hey, this is just the preparation, naughty boy. Don't you get woozy and wimp out on me, the Mistress has promised that you're going to show me a real man's set of balls tonight. If I disappoint her she'll put me up in your place, and we wouldn't want *that*, would we? Take a few minutes, get yourself together. Make sure you're really empty; you won't have another opportunity for a while. I'll be cleaning up a little." She disappears. I am regaining myself, but I am weakened and queasy.

Mistress Candy returns. "Try this." It is a slug of scotch in the bottom of a glass, straight-up and horribly fragrant. "Lower your hands and take it." I do, and throw about half of it back into my mouth. It is an explosion of taste, but it clears my vision. The second swallow helps even more, and I am recovering. I sit back, bump the porcelain lid of the toilet against the rim of the tank which causes a horrible noise. I jump. She laughs. I do as well, and interlace my fingers behind my neck. I straighten up my back, spread my knees wide. I am on display, on the toilet. The whiskey's fumes are in my nasal passages. I wheeze, try to speak. "Thank you, Mistress. I'm fine." My eyes are watering profusely.

"When you're finished return to the bench, Jeremiah. Mistress Mary will be ready soon, I've got to prepare you." She leaves me again, and I squeeze my flattened, lifeless abdomen muscles and expel another huge rush of liquid. Mistress Candy bustles in, wheeling the chromium I.V. stand. "Oh, I must say, you're smelling much nicer! Mistress will be pleased." It is not a compliment I cherish. I do not try to do more while she is in the small bathroom. Each outpouring is catastrophic and humiliating. My belly is shrunken and shriveled.

After a long while, it is gone. I am empty, cleansed inside, flushed. I take large strands of tissue to clean my arse. Three times! My anus seems to protrude, a bouquet of sensitive tissues bulging outward as if reaching toward more sensation. I know that this is part of the Mistress's plan, that she will aim her wicked sensations to more than satisfy my blooming rear orifice. I get to my feet at last, feeling surprisingly stable. The flush echoes; everyone in the building must have heard it. At the sink I see myself in the mirror, and I look tired and drawn. I splash cold water, two brimming handfuls onto my face, and again. Wash my hands. There is liquid soap, heavily scented of lavender. I have to pee. I face the toilet, do it like a man, and the sound of the cascade is deafening. The Hollywood Bowl, I muse. It is time to go back to the other room, to resume.

The darkness seems to welcome me, to enfold me in its indistinct sensual womb. The candles flicker madly as I close the bathroom door and dim the room drastically. Mistress Candy stands alongside the bench, holding the crossbar. I move tentatively, meekly, crouch forward and put my belly gently onto the leather pad, and then my neck and wrists into the cutouts. I feel the bar against the back of my head, hear the hasp close. The apple scent assails me again. My sex is hanging free, exposed, beginning to engorge again.

She straps my thighs into place but not my waist, then slips into the bathroom. The splash of cold fluorescent light disturbs the mood I am trying to establish. She returns, silently, closing the door to shut out the brilliance. We are alone in the darkness, and she is crouched at my upraised, naked ass. "Oooh!" I shudder throughout, tight as steel bands. It's okay; I relax. She has only put a hot, wet washcloth against my right buttock, down low where I am so extraordinarily sensitive.

"Sorry. I've got to wash you."

"I'm sorry, Mistress. You startled me."

"From here on, Jeremiah, I'll be preparing the seat of you for the flagellation that is scheduled. I'll be stimulating the nerve endings and attracting some blood flow to the area, to the surface. You should begin to focus your consciousness within. Do you know what I'm suggesting?"

"Yes, Mistress." It is a reverential whisper, as if I am in a church. I feel incredibly fresh behind, inside. Now that is done, and I am entering into more familiar territory. I am surprised that the enema wrought so much mental and physical havoc. Perhaps I am having an "off" night. I'll just have to increase my focus. Mistress Candy has warned me, and she is giving me time to gather and arrange my thoughts. Mistress Mary has told her about me, and I do not want to disappoint either of them. She washes me slowly with the hot wash cloth, with special attention to the more sensitive areas. Terrycloth can be quite abrasive, and she uses the rag like sandpaper across my anus, my inner thighs, up and down the crease between my buttocks. Next she rubs an ice cube over all the same areas, and clasps it tight against my scrotum. The contrast is maddening! I am goosepimpled again, in a far different manner from before. She massages me with warm scented oil, kneading and reshaping my gluteals, soothing me. This is a nice time, relaxing and invigorating, and I am able to refresh my mind. The chamber is silent, dark and intimate. Her fingers do not arouse me, but their deep manipulations attract bloodflow and sensations to the area, and my organ has become boldly tumescent. I have regained the desire, and I know I am ready to face the magic wand that is the whip. I am aware of faint new age music, Keiko Matsui, Kitaro. Now I am a spectator, viewing my own body, my captivity and impending torture as if from above. On the one hand I will feel it acutely, of course. But on the other I will know, intellectually, that I will survive this, and that it is necessary, and ultimately salubrious.

The door to the hall opens slightly. "I'm ready, dear." It is the Mistress Mary's voice, very understated. The door is immediately, silently closed. The soothing, slippery hands leave my flesh, and I am aware of how stimulated the under parts of me have become.

I am released, ordered to stand. "Put these on." She hands me the pettipants. They are, of course, a single layer of delicate nylon tricot, and designed to be a loose fit. They feel like gossamer over my glowing bottom, a sheer whisper in contrast to the heavy, glossy rich feel of the doubled satin panties. She gently takes my wrists behind me and fastens them, then attaches wicked metallic clips to my nipples. They seem to snap down onto my tender breast buds, and hurt like fury! She moves quickly in the dim light, linking the two clamps with a length of light-gauge chain, then attaching a leash so that she can drag me away by my flaming nipples. Finally, she picks up the luxurious ivory satin panty and turns it inside out. "This is your stain," she says, "and Mistress Mary will expect me to show it prominently. I'm sorry, Jeremiah." She puts the womanly garment over my head, the dried puddle full across my face. It is, of course, a blindfold. I am now helpless, shamefully naked except for the sheer, womanly lace-trimmed bloomers bulging like a tent over my sex, and the equally shaming feminine underpants masking my features. She tugs, and I follow blindly, shuffling cautiously but eagerly to ease the fiery hurt in my breasts. I sense that Mistress's hand is about four inches in front of the breast chain, and that she will guide me safely to my destination. This is, for me, the magic moment. I am being led to the whip, and I strain to appear dignified and serene. I do not struggle and I do not slouch. This is the first ritual of a long and arduous but meaningful ceremony. I am filled with pride and conviction, chest expanded, shoulders squared. I go to meet the Mistress, and only my carriage can express my respect and willingness. She is special, and so am I. I will respond well to her diabolical inputs. The young beauty who has prepared me pauses, knocks.

The hallway has a wooden floor, and then we move again, onto carpet. I can tell that we have entered another dimly lit room, but as we move I think we are moving into a spotlight's concentrated glare. There is virtually no sound except my breathing and an occasional rattle from the devices attached to my chest. She pauses, drops the leash so that it hangs heavy and drags at my functionless male teats. I am positioned, unseen hands adjust my calves apart, a finger glances over my anus and up the central crease of my behind. My head covering is tugged, smoothed over my face. I try to be as putty, to affect whatever posture the young protegee would create as an expression of respect for her mentor. I am proud in my bondage, ready to be tested. I am battling apprehension and raw dread, wishing I needn't be here. For a moment I am tempted to crumble to the floor, to dissolve into a puddle of tears. If I lose control, perhaps piss myself, become incoherent, might she pardon me and postpone the pain?

"Hello, Jeremiah." I recognize the voice immediately. All of the blasphemous thoughts abandon my head. There was never any question of what I must do, and the time is nigh.

"Good evening, Mistress." I must speak to her through the double satin panty which I wear on my head, the stain of my oozing a broad blemish across my face. I cannot see her. I am totally, shamefully exposed to her gaze.

"Nicely done, Candace. He has a major problem with erections and oozing. Very disrespectful."

"I tried to highlight it, Mistress. I knew you would be offended."

"Thank you. I'll break him of it. Twelve penalty strokes, Jeremiah. Masculine juices oozed onto fine feminine lingerie. Your disrespect surprises me. We've had this discussion before, naughty boy. The panty is exquisite, but the front of it seems to have been soaking all day, your puddle is obscene." I feel her fingertips at my swollen penis. "And you dare to come to me in this state! You *know* better! Make that thing wilt, Jeremiah. Immediately!"

I try to will it, but I am stimulated. My body is rigid. Suddenly the pettipants are ripped down to my ankles, nearly toppling me. A gloved hand comes up under my scrotum and catches my balls. The fingers lock tight around me, squeeze hard. My knees nearly buckle, and I grimace. The pressure increases, then again. I bend at the waist, fighting to contain a groan. The crippling pain is removed, and I struggle to return to my position.

She circles me, examining me. She opens one of the damnable nipple clamps. Blood rushes in, carrying along a heavy cargo of pain. As soon as it stabilizes she snaps the clamp onto my tender bud again, causing me to gasp. I feel her fingertips against my elbow, bumping down over my ribs, probing my navel. She cups my buttock cheek. "Doesn't he have the most incredible buns, Candace? I've always admired them, from the first time we met. If ever a pair were made to be punished..." I expect a spank, but it does not come.

Her fingers seem to wander into the central seam of my behind, to drum lightly against the tender little orifice there. I am grateful to be wearing the panty over my head. It will hide my blushing. "Wait till you see how they shudder and squirm under discipline," she whispers, her palm caressing my left hind gently. "They quiver in the muscles under the skin, most unusual. He seems to feel it so!"

"It is a lovely ass, Mistress. He struggled with the enema, especially the second rinse, and I thought I was a little weird because I enjoyed watching his bottom. But you're right, it really is a pretty one."

"Candace, take him to the closet and let him choose the instruments. A crop, a hardwood paddle, a rattan cane and a dressage whip. I'll begin with my hairbrush and finish him with the tawse; you know the one." Suddenly the thick satin panty is torn up and off my head. "Obeisance, Jeremiah!" I fall to my knees as I have been trained, and lean far forward in the dim light to kiss the toe of the Mistress's shoe. It is a stylish pump with a very tall heel, and I can see that she is wearing black stockings.

"Permission to speak, Mistress." My lips are lifted off her shoe only the slightest fraction of an inch.

"Permission, Jeremiah."

"Thank you for seeing me, Mistress."

"It is quite literally my pleasure, Jeremiah. It's nice to see you again, although you are very obviously in need of training."

"Thank you, Mistress."

"Anything else? You know you're going to undergo a very strenuous test this evening, naughty boy. Is there anything you would like to say before we begin?"

"Only that there is no other place in the world that I would rather be at this moment, Mistress." I am emotional, kneeling at this woman's feet, preparing to expose my inner self to her. There is a huge lump in my throat.

"We'll see in a few minutes, Jeremiah. Thank you for calling me. Your loyalty is appreciated even though your behavior is not. Take him, Mistress."

I am tugged to my feet by the harness attached to my nipples, hauled up painfully, impatiently, and the clamps tear at my tenderness. Mistress Mary hurries away, and I am rushed into the darkness, toward a massive cabinet along the far wall. Mistress Candy opens the slider and snaps on a bank of overhead track lights, and I am confronted by a vast collection of S & M paraphernalia and implements, all displayed in the most orderly fashion.

The equipment used in sadomasochistic play is always fascinating, and I am surprised that I can view an assortment of pieces and choose specific ones with which I would prefer to be tormented. Is it the shape, the texture? I know that my preferences are based upon some mysterious inner scene which has evolved from years of movies, books, and erotic dreams. If a dominatrix accesses those fantasies, my imagination immediately begins to form appropriate images of all manner of aspects; costume, equipment, and theme. This inexplicable chain reaction of images comes together into an elaborate "scene" which I must convey to the Mistress. She, of course, must be adept at recognizing key words and phrases, incorporating these as she "takes control and makes my dreams come true." As in any other arena of human interaction, a few individuals are on your wave length, and most are not. Mistress Mary knows the shadowy, cobwebbed nooks and crannies of my thoughts in such detail that I fear she is able to read my every thought. We are, while in session, able to communicate on some subtle, intuitional plane, and so she becomes a door through which I can exorcise my demons.

This is an extremely personal event, of course, and such a perilous journey requires strategic road signs and landmarks all along the route. On any given evening, the appearance of a whip or paddle pushes some uncanny button in my subconscious and, although it is an inanimate object, fulfills a murky, specific aspect of my script. Mistress Mary recognizes this, and so she sends me off to view her arsenal and choose precisely the implements which will cause me the most exquisite suffering this night.

I am trembling, searching my most secret reservoirs for the courage to see this through. I am prickly, sweating, but cold as stone. Silent and stoic, all of my senses at their maximum, inwardly screaming. I choose carefully, with pride and daring. I can withstand the bite of this crop, the streak of fire that must accompany the whipcord lash of the English dressage instrument. I will not be accused of avoidance. Foolhardiness maybe, but not avoidance.

10

The image of the fully erotic woman is one of unlimited wantonness, sexual hunger, and electricity so extreme that she gains the power to dominate men.... the sad fact is that there can be no equality with black-widow women, only domination or subordination. — James William Gibson, WARRIOR DREAMS: Violence and Manhood in Post-Vietnam America, Hill and Wang, 1994

"Wait here," Mistress Candy whispers. "Stare straight ahead at the instruments, Jeremiah. Make yourself ready. We will come for you in a few moments, and begin." She turns to leave me while she takes the collection of flagellatory tools to the place where I will suffer, but she pauses and turns back. She is close beside me, I smell her perfume and her leathers. She leans close and kisses my cheek. "Mistress Mary tells me I will see your soul tonight, Jeremiah. Courage! Good luck."

I stand alone, contemplating, just moments away from the pain. There is activity behind me, the room dims but then I detect the rich sulphur scent of matches, and the soft warm glow of candles. The music is perceptibly louder, still a far distant background but I recognize Danny Wright's piano, then Jim Chappell. I am a miner panning the gravel that has collected in my heart, searching for nuggets of golden masculinity. I have womanly pettipants stretched between my knees. It is a ridiculous situation, I muse, all of my own making. Like cloud cover on an overcast day the pain dominates everything, and I must be ready. I must. I close my eyes and sink deep into myself.

The room is hushed, steeping in soft music and the scent of the candles. Lily of the Valley, I think, and then a current of Sandalwood wafts over me. I am acutely aware of the flesh of my buttocks, the life forces flowing just beneath the surface. I can feel the hair from my scrotum brushing against my inner thighs. Fingertips at my left elbow. "It's time, Jeremiah." Mistress Mary's voice is calm and measured, as if she were summoning me to dinner. She steps in front of me, removes the nipple clamps. Blood rushes into my tender buds, hurting mightily. "Let the pettipants fall and step out of them," she orders. "You are to be completely silent." The delicate undergarment is as a whisper falling across the hairs on my calves, puddling at my ankles. I step out. She is alongside me, on my left, her both hands gently encircling my elbow. She turns me, leads me into the dim chamber. An enormous lump has lodged in my throat. My eyes have begun to tear.

We approach a straight-backed wooden chair illuminated by a halo of soft light from above. The room is large, and there are multicolored candles flickering all around its perimeter. It is impenetrably dark except for those flickering votives in their colored glass jars. "Kneel," she whispers. "Knees spread wide, back straight, palms up resting on your thighs. Eyes lowered, good boy." She moves in front of me, stands before the hard chair. "Why are you here, Jeremiah?" It is a whisper, but it resounds in this chamber. Mistress Candy is present, although I am not sure where. My thoughts are entirely focused on Mistress Mary and the impending torture. We are quite alone.

"I am to be punished, Mistress."

"You come to it willingly, Jeremiah?"

"Yes, Mistress."

"I am prepared to administer a prolonged session of severe flagellations, Jeremiah. Your behavior has made this necessary." There is a pause, a distant piano tune seems to embrace a theme of timid apprehension. "Look at me, Jeremiah." I raise my eyes. She is magnificent!

Mistress Mary is a mature woman, probably in her late forties. Her hair is honey blonde, thick and straight, with bangs across her forehead and full sides clipped evenly at her collar. She is a lively, beautiful woman who resembles the Linda Evans character from the old "Dynasty" television series. Her elegance seems to illuminate a room; she is used to comforts and yet she is innately kind. She has chosen a dark grey pinstripe suit, a snug, tailored waist-length jacket over a crisp white blouse, a gentleman's tie, and a straight, tight skirt. Her stockings are opaque black, and she is on gleaming black leather stilettos. The Mistress is a lovely mature woman, about five-feet-nine, healthy and athletic but also exceedingly feminine, with a full bust and a taut waist that flares dramatically to rounded, womanly hips. Her derriere is magnificent, and her legs incredibly beautiful. Dark, haunting eyes, ripe red lips that smile easily, a porcelain complexion. She is always composed, warm but confident and very, very sophisticated. Highly educated, although I know few details of her life outside the torture chamber. Mistress Mary has that certain something called "presence," the ability to command a room simply by entering it. A classic beauty, tonight she has costumed herself as a schoolteacher, a formal disciplinarian. She has large, round eyeglasses, and her lips seem somehow pouty. She is upright, strict and immensely proper, conservative and fastidious.

A busy woman taking time out from her hectic schedule to deal with this disciplinary problem, this slightly distasteful but entirely necessary ceremony of correction and counseling. I am but a boy before her, a student, and while I know she will be cruel, I am certain that she will be fair and that I will get my just desserts. I am frightened, almost quaking.

Even in the dim light, her eyes seem to bore through me. She recognizes my inner being, the core person beneath all the images and personae I have adopted to become successful in today's world. I am acutely aware of my infantile nudity. I am not a sex object to this woman, only helpless and unprotected. Which is as it should be, for this is not a place where physical comforts count for much. "Your safeword is 'bluebird', Jeremiah. Please repeat it for me." Her voice is tender and caring. She is wearing tight black leather gloves.

"Bluebird, Mistress."

"We will commence with a traditional boy's punishment, Jeremiah." As she speaks, she seats herself on the chair and bends to pick up something from the carpet. "A hard formal spanking, naughty boy, the hairbrush applied to your bare bottom until I think you've had enough." Mistress Candy approaches from my left and places the double satin panty onto my left palm, then silently retreats into the shadows. "You have chosen a wonderful panty, Jeremiah. Please place it between your male organs and my lap as you go over; we have already discussed your lack of control." I feel a blush heating my ears. She arranges her skirt, tugs down the hem, chases away a minuscule bit of lint. "Position!" My heart is pounding furiously within the tight confines of my chest!

I hasten to rise, bringing the elegant satin panty in my left hand. Mistress sits bolt upright, her right arm upraised at the elbow, brandishing the broad, flat wooden hairbrush. I place the satin insulation precisely at the hem of her skirt and then position my feet carefully and lean forward across her, catching myself with my hands on the carpeted floor. I feel her hands at my bottom, arranging me. "Soft as a baby's," she says, and I believe she honestly admires my bottom. "So lovely, Jeremiah. And Mistress Candace, it is very nicely prepared. Thank you, dear. Has he had his enema?" Her fingertip probes my anus! My sex begins to stir.

"Two, Mistress."

"And his behavior, Mistress?"

"Excellent for the first cleansing, Mistress. He had more trouble with the second. He asked to be allowed to empty himself before I had given the full dosage, and agreed to six extra cuts of the cane."

"I think you've been stretched over the years, Jeremiah, so that the Bardex is really necessary now. Did you feel he was *trying* to please you, Mistress?" I am arched high over her lap, and my thigh muscles are beginning to quiver.

"He tried very hard, Mistress, and his manners were superb."

"If only it could always be so, Jeremiah." It happens so fast I cannot prepare. Within a single terror-filled instant I feel her tensing, hear the stirring of her clothes behind my shoulder, hear the WHACK! like a pistol shot and feel the first full blast of hurt explode across my right buttock.

SMACK, SMACK, SMACK, SMACK, SMACK! Fast and furious she attacks me like a swarm of angry hornets, stinging, hurting, and in response I squirm a bit. The other buttock catches hell for that wriggle, the hardwood slaps down about a dozen times until I exclaim at the pain of it. Almost as if she is satisfied, she stops. I arch myself, hoping to lift some of my weight off her legs. CRACK! CRACK! CRACK! WHACK! Harder shots, individual stinging efforts applied one to the undercurve of the right, and then the left, and the right again, and the left as if mechanically. These are punishing blows, designed to hurt to the very depths of the musculature. Her aim moves slightly lower, spanning the crease where the bottoms become thighs. I struggle to contain myself, to accept it. It hurts like fury!

No amount of thinking can prepare one for pain. By its very nature, pain overrides all else, its wicked signals screaming up along the central nervous system to deliver the most frantic messages to the brain. This is the crisis, the moment of confrontation. I am crouched across a beautiful woman, naked and awkward, my fingers and toes straining to remain firmly anchored in the carpet so that my weight will not be too great a burden across Mistress's thighs. I am being soundly and systematically hurt! It is awful, and it has just begun. The dominatrix applies pain in the same way an artist applies paint to his canvas, and she will employ a variety of implements and techniques in order to create exactly the effects she intends.

I struggle to contain the hurt, gritting my teeth and fighting the groan, the desperate howl of anguish that my body naturally tries to emit. I must concentrate to do this properly, and so I begin to seek refuge within. I do not avoid the pain. The purpose of this exercise, this entire evening, is to experience the pain and control my reactions to it. To hold in the cries, to hold the positions, to overcome the urges. If I can overcome this, perhaps I can withstand the next corporate onslaught, the next personal setback. I grimace, and a small squeal of agony squeezes out from behind my teeth. I am about to cry.

"Good boy!" she whispers, signalling a change in cadence. Now she starts a string of smacks high up on the right cheek. Each application falls in perfect alignment, perhaps an inch lower but overlapping. Slowly, methodically, she stretches the fiendish sensations down my screaming flesh until the flat wooden hairbrush lands almost entirely against the upper thigh. I am frightfully sensitive there, and then she whacks the other thigh and begins to move her attentions up the other cheek. The contrast is maddening; it is as if she has split my bottom cheeks. I am breathless, desperate. She pauses at the top, then attacks again, harder, random blows in stacks like pancakes splatting and cracking wickedly all around my tortured arse. I am afraid I will begin to cry aloud, to sob like a child. My eyes and teeth are both squeezed shut as if that tension would somehow extract some of the pain from my behind, and my toes are dug into the carpet so hard that my calves are knotting. The hairbrush continues its terrible work. The blows come fast and hard, smacking loudly. Each impact causes a wicked instantaneous hurt, but then it leaves behind a residual heat that is cumulative. Now, after thirty or forty hard spanks, that heat has soaked into the deepest fibers and tissues of my behind and multiplied, and I am frantic to escape it! All of my willpower is required to hold position, to control the flaming need to squirm or buck or writhe. My self-control is unraveling!

At the critical moment she pauses. "Get up, Jeremiah, and compose yourself. Hands at your sides." Clambering awkwardly to my feet, I desperately want to rub the sting away. I am up on the balls of my feet, wrestling with myself to calm the furies that have devoured me. "Don't think of yourself, Jeremiah. Take your soiled panty off my lap, please, so that I might get up and prepare other delights for you." I have forgotten my panties. They are wet; a huge erection bobbles embarrassingly out of my loins. Mistress Mary gets up from the chair and busies herself behind me, but I do not dare to look. I stand now, in her absence, still sniffling, naked, clutching my panties in my left hand. Once a proud and meaningful icon, they now seem wrinkled and tired, and the emotion that propelled me at Macy's a few days ago has been spent. My seat is sore and swollen. There is a scum of dried tears on my cheek. Why am I doing this? How much further can she take me? Why did I agree to two hours? She can dismantle me in ten minutes! My arse is glowing, pulsing hot and tender. My erection has subsided. I am at a low state, dreading the rest. I must refocus my self-control, take advantage of this brief pause to make ready for the next installment.

I jump when she touches my elbow. "You have chosen well." She is brandishing the dressage whip, sending its slender whipcord tip shrieking through the air with just the slightest movement of her wrist and forearm. The instrument seems to hiss as it slices the still atmosphere of the room. It is a fine English implement, about four feet long with a braided black handle and a polished silver cap at its base. It tapers in a long and unbroken line, slimming gradually until there is only the last eight inches or so of coarse black cord. Does she wax it? The cord is stiff and unyielding, hardly conceding to gravity at all. It will, I know, hurt like fury when it slices over tender assmeat. The spotlight on the hardwood chair slowly fades, plunging us into darkness. Mistress Mary's gloved fingers are still lightly resting against my left elbow, anchoring me. Another light comes up behind us like an accelerated sunrise; I watch our elongated shadows crawl up and over the chair and carpet.

"Turn around." I comply, and see an ominous dark shape illuminated from above. It is a whipping post, a massive wooden T crafted from timbers that must be fourteen or sixteen inches on each surface. It seems hand-hewn and rugged, an uncomfortable primitive thing, and it is liberally adorned with dangling leather straps. Before I can determine more I am propelled toward it, and Mistress Candy steps out of the darkness to help fasten me.

The crossbar is just slightly above waist height, requiring me to bend at the waist to spread my arms out along its rough top surface. There are four straps for each arm, one at the wrist, just below the elbow, across the bicep, and above the bicep. The women are strong and they draw the straps down hard so that I am immobilized. My rear is throbbing, smouldering. They prod my calves and insteps forward until I am straddling the massive upright, and fasten each knee and ankle securely... causing my flaming arse to jut prominently out behind. Mistress Mary reaches in from the front and gently lifts my genitalia out onto the front of my thighs, while Mistress Candy wraps a broad leather belt around my lower thighs. Tugging it tight seems to swell out my buttocks, I can feel the change in muscle and surface tensions there and I know that I am positioned diabolically for the whip. My gonads are trapped out of harm's way, and my penis is engorging again.

"Twenty strokes, Jeremiah. Do you recall your safe word?"

It seems so long ago! I search... "Bluebird, Mistress."

"I expect absolute silence."

I am surprised to feel her fingers at my left ear, and then she inserts a tiny crushed foam earplug which expands and shuts out the sounds. She does the same for the right side, then slips the double satin panty down over my face robbing me of my sight. She smears the front of it against my face in an unmistakable gesture, rubbing my nose into my own disgraceful ooze. I am here to be disciplined. She misses no opportunity.

I am isolated, unable to hear or see. I can only wait and anticipate. Nothing occurs.

My right calf is cramping. I try to shift my weight slightly, but I cannot. I am completely immobilized, a set of prominent buttocks accompanied by helplessness.

I can almost hear my breathing. I strain to detect any hint of what the two women may be doing. Any hint of impending pain which would allow me to tense against it. I can hear nothing. I am available to them. Presented to the whip, awaiting its explosive kiss. Nothing more.

All of my attention is centered on listening, and on the exposure of my raw, red backside. Time moves, but it is fiendishly unmeasurable, a terrible obstacle without any definition except duration obscured by anxiety.

I wish it would begin. The first cut will introduce me to it, and then I can realistically prepare for nineteen more. It is vital information, the personality of the sensations I will experience from that first stroke. I am coping with the unknown, building my defenses behind an expectation that contains only random measures of hope and conjecture. I have not seen the damage already done to my ass. I have not experienced the cruelty of this instrument wielded by this woman on this occasion. What personal concerns might propel her arm tonight? What set of far-flung random coincidences might make her especially cruel this evening? Will she show off a little for Mistress Candy, impressing the neophyte because she knows I am a steady, experienced example? What possible role might their menstrual cycles play? These are women, subject to PMS and a myriad of other mysterious phenomena that make their dispositions, especially toward men, unpredictable. I am naked, so obviously male, and an extremely available outlet. Oh, I wish she would begin it! The cramp in my calf tightens again, and as I wriggle slightly I can feel the familiar after-spanking tension on my buttock skin, as if it has shrunk tighter over the soreness it contains. I am wracked with questions, and answers are not forthcoming. Waiting, thinking, expecting.

Opening my eyes, I can almost perceive the texture of the beautiful ivory satin blindfold. I see it move with my breathing. Is that a footstep behind me? My attention shifts frantically, my buttocks tense involuntarily. Still nothing occurs. I wait, hung out like laundry to dry. Nothing. Today's lifestyles do not prepare us for times with no stimulation of any kind. We are not comfortable alone with ourselves. I do so wish she would strike, that she would grant me some respite, however harsh, from this ordeal.

11

You cannot create experience. You must undergo it. – Albert
Camus, NOTEBOOKS 1935-1942

It is slender and straight and it cuts me as surely as a knife; a flaming
hard sharp shrieking input of sensation that covers perhaps one ten-thou-
sandth of the surface area of my body for approximately one-tenth of a second,
and immediately wipes one hundred percent of my thoughts away and leaves
my brain painted a ghastly, stark snowy white! I have seen references to
"blinding pain." Pain obliterates all rational thought, but it does not bring on
the darkness associated with blindness. Eyes closed hard to shut out the reality,
a poor soul experiencing excruciating pain sees vast swirling oceans of vivid
scarlet, yellow, or white.

Suddenly after all the waiting I have been thrust into the steaming
cauldron of pain. It subsides, finally, leaving me trembling and awash with
sweat, still blindfolded and immobilized, unable to hear, forbidden to speak or
cry out in my discomfort. I am waiting again, and terrified. There will be
nineteen more cuts across my agonized bottom! I am into it now, and although
this is familiar territory its reality is excruciating, maddening. I cannot allow
myself to go mad! I must collect myself, gather up my wits and focus myself on
enduring. I have to... OWWW!! The second cut seems to have landed on top
of the first, and it has stirred a thousand hornets across my bottom. AIIEEE!!
Before I can assimilate the second a third has landed and I am insane, fighting,
shaking and tearing at the immovable post in a mad effort to put my hands on
my burning ass and quench some of the terrible pain!

Three! I have had three. I wait, my poor arse outflung as if it invites
another. I wait, helplessly imprisoned, aching, trembling with fear. I strain to
hear her preparing to strike, to hear her foot move across the floor or the ripple
of her soft garments, anything! I cannot accept another stroke unless I am
prepared, unless... OOHHH!! That was four... NNNGGG!!! and five...
NNNOOO!! Six.

I have had six. They have striped me low, a few stretching full across my
ass, but one cut just the left cheek, the tip wrapping diabolically around the

buttock and stinging deep into the central valley. Oh, I am so sensitive there! And one, or was it two?, have come from the right, and swiped that cheek, and once again the tip has stung me deep between the buttocks, and so I am angry and almost insane. I have had six. Fourteen to go. I shouldn't think that way, I'll lose count, lose my bearings. Six. The next will be the seventh. I wait impatiently, tense, expecting that next stroke at any moment. I feel a wind current across my bottom and I lurch, rattling my bonds.

The clock is ticking, somewhere. I have accepted her challenge, two hours in session before we will go out for "field training" and then... AAAHHHH!!

My mind is wiped clean again! The strand of fire across my backside scrubs every thought from my brain, replacing them with only raw pain and desperation. I am sinking deeper into my reservoir, drawing upon my resources. There is a place deep inside me where I can take refuge. I am having trouble accessing that sanctuary tonight.

Seven. She leads me deeper, flicking that barbarous tail into the central seam of me, cracking it against my anus or even up underneath. I am riding on adrenaline and endorphins now, becoming more resigned to my fate. I have not made the transition to acceptance yet, but I'm gaining. Mistress Mary sees my progress, and she will not allow me any easy escape.

The first dozen are aimed from outside, the tip of the whipcord snapping home into the central groove of my behind. My mind screams in acknowledgment. Now Mistress adjusts her program, the lash falls full across the opposite hind and the tip snaps home on the outside of my hip. It is an all-new hell, and I have to strangle a scream that threatens to rise up from my gut.

Eighteen is a hard cut, slicing low into my left buttock so hard that my knees try to buckle. The hurt is fiendish, relentless, dragging me back from my near-reverie. Back to suffering. I try to breathe deep, to control the pace of my exertions. She waits me out, saving the nineteenth stroke. Eighteen. I am leaning on the crossbar, tiring. Eighteen. The number resonates in the vacuum that is my mind. Eighteen. Have I had it, or will eighteen be next? I have lost my bearings, stumbled over the count! Have I had eighteen? Have I? Again, I search my depths, the core of my resolve, my heart and soul. Have I had eighteen? The question batters me like the whip. Have I had eighteen yet? How can I lose track? Daydreaming under the whip? I am confused, almost disoriented.

Nineteen slices my right buttock. I try to dance, convulsing in my bonds. I hear a distant, plaintive wail and realize that it is my own voice. I am in a delirium of agony. Nineteen. I think, but I'm not sure. She strikes again, right on top of the last, and I think I am going insane! I fight, struggle, cry. My eyes are bulged open, studying the weave of the satin panties which are soggy and plastered to my face. Perspiration burns my eyes, and my nose is thickly congested. I writhe in the leather straps, wrestle with the enormous wooden frame that has become my replacement skeleton. I am tiring; I hang on the cross, sobbing. I am almost to the transition, almost able to find respite and enlightenment from the pain. I wish I could have a sip of water. I wish I could finish this soon.

I feel hands at my restraints, and the sodden panty is lifted off my face and head. The outside air is a cold slap in the face, clears my head. I am suddenly aware that my ass has been wounded, that the whip did real damage. My knees are freed, and I try to curl one foot up behind to comfort my flaming bottom somehow with my foot.

"How are you doing?" Mistress Mary leans close to my face, touches my forehead with a cold wet washcloth. I cannot answer; I am still on the border of insanity. "I'm going to free your wrists," she says tenderly. "You are not to touch your bottom, Jeremiah. Do you understand? Hands at your sides. The paddle is next." My heart seems to drop with a dull thud. The paddle? Isn't she done? Haven't I suffered enough? She frees me, leads me across the darkened room. I am stiff and sore, plodding. She smacks my rump hard with the flat of her palm. "You'll *prance* when I lead you to a discipline, Jeremiah. You're shuffling like an old man. Stand up and strut proudly or I'll add punishment strokes, and you're facing a healthy dose of those already!"

Eyeing something overhead, she positions me with care. There is a flurry of activity. Leather cuffs lined with sheep's wool are buckled to my wrists, then linked together in front of my waist. Mistress reaches to the wall and activates a growling electric motor somewhere above me, and presently a burnished metal hook at the end of a stout chain drops into view. My wrists are lifted and looped over the hook, and then the motor growls again and the hook begins to take my hands away. Higher and higher it winds, hauling my arms up overhead into the darkness, and still it hauls at me until I am stretched to my body's limits, up on the balls of my feet.

Mistress Candy has disappeared again, and now Mistress Mary approaches me. "You were stooped a long while, Jeremiah. This will straighten you out." She circles me, pats my fanny lightly. "You're very red back here, and streaked with vivid purple stripes. Are you getting what you wanted?" Reaching underneath me she grasps my scrotum again and squeezes!

"Yes, Mmm... Ugghh! Mistress." I lost contact with the floor for a moment, and I make a mental note to avoid swinging from my wrists at all costs.

"The hardwood paddle, Jeremiah. Two dozen may be sufficient. Present yourself." I am on tiptoe, but I strain to jut my bottom back and invite the paddle. "Nicely done." WHAP! WHAP! WHAP! WHAP! WHAP! WHAP! They come hard, low, full across the fattiest area of my poor bottom, and quickly as she can deliver them. The effect is almost like a pounding, the broad flat hardwood surface seems to compress my arse meat to the bone, igniting the tenderized skin but slamming far deeper than the whip's slender tail. If the whip cut me this instrument bangs broad expanses of my surface and compresses me, flattens my contours and spreads its awful discomfort evenly over whole buttocks at each swipe. WHAP! CRACK! SLAM! WHACK! What an incredible sound it makes, so vivid after the silent tranquility as I was whipped! SMACK! I am off my feet, kicking, swinging pathetically from my wrists, jumping and jerking like a fish hauled into the boat except that my torso is strung up immobilized so that only my ass and legs can dance the ill-fated dance. If I regain control for a moment my position is inevitable and she seizes the opportunity and smacks me again until I erupt in another frantic bid to spare my bottom the awful discomfort. I cannot dance long, gravity restrains me until the paddle ignites my struggles again. The blows are insistent, she takes advantage of every hesitation or pause, and the heat on my behind is rising to desperate, unimaginable levels. WHACK! SMACK! There is a blessed pause; I feel her palm cupping my right buttock, testing its temperature and consistency I suppose. "You're doing nicely, Jeremiah. Feeling it now, aren't you? Another dozen or so and we'll find another toy to entertain you. Present yourself!"

I am demolished, completely whitewashed by the accumulated pain, bone tired, drained. CRACK! SLAP! My soaking wet hair hangs plastered to my forehead. My eyes are awash with tears, my nose is running and I can taste salt upon my tongue. I have drooled down over my chin onto my pounding chest where the spittle mixes with the sheen of perspiration. Worst of all, I think I have to go to the bathroom soon, as if the remnants of the enema have settled and are burrowing out through the rubbery constriction of my anus! I dare not make a mistake here! Have any accident! The floor is carpeted. Mistress would destroy me! WHAP! HOOOWHACK! I hear the blade of the paddle roar through the atmosphere a split second before it scalds me anew, and then there are three more, and another, and another. My knees buckle, but I fight to stand erect. CRACK! She is merciless! WHACK! Cruel!

My ears are ringing, my eyes screwed shut. Nothing exists but the pain, the unholy all-encompassing overwhelming pain! It dances before my eyes in shimmering waves of Chinese scarlet or egg yolk yellow, it commands my hearing as I scratch to discern the sound of the instrument softly rending the air. Attuned to such a faint whisper because it has become so terribly important, my ears are simply assailed by the huge loud SMACK! when the paddle arrives at its target but there is no time to assimilate the sensation for a split second later my brain is overburdened by the exaggerated touch of the wood to my ultra-sensitive bottomflesh! As if she reads my thoughts the Mistress pauses and brings a flickering blue votive near my face, and the candle's flame flickers in the heavy air within the torture chamber, and the sweet scent of lilacs assails my nose. She moves away, brings a clinking, rattling glass to my lips. Cola! I sip hungrily, and she flicks the icy droplets of sweat onto my chest! I dance again at that, mindless, swirling in a kaleidoscopic mosaic space capsule of heightened sensations. She allows me another sip of the cola.

"Okay?" she whispers. Her eyes are enormous, incredibly sexy. I nod. "What is your safe word, Jeremiah?"

It seems so long ago, another place and time. I search my head. Oh, yeah. "Bluebird, Mistress."

"Are you ready to go on?"

I swallow. "Yes, Mistress." We both know the glorious freedom that transition can bring, and that it is elusive and not always attainable. We both know that I have come here tonight in hopes of visiting there, and that I will be painfully disappointed if I quit too soon.

Her fingertips circle my left nipple, tracing concentric little circles onto my flesh. "Breathe deep," she whispers. She goes away to my right, returns with a green candle this time. With a backhand wave she pushes a heavy strand of thick, sweet smoke toward me. "Breathe, Jeremiah." Lavender. "You're sure?"

"Yes, Mistress."

She puts the candle back, bends and moves the glass of soda. "I'm sweating, Jeremiah. Do you mind?" She unbuttons her blouse and shrugs out of it, unzips her skirt and carries them away. She is wearing a lacy white bra, one of those push-up low-cut models with the distinctive diagonal seam across her teat where the "secret" pillow bolsters her. Her panties are also white, but they are obscured by an incredibly lovely black lace garter belt. The black straps are eloquent statements in contrast to the flawless pale beauty of her thighs above the heavy black bands at the top of her stockings. She is still up on her heels, and she is more magnificent now.

"Ready?" She moves behind me. My attenuated ears hear the snick sound of her stockings as she bends to retrieve the paddle.

"Yes, Mistress." WHAP! SLAP!! CRACK! WHACK! WHOOOOAPP! I am insane again, my mind bloated and screaming against the hurt! Again, again, again, she hits low and full across and I cannot keep my toes planted on the carpet, cannot control my legs' reactions as they seek to avoid the paddle's kisses. Again, again, and then she changes sides and bangs away at the same terrible swath on the undercurves of my bottoms, but now the paddle's tip fiendishly scribes the other cheek. God help me!

12

To play the part of a severe but loving Superior requires an ethical and sensitive heart. Performing as the delicious one who yields up everything requires a great deal of strength. The point of these exercises is to leave you both feeling elated, pleased with each other and yourselves – to give you release, not resentment; affirmation, not despair. – Pat Califia, SENSUOUS MAGIC, Masquerade Books, 1993

Only the actual nature of flagellation itself prevents it from being classified as a bona fide form of therapy. – Edward Anthony, THY ROD AND STAFF, Little, Brown and Company, 1995

It has stopped.

I am hanging, stretched, my toes seeking to support my weight. I lost track for a while there. Seconds? Minutes? It is as if I fell asleep, although one cannot fall asleep while being tortured, nerves at the height of stimulation and sensation. No, my thoughts seemed to have wandered off, not to far distant peaceful places but inwardly, into the darker recesses and catacombs of my brain. It was not transition; I did not reach the sweet state of total acceptance and tranquility. Perhaps it was overload, the brain refusing to accept inputs beyond its established capacity.

Mistress steps in front of me. She is so beautiful, so sexy and regal! She attaches a clamp to my left nipple, screws it tight until I have to strangle an outcry and tears flood my eyes. Stretched as I am, my breasts are taut and the nerve endings are near the surface. Now the right breast; I see the chrome-plated device on her fingertips, I feel the alligator teeth sear my nipple as she cranks them down. I am very, very alert now!

Mistress goes to the wall, I hear the mechanical devices hum and I am slowly lowered. At first she only relieves the tension so that I can stand flat-footed; then she allows my arms to come down. The nipple clamps ache maddeningly, my flesh seems to balloon around them and magnify the compression of my little nipple buds. It is not an organ where men usually find sexual stimulation, and I can feel a re-awakening in my loins.

Allowed to stand for a few moments, I find many of my muscles are inflamed. Something in the back of my left thigh is fluttering uncontrollably, and I have a devastating cramp in the arch of my left foot. I try to stretch the muscles, press my toes hard against the floor, but as soon as I try to relax and stand in peace the pain is vicious. I try to tuck it back, placing the top of the toes against the floor and bearing down to stretch the cramping sinews, and I am caught in that peculiar position as Mistress Mary returns.

"Are you dancing again, Jeremiah?"

"I have a cramp, Mistress." I try to stand but the hurt won't allow it.

"I'm going to take you to another room. Try to walk it out. Would you like another sip of cola before we go?"

"That would be very nice, Mistress." She nods to Mistress Candy, who brings it and lifts it to my lips. Again, the cold bubbly liquid seems to explode in my mouth and throat. They are releasing my bonds, fastening my wrists behind me, attaching the leads to my nipple clamps.

"You're very red behind, Jeremiah," Mistress Mary says, and I feel her palm against my left bottom cheek. "You've still got to face the cane, the crop, and my favorite Scottish tawse. I'm going to be a little creative, not to spare you, of course, but to spread the sensations a little and perhaps avoid bursting the skin."

"Thank you, Mistress."

"Don't be too sure."

When I am properly harnessed they begin to lead me out of the chamber and into the hall. Mistress Candy has retrieved my panty and pettipants, and the instruments. As we shuffle up the hall Mistress Mary says we are going to the Victorian room which will provide me with a brighter, more cheerful atmosphere in which to suffer. My ass feels enormous, bloated and swollen, bulging with hurt to the core each time my pulse sends another wave of my life's blood through its arteries and veins. The cramp is better now, ambling slowly in bondage between these two beautiful women I am curiously lethargic and resigned. Beyond the terror, somehow, I am adrift upon the sea of this experience and far from land, and so I can only accept my predicament and marshal my endurance against the next onslaught. I search myself for dignity, struggling to stand tall in my bonds and go proudly. These are the moments that count most, I think. The moments of anticipation, chained helplessly, going to the ordeal watched by an imperious, beautiful woman. No other instant in all my life seems, to me, to be more sensual. I am a man, my genitalia bobbing and flopping unfettered as I shuffle. I am bruised but not broken, proud and strong, giving the finest account of myself that can be given. Behind me a magnificent young woman in tight oxblood leather, before me the mature older figure in her exquisite satin underwear. One leads me as if I am an animal to be tamed. The other carries the cane, the crop, and the special leather strap. They have appointed this house, decorated and equipped it to break the will of men like myself. They have, I know, seen many performances. I am prized here, my stoic endurance acknowledged. In this place I am truly masculine, and the tortures demand that I display my most primitive mating ritual, and the torturers appreciate every nuance of my dance. That I am forbidden sexual release is, after all, just another inevitable definition of the rules of life: a man's greatest exertions do not earn him any woman's favors. Learned early, it is a basic truth that has shadowed my existence, and more inescapable than the chains I wear.

Here, I am appreciated. Here, my strength and endurance earns a feminine smile, a whispered congratulation, a gentle fingertip's touch of encouragement. It is vital, and primitive, and so necessary. I go proudly, anticipating another dose of frightful torment. That I accept the inevitability is a good sign, I am well down the way toward transition. Mistress Mary is a craftswoman, and she is moving me to another venue because she senses that it might somehow enable me in my spiritual quest. I am an experienced, trained seeker. If I am compliant, Mistress will provide for my needs. I can feel my heart thudding in my chest. I am very, very much alive!

The Victorian chamber offers a totally different scenario for one's ceremonies of anguish. This room is larger, and brightly lit. The walls are covered in a joyous yellow flowered wallpaper divided into panels by moldings of snow-white painted wood. The furniture is rich and comfortable, white wicker upholstered in tones of dark or mint green. There are plants, sprouting majestically from earthen urns on the floor, spilling over in blooms from hanging pots along the perimeter. Mostly yellow blossoms to complement the wallpaper. The air is cooled by an elaborate ceiling fan swirling listlessly, silently. This could be a gentlewoman's sitting room alongside her conservatory, a sunny, private place to refresh oneself.

The implements of Mistress Mary's trade are inconspicuous here, and decorated in most unusual ways. I recognize a St. Andrew's Cross to my left, obviously built to rotate its spread-eagled victim. While most devices of the type are stained dark and fitted with black leather straps, this one has been painted and polished to an elegant off-white satin glow, and the restraints are of beige leather with fittings of gleaming silver. To the right of the cross I notice a lovely umbrella stand of wood and woven rattan, a most decorative antique that is wonderfully utilitarian here with its cargo of canes, switches, whips and crops. To my right I see a small table and chairs, framed in wrought iron and painted a soft shade of yellow. The table's top is a circle of glass tinted green, and the four chair cushions are covered in a gay floral pattern of hollyhocks and hummingbirds. Beside them I recognize a trestle in the off-white satin paint, a stout device where a man can be made to suffer as the ladies take tea.

The tiles underfoot are the color of thick cream, and I see casual throw rugs added, no doubt, for decoration. At the far end of the room the white woodwork simulates a huge picture window, and beyond it a mural depicts a lifelike formal garden abloom under a brilliant summer morning's sun. There is a cool, almost misty quality to the photograph, but not in such a way that the glorious excitement of the flowers is muted at all. No, it is a brilliantly joyous scene, bountiful and colorful and calming, a private park overflowing with life. The herringbone brick walkways are carefully defined, the clusters of plants meticulously arranged to highlight the various species and contrast their exquisite blooms, and all of this panorama is surrounded by tall walls of faded brick topped with a crowning shelf of white marble. There is a birdbath off to the right with sparrows fluffing up a spray to cool their feathers, and in the foreground I can see an ancient copper sundial tarnished to shades of green similar to the cushions on a wicker armchair and hassock to the left of the window. This formal garden contributes to the chamber's feeling of space and openness, but I suspect the strict architecture of the garden is also meant to convey another message, especially as it is framed, at least from where I am presently standing naked and fettered, by a pair of carved posts rising floor to ceiling and fitted with the hardware for restraint. They are thin columns, painted in the same soft satiny glow as the rotating cross, and there are white nylon ropes dangling from the ornate silver fittings near the ceiling. They are, of course, whipping posts.

The ladies are busy as I stand agape. "Do you like it?" Mistress Mary calls.

"It's wonderful!"

She comes for me, takes up the leash and tugs me away by my flaming nipples. As I stumble along behind her I cannot help but admire her tight, athletic body. Her curves are clearly defined, and I am mesmerized by the silk panty as it ripples over each of her buttocks as she walks, yet somehow it remains deep in the cleft between her bottoms. Amazing! Her shoulders seem wide, her waist is tiny, and the glossy white framework of her bra gives her upper torso a muscled, powerful look. Her body ripples as she moves, and I can feel my scrotum swinging, slapping against my thigh. I am brought before the St. Andrews cross. A quick chill of fear makes me shiver. She releases my nipples and I groan as the blood rushes back into them. There is little time to savor the pain; they are both upon me and propelling me backwards toward the cross. It is a sturdy device, two heavy planks fastened into the shape of an enormous X. There are footpads, I step up and backwards and they steady me. It is an ungainly maneuver and they are clearly concerned that I might slip and be injured.

They are at my ankles and calves now, securing the straps, and then up onto my thighs. Where the beams join, Mistress Mary fastens a waistbelt around me and hauls it painfully tight. I am drawn up tight against the cross at my midriff, and my wounded fanny is excited terribly as it is drawn tight against the wood.

They rotate the thing! I seem to fall to my right, but they stop when I am horizontal. There is a chest strap, and restraints to be buckled tight around my biceps and wrists. I can smell their perfumes, the leather of Mistress Candy's incredible outfit. I can feel their bodies as they brush against me, and watch them at their work. I am becoming aroused as they immobilize me, one peculiar part of me jutting out as if it wants to escape from crucifixion. When I am secured they right the thing, and then Mistress Mary fashions a slip loop from a black leather thong and brings it up around my scrotum and fastens it tight above my balls! I am unable to escape, and unable to see what she is doing. She steps away, then returns with a large grey weight that looks like an oversize version of a fisherman's lead sinker. This thing is the size and shape of a turnip, dull grey with a brass loop on to top, and as she carries it in her hand I can tell that it is hefty. She takes the leather thong which is dangling from my sex sac and attaches the weight, speaking softly as she fashions a knot just a few inches below my tender jewels. "Candy thinks your testicles are drawing up close to your body, Jeremiah. In a minute you'll be able to say you're well-hung, but I wouldn't wriggle much or your voice may change. Careful now, I'm going to let this swing free."

It is an altogether different style of pain, something internal and constant, and I try to arch out my pelvis to meet it but I'm too tightly bound. I am truly miserable, hard steel splinters of discomfort lancing up into my lower abdomen. "We're going to turn you now," she whispers, and I feel the cross begin to tilt to my left. They control it, letting it rotate slowly, and I feel the cold lead weight bump against my thigh, then over it, and it hauls my straining scrotum sideways until it bangs against my side. I am nearly upside down now, the weight is hard against my ribs hauling my balls up onto my belly, and I realize that my erection has shrunken and gotten out of the way. The blood seems to rush to my head, my body weight settles hard against the restraint straps in a whole new distribution that is disturbing and upsetting, but I am helpless. Helpless! I feel a quick flash of panic, but then she fastens the cross and I am hanging fully upended and the weight is almost to my chin and I'm desperately uncomfortable but I see her brandishing the black leather riding crop, slapping it into her palm as she smiles at my dilemma. Even upside-down I can assimilate these things, and so I set about to focus my thoughts and prepare myself.

She steps close, her black satin panties just inches from my face. She says nothing, just raises the crop between my legs and begins to flick it, stinging the insides of my thighs twenty or thirty times in quick succession and I feel as if I have been stung by a swarm of hornets! These are tiny, precise bites of pain, pinpricks, BAP Bap Bap Bap Bap Bap Bap like a machine gun and then there is a sudden break in the rhythm and her arm's attitude flexes slightly and HoooooWHAP! she strikes hard on the area between my scrotum and anus, between my thighs, and it is as if I have been bitten by a wild animal! I explode, hanging suspended, and the weight bumps my sternum, and I see the wicked cleverness of it all. My testes are hauled safely out of harm's way, and this tender little space on my anatomy, this terribly awfully sensitive area, is presented diabolically to her crop! WHACK! I am delirious, my head ballooning, SsssBAPP! WhoooAPP! I cry out at the seventh, and beg her to stop at the tenth. She pauses after a dozen, but strikes again when she sees me relax. "Thirteen's an unlucky number, Jeremiah." There is another pause, I struggle to collect myself but then there is an awful hurt in my groin and the weight is rolling off me and I realize I am being turned upright! As the weight bumps off my thigh Mistress Mary catches it, and she supports it on her palm as the cross is locked into place. I am blubbering, I can feel the blood rushing out of my cranium, and Mistress untying my gonads and the raw stinging burn between my legs, and then I feel the old familiar hurt all through my buttocks and I realize that it has been there all this time but my attention was diverted elsewhere, and now I have two sore areas and another couple of instruments still to face. They are turning me again, releasing my arms, standing me upright and loosening the straps around my waist and thighs, and I cling desperately to the cross until they have removed all the straps. They help me down, and I am ungainly and bloated and their assistance is entirely welcome, and then finally I am back down on the cold stone tiles and I find it necessary to bend my knees, and then to kneel and go to hands and knees.

It's not that I am groggy. I am overwhelmed, exhausted and lethargic, unable to control my body. "Are you okay?" Mistress asks, close by my side.

"I'm like jelly inside, Mistress."

Her hand comes under me, grasps my balls and squeezes gently. "You're doing fine," she whispers, and her hair tickles my chin! I have never been so close to her, I can feel her shoulder against my upper arm, and then she squeezes a little tighter and I lurch at the hurt and she giggles. "You're magnificent, Jeremiah. You know what's next, don't you?" Her tone is almost apologetic, but I know there can be no escaping it.

"The cane, Mistress?"

"The cane, Jeremiah."

"How many, Mistress?"

"A dozen, sweetheart."

"Mistress..."

"Yes, Jeremiah. Permission to speak. Go ahead."

"Is there more of the scotch, Mistress? May I...?"

She is crouching close beside me, holding me, whispering intimate little promises and now she stretches up and away from me and calls out to Mistress Candy. "Candace! Bring the scotch, and an ice cube." The girl hurries to obey. I can hear her in the distance.

"Mistress...?"

"Yes, Jeremiah."

"I'm not near transition, Mistress." It is as if I am admitting failure, and my eyes are awash with tears.

"You're closer than you think, Jeremiah. You amaze me, do you know? I will take you there, sweetheart, just trust me. You'll be there soon."

"Thank you, Mistress."

The younger woman returns with a pungent glass, and Mistress Mary puts it under my nose to let the scent of it clear my mind. I wheeze at a deep sniff of it, and then she puts it to my lips. It is just a mouthful of liquid, but it resembles a Fourth of July fireworks extravaganza!

"The cane, Jeremiah. Do you remember your safe word?"

I am surprised that I do. "Bluebird, Mistress."

"Can you get to your feet, dear?" She is close to me, steadying me. I get up, struggling to be proud. She hands me the glass. There is still about an inch of scotch, and I throw it back and savor the outburst of sensation in my mouth. I hand it back, empty, and straighten myself. I am ready to continue. She takes my arm, and although I am nude and she is in flimsy underwear we stroll like lovers in the park, arm in arm, toward the photographic garden and then off toward the wicker chair and hassock.

She leaves me then, standing alone and undressed in front of the great window, and then she returns with the cane. Mistress Mary stands before me in her bra and panties, sexy and seductive. She bends the rattan as she speaks, and it is a slender, whippy thing, flexible and cruel. I stare at it, and once again I begin to shiver with dread and terror. The cane is a wicked instrument. Six strokes across an unblemished seat can break a man. A dozen strokes on my wounded behind will be impossible!

"Twelve strokes, Jeremiah. Low and close, I'll make you pray! No restraints. I want you to bend forward at the waist and place your palms flat upon the hassock. Knees straight, feet a little bit farther apart than you've got them now just to separate the cheeks for me. If you lift your hand off the hassock I'll consider it avoidance and repeat the stroke, plus two penalty strokes at the end. You'll call for each cut, sweetheart. Over a minute since the last constitutes avoidance, so try to move it along. I'll do six from each side, so you can have a little longer after the sixth. Any questions?"

This is discipline in the formal English manner, and I am frightened. "Will you break the skin, Mistress?"

"Probably not, Jeremiah. You are tender behind, and I'm not sure it can be avoided. I hope to attend to each cheek separately so the tip will cut in close to the center groove. They'll be low, so an occasional one might tickle your anus, naughty boy. You'll know the difference from the paddle. Anything else?"

"No, thank you Mistress."

"All right, Jeremiah. When you're ready step closer to the hassock and assume your position. Again, you'll invite each stroke. Focus. You know you can do this. Focus."

"Thank you, Mistress." I am oddly eager to get on with it. To my right the garden scene is bright and cheerful. I step closer to the ottoman, spread my feet and bend forward. I can feel my ass, the residual hurt, the shrunken skin tight across the damaged musculature.

I adjust my feet slightly, heels out, toes in to increase the separation of my bottom globes. My palms are flat upon the dark green cushion, and perspiration from my underarms is coursing down the underside of my biceps. I am trembling slightly, especially at the knees. I breathe deep, concentrate on something simple.

I must not move my hands.

"Twelve with the cane, Mistress. Thank you for correcting my behavior. I will have the first at your convenience, please, Mistress." Am I insane?

WhiirrrrOPP! She has caught the left cheek, exceedingly low and the tip has landed within a fraction of the anus! The pain is deafening, my eyes run red with scarlet sensations, my knee buckles, and I think I have exclaimed something at the severity of it! Only the first! And now, as I struggle to control my reactions the pain of it wells up and multiplies in the same way that a mushroom cloud follows a nuclear blast, and I can only gasp at the discomfort! A dozen indeed! Eleven more, five more on this side, close upon that first. I search my soul for any molecule of resolve upon which I might base my preparations for the second. Oh my God... I must not move my hands!

"Thank you, Mistress. May I please have the second?"

FRRRACK! It is awful, frantic and earthshaking and perhaps the most intense moment of my life so far! But I begin to feel something; I begin to imagine that I might cope with it, overcome it.

I MUST not move my hands!

"Thank you, Mistress. May I have the third?"

WHOOOMP! She has scored a direct hit upon my anal bullseye; my knees bend involuntarily. The hurt is furious, my eyes see only yellow; I think I hear someone singing and realize it is me crying, even screaming. I rummage through my thoughts a long while before I remember that I must call for another.

I MUST NOT move my hands!

"Thank you, Mistress. May I have another?" I am not sure how many I have... HOOOWHAPP! Insanity! I am out of my head, swimming in a great crimson sea of agony and... I MUST NOT MOVE MY HANDS! I cannot take more than the twelve! "Thank you, Mistress. I... would... like... another... Please!" WHOOOACK! My hands! Did I lift them? I am beginning to go now, to test the gates, to seek solace in myself.

I WILL NOT move my hands!

"Thank you, Mistress. Would you please correct me again, Mistress?" I can arch my back slightly, go up on the balls of my feet. This is my forté, what I do, the essence of who I am and what I am.

WHAAAP! She is cutting me in half! I withdraw, shaking, trembling, blinded, frantic, unclear what it is that I must do next. I see my hands, the fingers spread upon the green cushion just below my chest. I WILL NOT move my hands! Oh! God help me, it is agony! "Thank you Mistress. May I have another?"

She makes me wait! The hurt seems to flame up a few seconds after each blow, and to magnify itself. I am struggling, nearing my nirvana, unable to escape the desperate hurt! From afar I hear something vague, someone saying something, I miss it but catch the phrase "from the other side" and I am wondering what that means when my right buttock explodes! It is altogether different now, a totally separate focus, a raw new target that cannot begin to withstand...

And still, I WILL NOT MOVE MY HANDS! "Thank you, Mistress! Please..." I cannot remember what I am supposed to say! How can it be?! It is my only hope of escaping this, of minimizing the damage! WHAAPP! Oh, sweet Jesus! Not again! I see my hands upon the cushion and remember something but I can't imagine what, but they are fastened there somehow and so I am comforted by that. I WILL NOT MOVE MY HANDS! "Thank you, Mistress, may I... ummm... Uhh, please..."

"May you please have another, Jeremiah." That's it! I feel her hand on my ass, like a spider on its web.

"May I please have another, Mistress?" I WILL NOT MOVE MY HANDS!

"Thank you, Mistress. Another..." I WILL NOT MOVE!

"Thank you, Mistress. I can, you know. Yes, I'd like another, Mistress!" I WILL NOT MOVE!

"Thank you, Mistress." I WILL NOT!

13

You must resign yourself. You must accept. It is the hardest lesson,
compared to which the pain is really nothing. – Anne Rice,
writing as A.N. Roquelaure, THE CLAIMING OF
SLEEPING BEAUTY, E.P. Dutton Publishing Company,
1983

She is very gentle, but insistent. She straightens me, and my ass has been
scalded! I kneel at the hassock, elbows and belly where my hands have been,
and I try not to lose my way. My ass throbs; it is as if I can still feel each and
every stroke of the cane! She whispers, close by my ear. "You're doing wonderfully, Jeremiah. Just relax and ride it. It's my responsibility to take you and
guide you. You're nearly there, and then it will be over and you'll be wishing we
could do it again. I've tried to excite your senses, and I still have some stimulations in store for you. Be brave, Jeremiah. You're awesome, and you'll make it
all the way." I am delirious, nearing my destination, angry at being interrupted.
The hurt is an obstacle, a huge barrier. I must overcome the hurt, and I can
only do it mentally. Her fingers caress me, encourage me. Mistress Candy
brings the glass, and it contains pineapple juice. It is good, refreshing. My
mouth was dry. From screaming? I'm not sure how well I have been able to
contain myself.

Up now, onto my feet. A bit unsteady for a moment. There are two of
them, and they lead me to the posts in front of the garden. It is beautiful, alive,
colorful. I become aware of New Age music, gentle rhythmic sounds too loose
to be considered melody. Calming, tranquil sounds that fill in the silent
moments and soothe the mind. I am almost trancelike, and yet I am acutely
aware of everything. So near to my goal! They take my arms, fasten something
'round my wrists, lift them, fasten them. And my ankles. They tug me, spread
me quite open, and I remember that I am completely naked and I hope no one
is walking in the garden. I am floating, just existing. So excited that my brain
cannot consider every detail, and so it has closed down like an eyeball's iris to
focus on what's truly important. They haul at the ropes, stretch me tighter, up

on the balls of my feet again, and then it begins. Mistress knows that I must move on, and she does not delay. The tawse!

It is a Scottish instrument. Basically, a leather strap about eighteen inches long and three across. There is a hand-carved wooden handle, and at the other end the leather has been sliced up about four inches, divided in half right up the length of the thing to give it more flexibility. Each of the tails can wrap individually, can conform and delve and excite with maddening fury, licking like a fiery tongue. Each of the tails has been soaked in brine, then seared over an oak flame to harden its edges. Once, I'm told, the tawse was found in every Scottish classroom. Pity the poor Scottish children. Perhaps that explains why Scottish men wear kilts. What's underneath is scarlet leather burned so hypersensitive that trousers are simply impossible to bear.

She begins with a series of broad applications, full across the seat of me so that the fingers snap at the outsides of my hips. Three from the right, then three from the left. It is a new variety of pain, and so different from what has gone before. The strap seems to lay over the skin and baste it with a coating of liquid fire. It paints with pain, I think, not denting or cutting like the paddle or cane. It sings more as it approaches, a deep bluesy mournful tone that erupts with a sharp slapping WHOPP! as the surface of the leather meets the surface of the buttocks.

She is relentless now, meting out her attentions in careful, rhythmical strokes that are concentrated upon my left buttock. She has started high, the fingers seeming to reach into the groove of me and burn me to the bone. The next stroke is an inch or so lower, overlapping but spreading the influence downward, and the next. I know the ultimate objective of her plan, and I can feel the crinkly little lips of my anus bulging in the aftermath of the enemas. So long ago, it seems, but all leading toward the crescendo. I am a tiny boat riding a heaving sea of discomfort, hauling at my ineffective wrists, struggling against the restraints upon my ankles. I am so close... so close... WHRRROPP!

The tawse kisses at the very edge of my rectal orifice and I arrive at the promised land. This is my destiny, the deepest truth in all of my existence. This is my fullest expression, the essence of my truth. In the brief instant between strokes of the tawse I present myself. Up on the balls of my feet I go, steeling the cords in my calves, straining. And my wrists. I drag at them, haul at the unyielding posts to gain a fraction, to allow me to stick myself out at her, to jut my backside defiantly and present it proudly in all its sacred, profane glory as the leather moans through the air and WHOOOOAPP! the hardened edge of the tail of the imported instrument scores a direct hit upon the most sensitive, private, nerve-engorged bit of my available anatomy, and I topple headlong into the sweet lagoon that is transition.

Here there is no dichotomy between pain and pleasure. In this place, this halcyon mental oasis at the end of the grueling journey, pain and pleasure marry and live happily. I am an honored guest here, allowed to visit briefly, to relax my mind and soul within the tranquil space they share, and I am aware that the strap is working the right buttock now and moving lower with each stroke toward that same sensitive button, and I hold my vividly strained position and invite it.

This is, of course, what I am. What I must do. There is no choice, no decision. I cannot avoid it. This defines me! I am Samson to her Delilah, shorn of my hair, my strength, my every material thing. I am alone, utterly alone in this chamber on the other side of the continent from my life. Nothing matters here except my heart. Not my job, my family, my money, or my car. Not my college degree, my professional experience, my annual bonus or my retirement plan. Certainly not my golf trophies. What matters here, of course, is what *really* matters anywhere. My heart. My endurance. My mettle. Mistress separates me from all but my essence. Here, I can only do it well, accept it proudly, perform my part with dignity and grace. Despite the pain, I have no choice. I cannot succumb to it. That realization sweeps over me like a cool, refreshing breeze. It is as if I have gotten the proverbial second wind. I jut my bottom back to her, rise up on the balls of my feet and strain to separate the buttocks, to provide her with a better, wider, more susceptible target. I can take whatever she's giving, and I will! It is not defiant, it is teamwork, my acceptance complementing her inflictions, an intellectual game gone spiritual. I am floating upon the breeze of ecstasy, flying as an eagle must, over hill and dale and all of life, looking down and recognizing the valleys but somehow immune to them. Everything is smoothed here, sensual and accommodating. I have left the obstacles behind. Yes, it still hurts! It hurts in the most fiendish way, but I can take it, and I can overcome it. This is the point! This is the essence of my manhood, and I show it best when the torturer and the spectators are women.

This is my ultimate statement; the woman sees my commitment and my heart, and I know that Mistress, of all women, will recognize it and appreciate it. Oh, how I must exert myself for her! And my thoughts spread like a summer evening's fog over a shaded pond. I do not abuse women. I adore women, place them on pedestals, suffer for them, exert myself in their behalf. I have always been different from other boys and men, less cruel, more adoring. I will kneel before a woman and kiss and lick her private parts and be grateful for the juices that grace my tongue. I will tongue her toes, her ass, her menstrual blood, and savor the opportunity. I have never raised my hand to any woman, never given anything but my best. Only here can I feel understood; only here am I appreciated, but my truth is real and I do not care to be like other men. I do not wish to be crude, to swagger and bully and demean femininity. I wish to be seen, to uncover my organs and be touched by a woman's gentle hands. To be tested and found true, as now, and to journey with her to this glorious magical oasis where I am reassured and reinforced, for having visited here I know that I can cope with anything outside, that I am truly masculine and capable and strong. I have exhibited courage this night, and purpose, and resolve. I have given free rein to my heart and soul, and so the sting of the leather brings my male blood to boil and it becomes a powerful sweet syrup which will sustain me.

All of my senses are at maximum revs and melted together. I smell the scent of oranges and cowhide and Chanel, my head reverberates to the sounds of the wind and birds chirping and the casual tones of an electric piano. My vision is overwhelmed with swirling bright colors, whites and yellows and streaks of red and green, a shifting kaleidoscopic tableau that is the most beautiful collection of images I have ever seen. I seem to taste sweetness, perhaps citrus, and all of it is linked inexorably to the sensations of touch welling up from underneath my rear. I have, I think, entered heaven, or achieved the ultimate psychedelic high, and I want to prolong it, to stay here, to rent a room.

But life is inevitable change. My ass hurts differently now, attracting my thoughts back. I cramp my eyes shut, inhale deeply trying to stay! "Jeremiah." Someone is calling from afar, a woman's voice from across the valley, perhaps on the wind. "Jeremiah". It isn't my real name, I know, or is it? I am being spanked again, and I am deathly sore! "Jeremiah." A siren's song drawing me toward disaster. My wrists are stretched high overhead, I cannot retrieve them! My bottom hurts! I dare to open my eyes, to view the sunlit garden, the brilliant flowers. Mistress is reaching around me now, wiping away the froth from my penis which is bloated and twitching. "Welcome back." She is beautiful in white lace bra and panties, blonde and smiling, inviting. She does not stimulate me to orgasm, but instead goes behind me and spanks my flaming backside with her palm and I realize that she has been handspanking me for a while, that this was the change that brought me back. It is all familiar now, and I begin to cry. I am back.

When I am fully aware she pauses and I become aware of the heat radiating from my bruised behind. "Mistress Candace," she calls.

"Yes, Mistress?"

"You have an agreement with our guest, Mistress. He is to take six with the cane for failing to accept the full second enema." I cannot!

"Yes, Mistress."

"In my opinion, Mistress, Jeremiah has performed admirably this evening. With your concurrence, I would like to suspend sentence and spare him those six. I don't feel they would have a measurable effect upon him, Mistress. He stands corrected, don't you agree?"

"Yes, Mistress."

I dare to relax, to anticipate the end of it. I am immediately hauled back to the reality of my situation by a volley of hard, stinging hand spanks! SMACK! SMACK! WHACK! CRACK! I bend a knee, twist my hips to avoid it. I can do no more, no better. She pauses.

14

*Social rules say that straight is better than gay. The rules also say
that vanilla is better than kinky. So there is hiding. And a part of
us is cut off from ourselves. – Guy Baldwin, M.S., TIES THAT
BIND, Daedalus Publishing, 1993*

*[Professional female floggers] must have a quick and intuitive
method of observing the various aberrations of the human mind,
and be ready and quick to humour and relieve them... when an
elegant high bred woman wields (the birch) with dignity of mien
and grace of attitude, then both the practice and suffering becomes a
real pleasure... – St. George H. Stock, ROMANCE OF
CHASTISEMENTS, 1866 (writing of "an establishment" at 7
Circus Road, St. John's Wood, London, where the poet A.C.
Swinburne, among others, was regularly chastised by two
outwardly respectable ladies)*

It is over. I am, in some strange way, saddened.

It is over, and I must exist again, for who knows how long, fueled by
what I have learned tonight. I must carry the secret elixir, telling no one, and
deal with everyday concerns like bills and voice mail and political choices.
Underarm odors and crab grass. I will have to be "normal" until the next time,
whenever that may be.

I sob as they take me down, fall to my knees and weep into my hands.
The younger one is concerned; have they done something wrong? But the
older woman, the saintly Mistress Mary, knows. "He has visited a better
place," she whispers, "and he wanted to stay longer." Her fingers rustle my
hair. "Come on, Jeremiah. You're supposed to take me out to dinner." I open
my eyes and through the swirling salty tears I see her foot to my left and I bend
forward to bathe it in kisses. She lifts me by my hair. "Now Mistress Candy,
Jeremiah. She was here throughout every minute." A maroon boot toe is
presented from my right, and I bend to adore it. It is fragrant with the scent of

leather and polish, further returning my awareness to the present. I kiss with heartfelt passion. Her cheeks are streaked with tears.

"I'm going to freshen up and get dressed, Candace. Take Jeremiah to the shower, and bring him his clothes. And don't you dare forget that he's forbidden to experience orgasm." Mistress Mary swirls away, still in bra and panties and those long, smoky gartered stockings. Her body is graceful in a mature, rounded way, and I am thrilled to watch her departing bottom wiggle, framed by the garters and stockings and her lovely white underpants. She is still on heels, and her derriere juts provocatively, but I think I can detect some fatigue. She has exerted herself in dealing with me. I will recall this vision of her in many, many dreams.

"That was awesome," Candy whispers, breaking my enchanted spell, taking my hand in hers. I am naked, she is clothed head to toe in glamorous dark red leather. "I thought you had had enough halfway through the paddle."

"I had." She surprises me by fastening my wrists behind me again, and then the clamps and leash to my nipples. "I thought we were finished, Mistress." She giggles as I grimace.

"Mistress asked me to take you to the shower. This is how we transport clients in this house, Jeremiah. I'm sorry. Do the clamps hurt too much?" She is sincere.

"No, not considering the last couple of hours. It's all right, Mistress." She screws them a little tighter, until she sees fresh tears in my eyes.

She gathers up the instruments and my underwear, extinguishes candles, and pops a tape out of the stereo. A strong whiff of orange scent assails my nose, and my mind reacts. "At one point I was overwhelmed with the orange scent," I tell her.

Mistress Candy is overjoyed! "Please, Jeremiah, if it worked for you, tell Mistress. When you were struggling so I brought the candle near you hoping that the scent might attract some small bit of your attention away from the pain. She wants everything flowery and sweet, and I like the earthy scents. They have one called Autumn Leaves, but she says it wouldn't be good. She's lived in California all her life. She wouldn't recognize the scent of autumn; they don't have autumn here."

"Where are you from, Mistress?" Do I dare ask?

"New Hampshire. We have real autumns in New Hampshire."

"I thought you were from the east coast!"

She takes up the lead and begins to tug me toward the door. "I've been here five years. I'm doing graduate work at UCLA. I got my bachelor's in psychology in May."

"And this is how you're working your way through college, Mistress?" She snaps out the lights and tugs me into the hallway. My hips and behind are very, very sore. My arse feels swollen, bulbous, as if it is hanging on me like freight.

"Yes, but I'm also studying psychology. This is a very well-equipped psych lab, don't you think?"

"Very! And what do you want to do as a career?"

"I want to be Mistress Mary when I grow up!" She laughs. "I want to work with abused women, spousal abuse, you know. Issues like that."

"I think you'll be terrific, Mistress. Will you stay out here?"

She shrugs her lovely shoulders. "I don't know. I suppose it depends upon where I get an offer, but I really want to go back toward home. You know, maybe Boston. I miss the cold weather, and L.A.'s such a phony, fast-paced environment." We have arrived at the first room. She drops the instruments and gathers up my clothes. I feel that I have journeyed back to reality, and I feel drained and leaden. A little over an hour ago I was taken from here, led away to a special vacation land. Now I must return, get dressed, go back to my office and the e-mails and phone calls. I must, at this moment, reconcile the experience I have just endured and put it into some perspective with the life I lead outside this place. This evening is simply a disruption in that existence, a holiday. "The shower is just down here. Where are you going tonight?" Mistress Candy's voice drags me back toward reality.

"I haven't a clue. Mistress has planned everything. What time is it?"

"About ten after eight. You'll be out the door by eight-thirty. Oh, and Jeremiah?" She has stepped close, and her eyes are dark and expressive. I pause. "I, uhh, want to tell you how much I appreciate what you did tonight. I know you don't know what other guys do, but I've never seen anyone endure as much as you just did. Mistress told me I could expect to see into your soul tonight, and I think that's true. Do me a favor, please?"

I am surprised. "Sure."

"Turn around, just for a minute." Puzzled, I comply. I am still in bondage, with clamps on my nipples attached to a leash. I offer her my wounded bottom, fully expecting her to hurt me again.

She is behind me, but I know exactly what she is doing. She goes to her knees and, leaning forward, she kisses my ass! First the left buttock, then the right. Her voice is wavering. "My little brother used to ask me to kiss his boo-boos and make them all better, Jeremiah. I've got to tell you, he never had boo-boos like these! I just want you to know, like, well... how very much I learned tonight, and how very much I admire you." She kisses me again, both cheeks of my ass, and then she remains kneeling and I think she is weeping softly. Her voice is choked and raspy. "So many guys come here, and they're so superficial. It's like they're defiant, you know. They want to prove we can't hurt them, but they wouldn't even imagine doing what you did tonight. They want a little spanking over Mistress's knee, or maybe a few taps with a crop. I don't understand why they come here, and most of them can't either. Mistress sees a couple of other guys, there's a guy named Michael from New Orleans, and Keith from Savannah, they like it heavy but nothing like you. You get so deep into it, like a religion or something. You made me proud tonight, if you can understand when I say that. I get a kick out of being here, but tonight was something very worthwhile and special. Thank you." She kisses me again, and I think she is weeping. She wipes her eyes, unfastens my wrists, releases my breasts. I recoil at the hurt, and she laughs through her tears, and I laugh too. "Get your shower, Jeremiah. When you finish I'll rub some cream onto those marks. You're going to be very uncomfortable at dinner! Please, go now. Don't keep the Mistress waiting." And then, before I hurry off to the shower, I kiss her cheek. I taste her tears, and I whisper a gentle "Thank you, Mistress."

It is over. The light is fluorescent and clinical, and I turn myself to the full-length mirror. Oh my God! My behind is dark and mottled in shades of maroon and scarlet, black, purple and blue. It is rippled and welted, striped, swollen and bulging so that the skin is stretched shiny. The sexy young Mistress closes the toilet lid and sits down. The shower curtain is translucent, and Mistress Candy will watch me to be sure I don't masturbate. I step into the tub and pull the plastic curtain closed. The water is refreshing, but when the warm torrent splashes onto my raw backside I leap and almost slip. When it is time to wash there I try to be gentle, but it is too sensitive. I am concerned. How will I sit in a business meeting tomorrow?

When I emerge from the shower Mistress Candy is still sitting on the toilet, and she seems very juvenile and curious. Her dark red leather outfit is snug and sexy, but her expression seems innocent, either bewildered or petulant. The towel is thick and luxurious. Her eyes are relentless, searching for answers to questions I don't recognize.

She thrusts out a hand. My panties. "They're very nice," she whispers, her eyes large and intimidating. "Did you choose them?"

"Yes." My thoughts return to the Macy's for a brief instant, but I cannot recall the saleswoman's name.

"Will you relieve yourself later?"

"Do you mean sexually? I suppose so."

"Me too, if Mistress Mary allows it. You have a beautiful penis, Jeremiah. The veins just bulge out of it. I can't believe you stayed erect so long. Isn't that uncomfortable for a man?" She looks like a little girl.

"Not really. Thank you for the compliment. I think you are very lovely too."

"Thank God I'm wearing leather pants. I'm soaked halfway to my knees. I'm forbidden to touch myself without the Mistress's permission. I'm twenty-two years old and I have a college degree and I have to ask permission to touch my own body, Jeremiah. Isn't that bizarre?"

15

More commonly, gentlemen patrons paid generous sums to receive
the disciplinary ministrations of "nurses," "governesses," or
"schoolmistresses," as flagellant prostitutes euphemistically were
known. There are a number of reasons why men sought out these
"services." A frequent side effect, or aftermath, of being beaten on
the buttocks is stimulation of the primary sexual organ. – Patricia
Anderson, WHEN PASSION REIGNED, Basic Books, a
division of HarperCollins Publishers, 1995

Mistress Mary's dress is the same as before, conservative and business-like, but also close-fitting and sexy. She gathers a few implements into a heavy black leather equipment bag, requires me to kiss Mistress Candy's toes and thank her for my disciplines, and especially the enemas.

"Bring my bag," the Mistress orders, and then, "We'll take my car." Out the door into the warm Southern California air, it is evening and I hear the sound from a neighbor's radio. I am incredibly sore, my ass feels like a balloon swollen with liquid discomfort. My entire body drags under the lethargy of fatigue. It is eleven o'clock by my body's clock, bedtime, and we are just going out. She leads me to a black Land Rover, a gleaming dark monster with a dented right rear corner. The heavy bag in the back, I clamber up and onto the passenger's seat. All of the evening's pain rushes back into my behind, and I lurch and exclaim with a hushed "Oh!"

"You recall *The Story of O*," she says, firing up the engine. "The touch of leather enhances your bottom, Jeremiah. Put your trousers at your ankles and your panties at your knees." An uncomfortable task, and my ass resists. I feel ungainly and ridiculous, and when my clothes are finally positioned to the lady's liking my cock is standing proudly again, out from under the waist belt of the safety harness, and I feel the blood rushing to my neck and face. Thank God it is dark! She watches my efforts, smiling, and when I am settled she touches my wrist and says, "Good boy. I have not released you from your disciplines, Jeremiah. Remember, this is a field trip. I expect your full obedience at all times. Is that clear?"

"Yes, Mistress." My erection is dissolving, and I can feel its wetness. I hope it does not seep down to the costly leather seat. She reverses out of the driveway and accelerates up the street, switches on the radio and pushes a button to call up an oldies station. The Bee-Gees are singing "Holiday."

We are on a major artery, three lanes of traffic each direction, a myriad of lighted signs, suburban automotive pandemonium. Paused for a red light, she says, "Hands alongside you on the seat, Jeremiah. You are forbidden to cover yourself." Billy Joel whistles a mournful introduction to "The Stranger," then sings of secret faces in satin and steel, silk and leather. A most curious song! At the next red light a furniture truck pulls up alongside my window and I struggle to maintain my position.

Mistress accelerates away, touches my naked thigh lightly, shifts to second gear. We turn left, then right into a K-Mart parking lot. She parks in one of the diagonal rows, grabs her purse and climbs out of the truck. I hold position. We are under a huge ultraviolet light, and my nudity is clearly illuminated.

She opens my door. "Dress yourself." I scramble to do so, wincing as I stretch and buffet my behind. She closes the door and punches a remote button to lock the vehicle. As we walk toward the brightly lit iconic store she takes my hand in hers. "I love the panty you wore tonight, Jeremiah, but it is wet and stained with your discharge. I want you to be obedient and cheerful as I deal with your habitual oozing. You're a naughty little boy. Do you understand?"

"Yes, Mistress."

K-Marts are the same everywhere, and it is oddly exciting to walk into the harsh fluorescent lights holding hands with this exciting, beautiful woman who is not my wife. I am on the opposite edge of the continent from home, but still there is a chance that I will be recognized, discovered. The Mistress is dressed in conservative, professional clothes that seem to magnify her beauty, and she turns heads. She walks with a stern, purposeful gait and takes me directly to the lingerie department. It is a strangely sad area densely displayed with intimate feminine garments, but so different in ambience from lingerie in the more upscale stores. These are utilitarian clothes, and the manner in which they are presented is neither erotic or exotic. Huge assortments are jumbled on rickety plastic hangers, often askew, sometimes rumpled or even soiled. The colors and prints are harsh, even bizarre. In the interest of economy, the prevalent packaging is cardboard or clear and rattly plastic with garish yellow or red lettering, often festooned with day-glo stickers or sale tags.

"May I help you?" The salesgirl is a mildly attractive young woman in glasses. She has a sincere look, a ready smile under a heavy mane of curly dark hair and is wearing black slacks and starched white short-sleeve blouse with a plastic nametag that boldly invites us to call her Sally.

"Hanes Her Way," the Mistress responds.

"Right over here." She leads us to a tall display. "What size?"

"You're a six, aren't you?" Mistress squeezes my fingers in hers. I feel the scarlet blush envelop my face instantly.

"Yes, Mistress." It is a low whisper. I look at the floor, at the two sets of ladylike feet.

"Six. Is there something pink?"

The young woman seems to be ignoring the previous exchange. "Yes, ma'am. Briefs or high-cuts?"

"Briefs, please."

She takes down a plastic package. "This set has pink, purple, and blue," hands them to the Mistress, then steals a quick glance at me. Of course, Mistress has released my hand, and I feel somewhat adrift.

My beautiful accomplice holds the package toward me and speaks in a low, conspiratorial tone. "Look at the lettering on the waistband, Jeremiah. You're going to wear a bold HER WAY label all around you so anyone who sees your panties will know that your Mistress has chosen them for you." Without pausing she turns toward the sales clerk. "I'm a professional disciplinarian and trainer, a dominatrix, and Jeremiah has been assigned to me for lessons in deportment in the company of ladies." The woman seems amused. Her quick smile multiplies my humiliation.

Now the Mistress takes a half-step toward the other woman. "Thank you so very much, Sally." It is, once again, conspiratorial in tone.

"You're welcome." She smiles.

"Thank the lady, Jeremiah."

"Thank you, ma'am." I keep my eyes respectfully lowered.

"You're welcome."

"I want you to carry these, Jeremiah." She thrusts the crackling plastic package into my right hand, seizes my left and tugs me away. I am scarlet as we head toward the crowded checkouts. Mistress grips my bicep now, and whispers close to my ear. "You did very well back there. Keep up your good behavior. Does your bottom tingle?"

"Terribly, Mistress."

"Good."

We are in line to pay for our purchases. I am blushing maroon, steaming from the neck up, trying to hold a crinkly package so that the women around me won't notice. Mistress, of course, wants it prominently but naturally displayed, and so I hold it in my hand instead of under my arm. She makes a point of talking to me, openly discussing the comfort I will experience in cotton panties. The lady ahead of us in line glances at me nervously, her eyes avoiding mine. She knows, at the very least, that we are together and I am the only one holding merchandise, and that the merchandise is a package of panties, and that I am blushing scarlet.

Mistress notices my consternation and takes my arm again. "You're doing fine, Jeremiah," she whispers. "Are you proud to serve me?"

"Yes, Mistress." It's true. I try to hold my head up high. I am with the most beautiful woman in the store, and she cares enough to deal with my needs. The checkout clerk is a youthful Latino, probably Mexican. She has smouldering dark eyes, long hair and a thick accent. As she records the other woman's purchases I put my meager package onto the counter. The woman bustles off and the conveyor hauls my embarrassing package to the girl. Her eyes flicker up toward mine, and I see instant recognition alter her face. Mistress leans close to me and says," Do you have enough money, sweetheart?" It is just enough to confirm the girl's thoughts, her eyes dart to Mistress and back to me. I am holding out a ten dollar bill.

"Are you sure of the size?" the girl asks, her eyes boring holes in me. "These cannot be returned after they are opened."

Mistress leans close behind me. "He's very sure of the size, Miss. Thank you, but it's not his first time buying panties. Is it, Jeremiah?" I want to crawl.

"No, Mistress."

"And you won't ooze your disgusting slime into your pretty new pink panties, will you, Jeremiah?" I fear I might dissolve of humiliation!

"No, Mistress."

"No, sweetheart, because what happens to your little bottom when I find wetness in your panties, Jeremiah?"

"I... uhh, you... spank me, Mistress."

The girl has taken the bill and recorded the sale. She is counting out my change, paying huge attention to the drawer of money as she listens to our exchange. "Yes, Jeremiah, "Six forty-one," she says. "Your change is three dollars and fifty-nine cents... Jeremiah." Her eyes are black and hard, and they see through me. She looks down at my hand and carefully counts out my change. "Sixty, seventy, seventy-five, that's seven Jeremiah. And eight, and nine, and ten. Thank you for shopping at K-Mart, and have a nice evening, Jeremiah. And you too, Madame. Spank him hard for me." She hands me the package and my receipt, no bag. I almost stumble as I move away from the cash register.

"Just a moment, Jeremiah." Mistress touches my arm, halting me. Clutching my arm now, she leads me to the information desk near the broad doorway. I am acutely aware of my cargo, my panties, and it seems that every eye is upon me.

"May help you?" It is an older woman, very heavyset and unkempt. A red swatch of label tape on her plastic nametag tells us that she is a manager. Her eyes are riveted to my package of panties. The receipt is obvious; she is not accusing me of stealing.

"We've just purchased some new underpants for my gentleman friend, madame, and I'd like him to slip into them as soon as possible. Is it possible that we might use a changing booth, or perhaps the ladies room?" I want to disappear!

The woman's eyes devour me, flashing from my package to my face and back. "Is there some kind of problem?"

"Only that I have him in a very expensive satin panty and he has become aroused and has oozed across the front of it. I want to put him into the more absorbent cotton." I can feel veins bulging in my forehead and my neck.

"What is he, some kinda pansy?" She is chewing gum!

"No, ma'am. He's in training."

"We've got maxipads on sale. Aisle seven." She chuckles.

"Thank you, we have them in the car." The woman's eyebrows arch. She picks up a phone, pages someone in lingerie.

"You just wait on a couple, pack of three panties for the guy? Yeah, well, she wants him to wear them home. Yeah, that's right. You got a changing booth open? Yeah. Yeah, I'll send them right back. He's got a receipt. Yeah, thanks, I owe you one." She hangs up, looks at Mistress with a tired, cynical expression. "See the girl in lingerie. And when you leave, I want to examine your package." She swivels her greying head in amazement.

Sally greets us at the perimeter of her department, obviously worried. "They're supposed to be for women, but it's slow tonight. If he doesn't attract attention." Her eyes mock and humiliate me, and Mistress Mary swells with pride. We follow her through the maze of racks and displays to a row of locked doors. She has keys attached to her belt, and she unlocks one door and drags it open to reveal a tiny closet littered with discarded underclothes, plastic hangers, and approximately forty thousand straight pins.

"In you go, Jeremiah. I'll expect you to knock when you're in the pink ones, so we can see how they fit you. Hurry up, we have dinner reservations." I have never been so glad to close a door on two attractive women!

There are beads of sweat on my forehead. I hear Mistress say to the young clerk, "He will do anything I ask!" I try to change quickly, but to do so requires considerable exertion! My ass is stiffening, hurting viciously when I bend at the waist. When I am safely settled into the humiliating panties I tap upon the door.

There is a pause. "Open it, Jeremiah. Come on, we haven't got all night!" I comply, but with hesitation. Mistress yanks the door open wide. Sally is blushing now, but she stares at my loins. "Turn around," Mistress orders, although it is just a whisper. I do, and then I feel her fingers at the leg opening under my right buttock, and she tugs the fabric back. "This is why he obeys me, Sally. If he doesn't, he doesn't sit down comfortably for a few days." I hear the woman gasp. "Get dressed, Jeremiah." Mistress closes the door.

16

Here is a rule to remember in future, when anything tempts you to feel bitter: Not, "This is misfortune," but, "To bear this worthily is good fortune." – Marcus Aurelius

The restaurant is on Slauson Avenue, which my mind somehow associates with a Johnny Carson comedy routine. It is a tiny place, and there are only six cars in the parking lot. I am once again naked below the waist, trousers puddled at my ankles and the bright new pink panty with HER WAYs stenciled all around the waistband is stretched between my knees. "Get dressed," she says softly, and while I am struggling to comply she takes my beautiful ivory satin panty out of the crackling plastic package and examines it. "It's really wet," she whispers thoughtfully. "Maybe we should get you some maxipads!" My ass hurts terribly, I am hungry, and I am getting tired. She hangs the sodden briefs from the rear view mirror. "The kids will think it's some guy's trophy," she jokes.

"It is, Mistress."

I feel her touch against my left elbow. "Jeremiah, look at me."

She is beautiful, perhaps the most lovely woman I have ever seen. The light is dim in the Range Rover's front seat, but she is ravishing! Her eyes seem to penetrate me. "Jeremiah, I have never done this before tonight. I have never taken a man into K-Mart to buy panties, and I have never asked to use a dressing room so he can change, and I've never taken a client to dinner. There are a couple of reasons why I'm doing all this tonight, and I'll tell you some of them later. Right now I want you to know that the primary reason I'm doing all this with you is because you exert yourself so for me. Your performance tonight was simply awesome, Jeremiah. Simply awesome. I watch you and I marvel. If this business is about pain and pleasure, then I owe it to myself to spend a few pleasant moments with you while your ass is in tatters. I hope you will enjoy dining with me, too. I'll work you, silly boy, even here, but wouldn't you be a little disappointed if I didn't?" I nod in agreement. "This is a wonderful little place, Jeremiah. I come here often. It's dark and intimate and quiet, and the food is delicious. It would be my very great pleasure if you would accompany me, sweetheart. And Jeremiah, you are still in discipline. Thank you!" She leans far forward toward me and kisses my cheek, then opens her door and steps down.

When she opens my door and I alight from the truck my arse is agonizingly stiff and sore. I walk awkwardly the first few steps, almost like an old man. She pauses outside the door. "Kneel and kiss my toes, Jeremiah." I comply, but carefully. My behind does not bend well. "Good boy. Come on up, let's eat. I'm famished."

I open the door for her, of course, and the interior is darker than the outside. The maitre d' recognizes her, and she sparkles. I cannot hear his words, but I hear her say, "... something along the wall. My friend has had a terrible spanking tonight, Alfred, and he won't be sitting for dinner. I hope we won't attract too much attention, or be in anyone's way."

"Of course, madam." He leads us into the depths of the dark, past tables bathed in soft candle glow. The piped-in music is gentle, strings and piano, romantic. We arrive at a back alcove, and Alfred seats the Mistress and then drags away a chair from along the wall and bows slightly to encourage me to slip into the opening. She accepts a heavy leather-bound menu, but when Alfred offers one to me she dismisses him with a hand gesture. "I will order for us both, Alfred." He retreats.

"Alfred is the owner, and also one of my clients, Jeremiah." He is a solid, European-looking man, dark squinting eyes and a jovial smile, black hair turning to grey at the temples. He obviously adores the Mistress, but who wouldn't? Her features are softened by the flickering candle, and very lovely. "Bring some Moet et Chandon, Albert. And a glass of water for the gentleman. Thank you." He bends at the waist, then scurries away. "I thought you would be more comfortable standing," she smiles. "Do you mind?"

"Not at all, Mistress." In fact, I like the idea immensely.

"And how are your new panties?"

"I am very sensitive in that area just now, Mistress, and they don't bring me any undeserved comfort. But they fit well, and I wear them proudly."

"A splendid answer, Jeremiah. Would you enjoy lamb?"

"That would be fine, Mistress."

Alfred returns with champagne, and my water. She orders appetizers, abalone with orange sauce and shallots, and then a main course of Grecian lamb. Alfred pops the cork and other diners begin to notice that I am remaining standing.

When we are alone she invites me to kneel at the table, or to stand close by and stoop so that she can speak to me in a normal voice. I am unbearably sore, and I choose to stand. She pours champagne for herself and for me. She lifts her glass and tips it slightly toward me. "To honesty," she says, and her smiling eyes are as bubbly and joyous as the wine. "To freedom, Mistress," I add, and we sip. With the champagne the woman changes. The studious, strict Mistress Mary (quite contrary) becomes insouciant and abandoned.

"Thank you for the gift, Jeremiah. Candace brought it to me, and it was very thoughtful. I, uhh... have to tell you something," she beams, her joyous eyes defying mine. "I won't see you again, Jeremiah. I'm going to be married. We've purchased a horse farm in Oregon and I'm going to train Arabian stallions."

"Oh, Mistress." I am stricken, unable to mirror her joy. What a loss! I go to my knees at the table and lean close to her.

"Hey, come on!" she exclaims, surprised at my reaction. "Be glad for me, Jeremiah."

"I am glad if you'll be happy, Mistress, but I can't help but feel a loss. I'm sorry."

"That's very touching, Jeremiah, especially from you. The reason I wanted to come here tonight was to tell you about my plans, but also to tell you what you've meant to me. How many sessions have we done?"

"I think this was the sixth, Mistress."

"And how long have I known you? Three years?"

"That's about right, Mistress."

Her fingers creep across the tablecloth and lightly capture mine. "Well, I want to tell you, Jeremiah, that of all my clients, you stand out. You understand this activity, Jeremiah. You exert yourself, both mentally and physically, to find enlightenment and fulfillment in the disciplines. You actually take lessons from the rod, dear boy, and then I learn from you, and I want to say that I admire you. You're inspired. It has been my very great pleasure to work with you, to assist you in your quest. I only hope... well, I hope that I've helped you." Her fingers leave mine, and she lifts her champagne again. "This is a celebration, my dear friend, and I want to celebrate you! You're one hell of a man, Jeremiah. One hell of a dreamer, one hell of a daredevil." She pauses, her eyes visibly misting. "I recognize the significance of what you've done with me." Her voice is a strained, cracking whisper. "I can't find words to tell you how I have marveled at your heart. The thought and significance you put into every gesture, every sentence, and that you wring out of every stripe I've ever put across your flesh. I wish I knew what you know, Jeremiah. I wish I under-stood, that I could go the places you go. I've enjoyed sharing your fantasies, Jeremiah. You're an inspiration. I hope your bottom is on fire." She tries to force a laugh, and tips the rim of her glass again. "Thank you." Her voice cracks with emotion.

"You took me to those places, Mistress. You hold the key that unlocks the door, and you have always brought me back again. I've seen other dominants, Mistress, but I swear, never anyone else as insightful, as understanding and... effective as you. I thank you, Mistress." I am on my knees, and my eyes are flooding. It is all too easy to slip beneath the table's edge, to kiss her feet.

"Come up here!" she hisses, almost laughing. "People are watching!" I couldn't care less.

Dinner is delicious, but all too brief. We talk as old friends, discussing topics that range from marriage to Oregon, seamed stockings to the Santa Monica pier, the stock market and the Dodgers. "What do you think of Candace?" she asks.

"She's very good, Mistress."

"Her father is a client. She knew that he was into S&M, but not that I was his Mistress. She saw my advertisement in a magazine and called me. We talked a few times, and then she came by and watched a couple of sessions. It was weeks before I discovered the connection with her father. She's a natural. She will be carrying on after I'm gone, Jeremiah. Your next session in L.A. will be with Mistress Candace."

"She tells me she's a college student?"

"Yes. Her dad's buying my equipment and renting the house for her. Putting her into business, as it were. She graduated with a 3.4 from UCLA. She's very, very bright."

"So her father knows?"

"You haven't seen our ad in DDI? Yes, he knows. Isn't she beautiful?"

"She's very attractive, Mistress."

"You're such a gentleman. The last guy I asked said she had the prettiest ass in five states!" She laughs.

"She didn't show it to me, Mistress."

"In that outfit? Come on, Jeremiah. Did she explain to you that all of the enema equipment had been sterilized to hospital standards?"

"No, Mistress. I just kind of assumed..."

"Jeremiah!" She erupts. "This is very important! Are you certain that she did not mention that the equipment was clinically sterile?"

"I'm certain, Mistress."

The beautiful woman searches the depths of her purse, extracts a cellular phone and punches the buttons. There is a pause. "Candace?" Her voice is hushed but insistent. "Is everything done?" ..."Your studying?" Mistress pushes back her hair, tugs an earring, checks her wristwatch. Her voice is an octave lower, and cold. "At ten-thirty, Candace, I want you to go to the studio and illuminate only the wooden trestle. Put out my cane, remove your clothing and fold it neatly, then stand with your hands at your sides and contemplate, and wait for me. You'll have eight strokes full across, and next time you'll remember to assure my client that the enema equipment has been sterilized. There are diseases out there that can kill, girl. Do you understand?" "...We'll be home before eleven. You're going to learn a lesson from this, girl. Concentrate." She punches off the phone. "I'm sorry, Jeremiah. It's the only way she will learn. She hates the cane!" I feel horribly guilty.

"May I say something, Mistress?" I am kneeling again, the table's surface is at the level of my chest. I sip from my coffee. The pain from my seat is seeping into the musculature almost as tea soaks out from a teabag into the surrounding hot water. She allows me to speak. "Isn't it sad, Mistress, that we cannot be friends with this common interest? If we shared any other interest: tennis, boats, bowling, flower arranging, horses, whatever it may be, we could be friends. I mean, if we shared an interest in assault weapons and machine guns we would be considered less of a threat to society! I understand that it has to be this way, but I can't even send you a card or a present when you get married. Because your treatments require that I take my pants down they are colored with a stigma, and I can't even express my joy or my hopes for your future at a time like this. If I multiply what I'm feeling times all of the other clients who care for you it becomes a very sad commentary, Mistress."

She looks at me with great tenderness and caring. "Thank you very much, Jeremiah. My clients have expressed great love for me, and that isn't a sad thing. I feel like an athlete leaving at the top of her game! I have to mention that I don't know your real name, either. There is a price to pay for freedom, of course. But don't say we can't be friends. You are one of my dearest friends, and if you like I will take your name and address and invite your wife and yourself to my wedding."

"You cause me more pain with that statement than anything you have done tonight, Mistress."

"I have a reputation as a cruel person, Jeremiah. In truth, I am only a realist. You hurt yourself by living a lie. You cheat yourself by saying you cannot when in fact you can. If you can withstand my tawse you can withstand any discomfort associated with accepting honesty into your life."

I know she is right, from her perspective. I have taken another path, and I am not unhappy. "I have been married to a beautiful woman for almost twenty years, Mistress. She doesn't understand S&M, but she is a good, loving woman and my life's companion, the mother of my children. She cannot see it, and I cannot say it in so many words, but I am her slave. Except for occasional moments like tonight, I set aside my needs for something more important. I do without so that I can share life with her. It is, in my mind, a dominant-submissive relationship. I hope that you will be as happy with your new husband as I have been with my wife."

"Thank you, Jeremiah." Mistress Mary squeezes my fingers, her eyes awash with emotion. I lift her hand to my lips and kiss her fingers, close my eyes and savor her presence for a precious, fleeting moment.

"Thank you, Mistress." She sips a little more champagne and smiles radiantly, basking in the warm and intimate moment. That's her secret, I realize. Mistress Mary lives in the moment, squeezing the essence out of life, getting it all.

She recognizes sensation as the essence of life, be it sight, sound, taste, or touch. She finds the most vivid or exquisite sensations and takes big, bold helpings for herself. She accepts others and invites them along on her adventures. I wish we could attend her wedding. I am very privileged to know her, and I hope that the marks she has engraved across my seat will last a long, long time. I feel them deeply, and will wear them with pride.

It's getting late when Alfred brings coffee and the check. "Jeremiah," she says, "show Alfred what I've done to your bottom."

"How, Mistress?"

"Well, I don't think he'll want to get a flashlight and look up your pant leg, silly! Bare yourself, bend forward and put your hands on your knees."

"Mistress, I have other customers..." Alfred objects.

"You have only one other couple, 'way over there. They're paying absolutely no attention to us, Alfred. They're nuzzling and whispering, lost in their own conspiracy. She wants to see more commitment before she'll sleep with him again. They don't know we're on the same planet. Do it, Jeremiah."

I loosen my belt. "Turn to the wall so the candle will shine on you, sweetheart." She is whispering. My pants tumble to my knees. She touches me, points out my special underpants to the startled waiter. "Display, Jeremiah." Her fingers leave my thigh. I am so sore! I shrug down my panties. "Up on the balls of your feet, Jeremiah."

Alfred whispers, "My God!"

Part Two

17

As children we feared that the sexual feeling would lose us the love of someone upon whom we depended for life itself; the guilt, planted early and deep, arose because we didn't want the forbidden sexual feeling to go away. Now it is fantasy's job to get us past the fear/ guilt/anxiety. The characters and story lines we conjure up take what was most forbidden, and with the omnipotent power of the mind, make the forbidden work for us so that now, just for a moment, we may rise to orgasm and release. – Nancy Friday, WOMEN ON TOP, Pocket Books, 1991

How had it come to this? It was the nineties, I was in my mid-forties, battered and scarred by life. My marriage was unraveling, my home a battle-field. In a moment of utter frustration I had blurted out the truth to my wife, told her of my masochism, my visits to the dominatrices. More than twenty years of marriage exploded at that instant. We were trying to put Humpty Dumpty back together again, but the focus of the guilt and blame were certainly upon me. I had gone outside the marriage for sex. My wife could hear nothing more. I had been seeing another therapist, searching for answers, hoping to make sense from all the confusion and loss. I was distraught and depressed, nearly suicidal.

There was soft folk music in the Taurus, and the whap-whop of the wipers on a drizzly autumnal morning. The trees thrust their bony bare limbs up into the thick fog and the clutter of dead brown leaves in the ditches alongside the road seemed glossy as plastic. Shoots of dried, bleached grasses stood like bristles in the darker brush, lifeless as the winter approaching but glistening with pearls of rain. Driving leisurely, I reviewed the fragments unearthed in my latest session with the counselor, the clues we had followed today. Although I was skeptical, the therapists seemed to think my childhood held the key.

I'll never be sure where my fascination began, or why I was chosen, or susceptible, to it. My earliest memory of these feelings was at the age of about five. Many afternoons I would lay on the floor of my bedroom, on my tummy, and leaf through the great dark-blue book until I found those special pages, as if they addressed some inner calling. It wasn't the same in the night time, when my father would read to me from the very same book, trying to convey the wonders of its story. I felt no wonder; I couldn't comprehend miracles or magic, but later, alone on the floor of my room, I could look at the simple line drawings and feel my being flooded with a cold-splendid wonderful rush of excitement, pleasure and purpose so intense I often shivered and my heart thudded in my chest. Too much truth was lost in the changing currents of time, but I know that my interest in S&M began with that big dark-blue book about Jesus, especially the special pictures in the back. There was fascination in the drawing of the crucifixion; I thought the women were especially beautiful as they watched Christ up on the wooden cross, but the key clue, the spark that ignited this obsession, was another drawing a few pages previous. It was a simple black-on-white line drawing, almost like a picture in a coloring book. Jesus was placid, stripped to the waist, His wrists bound in ropes and lifted just face-high to expose His back. There were thin lines wrapping around His torso, and in the background the Roman soldier with the whip, athletic as a pitcher delivering a fastball, eyes intent upon his target. Christ's eyes fascinated me, even at age five. He accepted the suffering, and transcended it. It was as if I understood, even then, the importance of that acceptance, that serenity under torture.

I know my life's obsession began with those simple drawings, with that book. If there was anything before, it is inaccessible. Why, as a little boy, would I respond so emotionally to pictures like that? Whatever this fascination may be, it's in me. It may be inherited, or congenital; it is inextinguishable as any hunger but so much more satisfying, and primeval. I don't really believe in such hokum, but perhaps I was whipped or tortured in a previous life, and perhaps beautiful women watched my suffering? It is not something I can explain; it simply is, and I have had to learn to live with it.

There is a deep void from the memories of the dark-blue Jesus book until anything else sexual occurred in my life. I grew up outside, playing cowboys or soldiers with the neighborhood guys, riding my bicycle with reckless abandon, and usually surrounded by animals and pets. These were relatively uneventful years. My school marks were above average, although my report cards invariably suggested that I didn't apply myself as I should. My mind raced over a thousand subjects, and I was a voracious reader. But school textbooks rarely touched upon the subjects I was studying at the moment, and so I tended to disregard my homework in favor of a spirited investigation into the Aurora Borealis, Indian culture, airplanes, the Civil War, baseball, hot rods, or my crystal radio with the wire antenna strung out to a nearby tree. I had a paper route, and I mowed lawns. I fought when I had to go to the dentist, or for an immunization shot, and so my parents were forced to find a dentist who would routinely give me gas to put me to sleep.

I think I was twelve, it was a Saturday morning and my mother had just emerged from another doctor's appointment, groaning pathetically about her latest ache or pain. We were at a drug store in the city, waiting for a prescription, and I wandered to the crowded news rack looking for hot rod magazines.

What was it about that particular magazine? I don't remember why, but I took it off the shelf and thumbed through it, and found a full-color picture of a naked woman, her breasts boldly, proudly displayed, and (strangest thing) I wet my pants! It was an incredible thing, I hadn't wet myself in years, and it felt oddly different somehow, uncontrollable and shivery, like a pumping off-and-on sort of motion that I didn't understand, and when it was over I put the magazine back and memorized the title, and put Kleenex into my pants to hide the mistake but it wasn't as bad as it had felt and so it didn't show, and I was puzzled. Later, at home, I rode my bike down to the corner store and searched through the magazines until I found that same one, and there was another one nearby with more appeal (I couldn't define how), but I slipped the two magazines into my jacket and pedaled furiously for home, retreated upstairs to my room, closed the door, and investigated. Until that day I had never realized that women had bigger breasts than men, that they were constructed all curvy and pretty and different, and then I felt that odd excitement in my underpants again and clutched myself, but before I could even get started to run for the bathroom downstairs it started and it was unstoppable. But this time I stared at the pictures and just experienced it, and it still pumped, but it wasn't really wetting my pants exactly; and it was good, very good. A warm, electrical feeling, and I felt sort of weak when it was over, and sweaty, feverish, but it had been incredibly pleasurable. Late that night, before bed, I took the magazines out of hiding and tried it again, and it took longer to begin, but by squeezing my little tinkler I encouraged a less intense one, almost glorious, sort of disappointing, and then I fell asleep, after hiding the magazines first, of course.

Surreptitiously, I began to collect those magazines. I kept them hidden among my hot rod magazines, in the darker corners of my room. I devoured each new issue, every stimulating photo or exciting article. I remember a small piece, about four column-inches, at the bottom of a page near the back of a

"True" magazine, about a primitive tribe that celebrated a boy's passage into manhood with an elaborate ceremony of pain in which all the young women of the tribe pushed thorns into every inch of his naked body. I imagined myself in the school gymnasium, suspended by a long rope, my hands stretched overhead so that my toes just barely grazed the floor. All the girls were standing on line in their abbreviated blue gym suits, clutching straight pins or wicked thorns, smiling their contemptuous, mocking smiles as they watched my suffering and tried to decide where to insert their personal contributions. The majority of the thorns were clustered around my groin, my buttocks, and my breasts! I was terribly ashamed, and enormously stimulated.

Why? Why did I steal the magazines? I had never stolen anything before. And, how did I realize that I had to hide them, that neither of my parents would allow me to see them? Why was I so unable to resist them? It did not begin as something subtle; it was never, ever subtle. I went from discovery to obsession at the speed of light, and my urges seemed to control me. From the very first, I was preoccupied with sex, unable to help myself. I masturbated often, and I began to collect things. I created harnesses from lengths of dog chain and rope, imprisoned my genitals and then fastened myself to the bedpost, and I crawled against the immovable object. I dreamt I was an ancient Egyptian slave undergoing punishment, chained to a huge block of stone by a loop around my scrotum just above my balls, and I must drag the stone toward the pyramids under construction. I tried to crawl, to drag that enormous weight, and I fantasized that a beautiful woman stood over me with a whip. She was cruel but beautiful, and I struggled to please her.

I was a good student, but always seeking attention. I had never been an accomplished athlete, but my boyhood passion was baseball. We lived a long ways from the centralized school and the fields where Little League teams played, and in those days common folks didn't have second cars. The teams were everything in our rural town, and without transportation home I couldn't be on them. Too often, those of us who didn't play sports were ridiculed as "nerds," hounded, picked on, vilified, or shunned. I hated school, and my stomach began to tighten and cramp at the thought of it. The doctor assured my mother that my problems were entirely emotional, that I was only tense and frightened, and that I should learn to relax inside. I was eleven, maybe twelve. Gym class was awful; many of the other boys were developing their adult body hair, and they mocked me in the shower. The girls had begun to blossom, and they did not recognize my hunger. I was very alone with my fantasies and my magazines, and troubled.

Mother knew what to do. At the end of my Sunday night bath I was required to knock on the door, then dry myself and wait. Sometimes I could hear the water rushing through the pipes, and then footsteps approaching. I stood in front of the toilet, unclothed. She came in quietly, spread a towel on the floor at my feet, and nodded. I had to lie down on my side and bend my left leg at the knee. The metal lid gave off a distinctive sound as it turned on the vaseline jar; she spread my buttocks and greased me thoroughly. There was never much conversation, but I was made to feel that I was inconveniencing her terribly. Finally, when all was in readiness she would stand and take down the pink-red bag from its hook. She knelt behind me, spread me again, and carefully inserted the hard plastic nozzle, wriggling it to find my opening, then sliding it home impatiently. When it was seated deep she would release the clip, I learned to recognize the soft metallic "ping," and the hot soapy water rushed into me like a terrible tide, scorched my insides, distending me, sometimes cramping me until I groaned. She made sure I took it all, rolling the top of the bag and squeezing the last of it into the hose. By now I would be quivering on the cold floor, frightened to move, straining to hold it in, and she would take the nozzle out of me and settle herself onto the edge of the tub, and light a cigarette. She looked down upon me with disgust painted clearly across her face, and she stared mercilessly as the cramps battered my abdomen. I waited, forbidden to move, miserably uncomfortable, for the command "Get up." With the blessed order I was approaching relief. I clambered carefully, oh, so carefully, to my feet and stood at the toilet, the backs of my calves hard up against the cold porcelain and hands at my sides, awaiting permission. The water surged and seethed inside me, the soap scouring my bowels as the heat caused them to clench and cramp painfully, desperately, sometimes so hard that I felt tears in my eyes. My body wanted to squirt out the foreign flood, but I had to resist those moments, to stand motionless, listening to the frightful groaning and bubbling roll out of my bowels, and feel her stare. She sat motionless, smoking her cigarette, her legs crossed, staring at my ordeal. It was an unusual expression, all-powerful, and there was no question of my failing to please her. I stood naked, squirming, displaying any progress I might have made toward manhood, but feeling like a very little boy. Finally, she would crush out the cigarette with great ceremony and turn her eyes back to me. "Sit." It was like a dog's command, but welcome. She listened, but I would not disobey. I sat, shivered, eyes watering, struggling to contain it all, waiting for permission. "Release." The boiling cauldron seemed to rush from me all at once, filling the small room with a pungent odor of soapsuds and soil, and I felt weak, empty inside. She rose then, gathered her things, and left me alone. God, I hated Sunday evenings!

There are fragments of memory, like pieces of a jigsaw puzzle laid out upon a card table. Odd bits of accumulated data that I sense are pertinent, but to organize them and create a realistic, complete picture may require more time and energy and dollars than I am prepared to invest. And, to what end? I am the person I am; I cannot be undone or remade into another. I am not uncomfortable with myself, except that I have been guilty of poor judgment and sometimes my actions have caused pain, especially to my loved ones. To my wife. I am very sad about that, but I had so few choices, so few opportunities to direct the main flow of my life toward other channels. This is my life, my work, my history. I have a career, a family. When the possibility of divorce loomed large at least I could take some sanctuary in my work. I am regarded as a professional, a success. To re-examine every fossil of my childhood and reinvent myself might jeopardize that, and so I venture to the scenic overlooks and I gaze timidly across the harsh landscapes at the Grand Canyon, but I do not jump into the chasm. I search for footpaths and trails where others have gone before, for railings and flagstone walkways, tour buses and sturdy guideposts.

My adolescence was made up of bold, enormous incidents, vivid crazy dangerous confrontations. My parents never talked much, about anything. Certainly, never about anything even remotely related to sex. That old scenario of the father talking about the birds and bees? Not at our house. It just never happened. And so I investigated any way I could, propelled by a huge thirst for knowledge, a need that was all-powerful and inescapable. Did other guys feel these things? Did they masturbate? I couldn't imagine it. I couldn't stop myself.

In the summers, the neighborhood ladies gathered their aluminum chaises and sunbathed together. In those days wives rarely worked, and so three or four of them would gather every afternoon to sun. Invariably, one or two wore swimsuits, and the others wore shorts and their bras. I knew better than to come close unless there was a *very* good reason, but I couldn't help but notice. It was all very natural, they just laid out their chaise lounges and unbuttoned their blouses, and shrugged them off. Mrs. Rafferty wore the sexiest bras, all the guys in the neighborhood agreed, but Mary Rhodes had the nicest breasts. I was fascinated, of course, but I was more interested in their bottoms and thighs. Marjorie Killian, Ellen's mother, had an incredibly prominent rear, I loved to watch her walk. Ellen, of course, was only two years older than I, and developing into a beautiful young woman. I thought I might be in love with her, but she rejected all of my initiatives. Sometimes, on a sunny summer afternoon, I liked to imagine that I was a flyer shot down in combat, and Ellen had rescued me and was keeping me in her bed, nursing me back to health. I watched her bedroom lamp come on sometimes, and imagined her getting undressed, stripping to her bra and panties. I longed to see what she looked like, and one afternoon as I was using their bathroom, I peeked into the laundry hamper and found a fragrant pair of her panties. I stuffed them down into my own underpants and took them home, and examined them. I found a pubic hair, which I saved, and incredible scents, and I masturbated with youthful vigor.

They discovered my magazines. I suppose I'd always known it would happen some day. Calling them "smut" and "trash," they gathered them up into brown paper sacks and carried them away. We would deal with them on the weekend. I could hardly walk for the trembling. Late Saturday afternoon I was finally summoned, and led out into the garden. I followed my father, quaking with the anticipation and the fear. We were followed in turn by my mother. The snow was brittle under our feet, crunching at each step. The sun was brilliant in that golden, late-afternoon way, the crisp air still as if in some hushed expectation. "Don't ever let me find anything like these again." My father soaked them in gasoline from the can that fed the lawn mower and struck a match. He hadn't spoken until now. My mom had registered her disgust, but for three days Dad had only glowered or looked bewildered. I thought he didn't know what to say, and I hoped the old man might even silently approve, or understand, at least a little, 'way down inside somewhere. No. The flames absorbed rich hues from the photographs, but it was a laborious process. Pages curled and wrinkled, became delicate black membranes that leapt skyward, then fell to litter the snow. I stood silently, watching my fantasy world disappear. It was bitterly cold, my mother went into the house, but just moving my feet to encourage circulation in my toes brought a harsh reprimand from my father. The sun began to lower in the sky, the wind had penetrated my coat. He worked at the dwindling pile with a rake, and not a single page escaped. I asked to go inside, to use the bathroom. Denied. I must stand and watch every moment, every word burn. And so I stood, shivering, unmoving, watching but never comprehending, just standing silently because it was required. There was sadness, loss, but more. There was resentment.

About a year later they found the female underwear secreted in my room. There was less said this time, and they did not make me watch the fire. Obviously this had upset them more, there were whispers and exclamations and arms waving, but I was not allowed into the conversation. One afternoon my mother took me out of school and we traveled to a hospital, to a psychiatric clinic. She hardly spoke in the car, perhaps the traffic required her attention. The doctor was an older man, very formal in a suit, and we went into his office, leaving Mother to study her magazine. "Do you wear the ladies' clothing?" The doctor was gentle, smiling, even encouraging. I nodded, yes. "Do you know what they call this condition?" the doctor asked, and I knew, but I wanted to see if there might be a newer term. "A transvestite. One who wears the clothing of the other sex. A transvestite." As if the kid might find the word on next Friday's vocabulary test! Nope, I knew that one. There was not much more to the meeting. No one ever asked about the other things in the box, the ropes and C-clamps, twisted handkerchiefs or the candle. No one ever mentioned the incident again. I was cured.

It is Saturday morning, I am slouched in a soft chair, struggling to explain to the therapist. For more than forty minutes I have responded to her questions, getting edgy, hoping to be offered some new avenues into my wife's psyche, bridges to rebuild all that has come apart in our lives. There are great costs to loving, and careful accountants have called for balloon payments due, past due, that I cannot afford.

"You're so distant today," she says. "What's bothering you?"

"My wife saw a lawyer again, about starting divorce proceedings. He told her she wasn't ready and sent her away! Can you imagine that? I'm trying to tell you that we're in a crisis situation, and I need help. I desperately need something to say, some suggestion of how I might break the logjam and prevent a disaster." I'm not slouching now, I am upright and swelling with tension, as if to pounce upon her.

She scratches at her ubiquitous spiral bound tablet, chronicling my desperation. "What do you think you should say? What would fill the cracks, or cement them? You know, someplace deep inside you. Let it out. It isn't healthy to hold it all within."

I rise, stooping far forward to the endtable beside her chair, under the lamp, where a decorative brass holder cradles her business cards. Taking one I retreat awkwardly, my rump upraised, back onto the safety of my chair. My refuge. This place is full of requirements and obligations, so parallel to the other places. Places where I would go to bare myself, to accept pain and humiliation, even verbal chastisements. This is voluntary, necessary to gain insight, and as expensive as an hour with a good L.A. dominatrix. Why can't anyone else appreciate the similarities? She is watching me, looking over the top of her half-lens granny glasses, and she puts the upright end of the pen to her lower lip. Her head twitches a bit, sideways, and her eyebrows arch to say she is puzzled. "Have you looked at your own business card lately?" I ask.

"Not in any great detail. Why?"

"Because it says you are a counselor, specifically a marriage counselor. How do you get away with advertising like that? I come to you for advice, for counsel, I've looked up the word in the dictionary and it centers around advice, suggestions, a plan. I get up on Saturday mornings and drive here, and pay you ninety dollars an hour, and I've been coming here for weeks while things get more desperate, and you haven't counseled me! You ask what I think. Jesus, if I knew what I think, and if it had any real value, I wouldn't be in this situation! I believed your card, believed you could offer advice and counsel that would rescue me. Instead, you're creating diversions, fiddling while Rome burns!"

"The answers are inside you. I cannot tell you how to live your life. You've consumed twenty years building this problem, and you expect me to unravel it in an hour? Therapy doesn't work that way." She is too calm, moving only her lips, watching over those damned glasses for my reaction. I lunge to the book case at the end of the couch, find the dictionary and busily thumb it, my back to her as if she doesn't matter. She is saintly in her patience, pushing up her lower lip with the upright end of her Bic pen, lodging it right in the depression in the center of her chin, precisely at the lower edge of her lower lip, and pushing up to create some type of pseudo-scowl, some distortion to express her discomfort.

"Here," I say, spinning to confront her. "Read this." My index finger underscores the word THERAPY, the allusions (illusions?) to treatment and cure. She considers my offering, closes the book with finality and purpose, surveys me again across the half-lenses, measuring me.

"Are you quite done?"

"Not quite. I have about eleven minutes remaining."

"That isn't funny."

"Look," I say. "We have cable at home, about thirty-six channels. Any night, every night there are a crowd of so-called comedians. There's no need to come *here* to hear something funny."

"Why are you so antagonistic?" The pen pushes at her lower lip again.

"Because you're not performing. In my job I have to perform, make a difference, fix things, leave with a situation better than it was when I arrived. You're so fucking content to just sit and absorb all my history, to hear all the lurid details, and nothing comes back. Nothing! It's like shoveling my life into a big dark hole, and it just disappears, meaningless." I glance at my watch. "Seven minutes. I don't plan to come back."

"How will you cope?"

"You cannot think you're helping?" It is a statement disguised as a question, or perhaps a question tossed out as bait hoping she will bite, and offer up some tidbit of advice before I walk out into the parking lot and get into the Taurus with no place to go but back to the battlefield. I have delivered everything honestly, investing shame and humiliation into the process. With the dominatrices shame and humiliation counted for something, my discomforts led to pleasure. Here there is no return, the bank is bust, another S&L overinvested in property. I prefer S&M, investments in feeling, emotion, accomplishment. There has been a tense pause while she writes in the spiral-bound notebook, and the thought process has delivered opportunity. I can express myself to her, she may understand, it doesn't matter any more. "I was hoping to accomplish something. I have so little measurable accomplishment of late, just crumbling and disintegration. I need to make some small progress." The sounds of the next client's arrival seep through the door. She scribbles the receipt so I can ask the insurance company to reimburse half her fee, writing unintelligibly as if to reinforce her ties to medicine.

"Same time next week?" She has heard nothing I've said.

"I doubt it. My conscience is bothered."

"By what?" She opens the door, as if my answer does not concern her, or to display me to the next client, I cannot be sure.

"I submit these to the insurance company." I hold up the receipt, whispering to spare her from any embarrassment, "and I feel like I'm taking advantage of them. We're accomplishing nothing here, and it's expensive."

"Don't be so sure we're accomplishing nothing. You're learning to be honest about your feelings. That's significant. I'll look for you next week."

I shake her offered hand, getting just a cone-shaped bundle of fingers. She feels noncommittal. It is the last time I will ever see her.

18

The fact is that sadomasochism did change my life. Never have I experienced anything so psychologically potent, so physically powerful, so emotionally satisfying. Never have I felt as free, and the freedom is longer-lasting than just the duration of my SM play. It is a continuing freedom and courage to explore myself, the people and the world around me from a position of inner strength that, before SM, was lacking in my life. Since SM has come into my life, I have been freed... – JJ Madeson, from the book BOUND TO BE FREE: The SM Experience, by Charles Moser, Ph.D., M.D. and JJ Madeson, The Continuum Publishing Co., 1996

We heard the Chevy sedan crackle over the driveway, and rushed to settle our clothing. The car door thumped shut, the porch door opened, then the inner door, and her mother called out a greeting. I was apprehensive this afternoon, having earned another D on a geometry quiz. Inevitably, Mrs. Bivens hung up her jacket in the hall closet, poured a tall beer, and asked to see our school papers. I was proud of the A in English, and the teacher's remarks at the top of my poetry.

Mrs. Bivens had heard the drone of German aircraft as a child, and endured the air raid nights clutched feverishly close in the cellar, wrapped in blankets against the damp. Today's American kids couldn't appreciate evil. Their wealth and a ubiquitous trend to permissiveness had left them soft. She turned the papers and came upon the bold Geometry D, with the hasty admonition, "You're not applying yourself," scrawled in scarlet.

"I thought you were studying." She said it softly.

"I was, ma'am. I studied hard. I just don't get Calculus." She frightened me at these moments.

"You don't get Calculus or Physics. You'll fail, Jeremiah. What are you going to do with your future? The world is revolving around space travel, and you think the ultimate expressions of our civilization are rock 'n' roll and drag racing! I won't have your failure on my conscience, dear boy. Fetch the ruler." She replaced my shuffle of papers on the counter and picked up Molly's.

The ruler. She kept the old wooden ruler in the desk, just to the right as you entered the living room from the foyer. Twice before she had sent me to get it, to bring it back to her and stand at attention before her. She would take my wrist, I knew, and draw it out before me, palm up, and she would bend my fingers back to accentuate the curvature of the palm. Fingers together, thumb precisely alongside, she would pinch and plump up the thick roll of muscle just below my fingers, the cushion that would be the ball of my foot if I were a quadruped, and then, with it properly displayed, her eyes would lift up to mine, peering out from under her fashionable blonde hair, and her lips would move, those lips so carefully lipsticked to a rich, wet gloss. Her eyes seemed to penetrate me at times like this, to create chill in my lungs, and trembling in the corded muscles at the back of my knees.

I returned to the kitchen, saw Molly's downcast eyes. She had hoped a B in Physics would be good enough to escape the discipline. Obviously not. I offered the ruler to her mother, Mrs. Bivens. She swallowed heartily from the beer, leaving a thin, curious scum of white froth on her lip just above the glossy off-pink lipstick.

"Jeremiah."

"Yes, Ma'am." I dutifully moved in front of her.

"Left hand." I bent my left elbow, presented my palm. She worked it like a sculptress would work clay, fashioning it until it seemed the target roll of flesh was erected, standing near-orgasmic above my fingers, palm, and wrist. Her eyes loomed up, studied me. I felt helpless, but also determined.

"You're eighteen now. The penalty will be six," she announced, her eyes wilting my resolve. Six? Last time, at four, I nearly pulled away. How would I stand six? As if she heard my thoughts, she said, "You may grip your forearm with the other hand." Her arm rose, the ruler flashed down and cracked flat precisely on target.

Molly shed her heavy coat and blew onto her fingers to warm them. I dropped my coat over the square post at the base of the banister and swept her up into a prolonged and provocative kiss, inviting her to warm her hands in the depths of my jeans. There was giggling and then we parted, she made hot chocolate, I tuned the radio. There was a note, Molly took the meat out to defrost, and we spread our books onto the dining room table and began to study.

After dinner and the dishes, after our homework was done, Molly's mother was in the cellar doing laundry. Molly and I had cuddled up on the living room couch to pet and watch television. She was still dressed in her school clothes, a red tartan jumper over a white blouse, a childish uniform that looked inappropriate on her mature figure. We were not entwined. She stretched out, her torso supported on the pillows at the armrest, her feet on my lap. I sat upright, watching Broderick Crawford in "Highway Patrol," the antiquated '54 Ford police cars. My right hand absentmindedly stroked Molly's calf. "Honey," she whispered, "Would you do something for me? Something really special?"

"Mmm-hmmm."

"Do you love me?" Her eyes twinkled with playful promise.

"You know that I do."

"Will you kiss me?"

I moved toward her, but her arm halted me. "No, not yet. Something really special. Sweetheart, I left my panties in the bathroom. Touch me." My fingers moved up under the heavy woolen tent of her skirt, to her belly. I felt the silky drape of her slip, the cushion of her pubic hair, her slippery damp privacy. "Kiss me there, Honey. Would you? I heard about it today, some girls were talking at lunch and they say it's sooo special. Lick me, put your tongue right up... oh, I'm embarrassed. Would you? Please?"

I had seen references to this in the magazines. Once, late last summer, inspired by a magazine, I had asked if she would allow me to kiss the panties of her white swimsuit. At the time, Molly had seemed puzzled, if not annoyed, and said "Not now." The summer ended, the swimsuit disappeared, and there hadn't been another opportunity. Now, suddenly, it had become her idea, her request. I dared!

It was necessary to kneel on the floor, to rest my elbows and torso on the cushions. She spread her feet wide apart, I nuzzled up under her skirt, up along her thigh. It was dark here, humid and fragrant. Her thighs opened blatantly to grant me admittance, she had perfumed herself, I felt her silken slip fall like a curtain over my forehead. I had one hand on her hip, on the soft resilience of her bottom, really, and her scent was rich, musky, tinted with gentle flower fragrance but so tempting, so intimate. My lips played over her inner thigh, her hand touched the back of my head through the thick wool dress and slip, just the faintest pressure, encouragement. I was almost reluctant, I was familiar with the concept from my magazines, but now, with my face inches from a moist vagina, I didn't want to do it incorrectly and lose the privileges I had so patiently earned. I could feel her curls now, and the dark shadowy cleft! I leaned forward just that extra couple of inches, and I kissed her. She stiffened, tremors sizzled under her skin, I kissed harder, she rearranged herself to grant me access, and she seemed to thrust herself to me. I rasped my tongue across her tangled, fragrant hair, then lower, until I found her slippery sweet channel. Exploring, I pushed into her, the taste was salty and wonderful and...

"What are you... Oh my God, get up! Get up from there!" Strong hands gripped my shoulders and ripped me backward, tossed me to the floor like a wadded paper scrap, there was a great fury and confusion, screaming filled the room.

"Mother! Mother, no, Mother, I... Ohhh, Please Mother!" I was in the light now, there was frantic pushing, scrambling, tearing, shrieking hysteria, a fast-motion kaleidoscope of anguished motion and wails. I was sprawled, confused, having risen to a half-sitting position so I could see over the coffee table, and there was a struggle, a cacophony of two battling voices, "Molly, Molly, oh my God Molly," versus, "Mother, please, we've never done it before, Mother, don't punish me Mother, please!" and the maelstrom moved away around the corner into the foyer and then the kitchen and Molly was being banished to the cellar, and then Mrs. Bivens was back in my face, furious, scolding, threatening, screaming eyes agog and spittle flying, that I'd better wait for her, just wait here! She started away, halted, screeched that she needed to... to talk, to talk to me, but first... she needed a few minutes to decide what to do, and I got up kind of awkwardly and sat dumbfounded on the couch to watch Broderick Crawford and the '54 Fords in a dazed, detached, utterly remote way. The events seemed to reverberate in my head, a confusing blinding mosaic, and I knew I was in dire trouble again, that my parents would just view this as another act of depravity, and probably tell Mrs. Bivens all about my outrageous behavior before, or behaviors before, that I stole panties and wore them to masturbate, and they would search my room and find a pair of Molly's, white cotton, never appreciating the subtle scent of her juices still lurking in the double cushioned gusset. No one would understand this, they would forbid me from seeing Molly, there would be crazy accusations and maybe psychiatric examinations, and far too many questions, and maybe I would be labeled a pervert! In this new town, where my classmates liked me, and where I was accomplishing so much, it would be a disaster. I could look forward to more lonely hours of solitude, more restrictions, strict rules, supervisions, as if my mother's controls weren't already more stringent than anything my friends had to endure. I was, as I waited, anticipating my own total destruction. A few moments before I had seen a vagina, tasted and smelled it. My ultimate fantasy had come true and now I was disconsolate and destroyed. Go figure.

I waited, trembling inside. She was downstairs with Molly, and I couldn't hear anything but the meaningless voices from the TV. I waited, dreading, but also silently filled with wonder at the glorious gift my lover had given me, the intimacy she had afforded, the scent and even the taste of her, and I was sorry it was interrupted. Would we ever have another opportunity? There was sadness, a weighty depression around the fact that my great fantasy had nearly come true, only to be interrupted and it may not be possible again forever! I waited. How would I explain this to my parents? My mother? I could just hear her. "You're spending a lot of time at home lately, Jeremiah. I thought I would just check with Molly's mother to see if anything was wrong, and she thought you had told me." I stood up, just to escape those thoughts, but the house was silent and I didn't dare move, fearful that the sound of my footsteps in the cellar below might signal that I didn't truly appreciate the gravity of the situation, and so I just sat back down again, sagging, limp with helplessness. Ahh, but I was also alert, my temples were pounding, I felt like a rabbit caught in onrushing headlights. I waited, impatiently.

Finally she returned, I heard her feet shuffling on the wooden cellar steps, the door open. Terror froze me, her steps rang with determination. She was tousled, sweaty. "Still here? I'll deal with you in just a moment, don't go away." She spun on her heel and climbed the stairs, and I had to wait again. The stairs squeaked as she returned, dressed in her rich black velvet robe. She had changed, not only her attire but her persona. Mrs. Bivens was an exciting, attractive woman. Robust, I suppose; she wasn't taller than other women, and not heavy, but she seemed strong and powerful. Voluptuous! I had seen her in a swim suit, she was shapely and she moved with a sexy, liquid swing to her hips. She was on tall black heels now, her stockings near dark as midnight, but it was her manner that intimidated me. I was so tense my eyes threatened to dissolve into tears, and now she confronted me, sitting on her chair with a tissue to her nose, her eyes were wide but there was also something extraordinary there, something beyond disappointment or anger. She fussed with her glamorous robe, avoided looking at me. She seemed almost afraid, and I was puzzled.

"Molly tells me you have never done this before." She didn't seem to be speaking to me, just tossing the thought out into the cold room to try it, to test its resilience.

"No, ma'am, never before." It was a whisper, the bitter, ironic truth. Nothing so daring, so intimate. I had never glimpsed a woman's sex before tonight, and now the grand accomplishment lay in tatters at my feet. My head was lowered, but I was acutely, warily studying her. She rose, turned the TV's volume off but allowed the flickering pictures to remain. Now she sat in her favorite chair, upright, taking no comfort from its familiar pillows. There was a palpable tension in her, too, and the rhythmic movements of the antique clock on the mantle seemed to fill the room. We were unsure, both of us, and it did not bode well for an inexperienced adolescent boy. The guilty one.

"You know what I should do, don't you?" She whispered it, but in the silence her words boomed like a cluster of fireworks over a country fair audience in the night.

"Ma'am?" I was simply devoid of knowing, a vessel uncorked and spilled carelessly, damaged, all lost but being examined in its emptiness, played with as if to add shame to failure. It was not a time for bold statements.

"I should march you over to your mother, tell her what I have seen, and ask her to keep you away from my daughter. Forever. To pen you up, I don't know. I cannot allow you to ruin Molly's life, Jeremiah, even if you don't value your own." Her tone was angry, and yet I expected to hear her say something starting with "but..." She paused.

I was expected to respond, but nothing I could think of would make anything better so I simply waited. "What do you have to say?" Her eyes were drilling into me, examining my heart which was thudding relentlessly in my hollow chest. I could only shrug cheerlessly, and wait. She shifted on her seat, and seemed to fill her lungs with the terrible close pungent air in this room, she swelled and, by simply breathing, assumed control. Nothing was said, but a decision had been rendered and my fate sealed, and the clock continued to measure out the increments of loss, but I was utterly powerless.

"I've encouraged you to court my daughter, Jeremiah. I have never objected to you, you know that."

"Yes, Ma'am."

"You're good for her, good *to* her. You are kind, and respectful. You don't hurt her. You are an intelligent boy, if not particularly motivated, and I feel you have promise, that you deserve a girl like Molly. I admire you, Jeremiah. Take comfort in that." Her voice retreated, perhaps regressed, to its English roots.

She was from Cheshire, just a few miles from Liverpool, and her near-Scouse lilt was wonderfully in style, as current as Beatles, Rolling Stones, or Peter and Gordon, mellow as Gerry and the Pacemakers or the Searchers, and I raised my eyes to look at her. Our eyes met, and I nearly jumped up and fled. She devoured me, her countenance rich with olde English propriety and tradition, with some formal code of ancient etiquettes and exotic snobbery. I had seen it before, of course, but never like this. She had boiled her womanly sweetness down to thick jam; I must shrink myself to the bone, impress her. I would have to earn forgiveness, performing somehow I didn't understand, to regain her respect. It was fact, a sealed bargain; and now I waited as the old clock ticked away, for her decision would be announced next and I must be attentive.

She made me look up and find her eyes again, searching. Asking for it.

Her eyes belittled me. "There is an alternative," she said quietly. She pushed at her luxurious blonde hair, so sexy in her black velvet robe. The tall heeled shoes were part of it, but I didn't understand their significance. I had to wait it out, awash in the thick silence. "In England, growing up, we were required to excel, Jeremiah. I went to a private school, a very strict institution. We were taught to be proper young ladies. There are great traditions in the U.K., behaviours are watched carefully and failures are dealt with rather severely. There is a bit of a formal decorum, you see, but it is not a cruel atmosphere. Humans are fallible. We failed, each of us at one time or another, took our medicine, and went on. Once the slate is wiped clean all is forgiven, you see, and so lessons are learned and the young adventurers become solid adults. Do you understand what I'm saying, young man?"

"I think so, Ma'am." I didn't. I wished I knew where she was heading.

"In the better English schools, Jeremiah, misconduct is dealt with immediately and harshly. Every schoolteacher keeps a rod or cane prominently displayed, and they take immense pride in their abilities to administer corporal punishment. I speak from personal experience, I assure you! It is a very solemn occasion, to be summoned before the class for a flogging. I recognize the fear you're experiencing tonight, boy, because I've felt it myself. The awful dread! More than once I've stood in front of the entire class, the young boys as well as the girls, and raised my skirt and exposed my knickers and my fine feminine seat to the instructor's rod. Then, on top of the humiliation and the shame comes the discomfort. Damned awful it was, too, every lick, every time. And then, to go back to your hardwood desk and try to be seated without express-ing the hurt, and turn your attention to your studies... But I survived it, as we all did, and I believe it has stood me in good stead all my life." She paused, looked away. Lit a cigarette, blew out the first hard hit of sweet comforting smoke with great force. The room was frozen in still anticipation, a closed box of dangerous electric currents. I tasted hard metallic fear coating my dry tongue. I wished I could disappear, but no. Mrs. Bivens had spoken to me quietly, intimately, drawing me close by calmly stating the facts. Her gaze rooted me to the spot, and the accumulated dread of the moment threatened to flood my eyes with tears. If sincerity counted for anything, I was truly, sincerely sorry for what I had done.

"I've punished Molly tonight, Jeremiah. She won't sit comfortably in school tomorrow, but she'll think hard before she lets you take liberties with her again. If I report you to your mother and keep you away from my daughter, nothing would be gained. Molly would probably rebel against me, try all the harder to see you secretly and so defy me, and fool herself into thinking she loves you more when all she would be feeling is the normal rebelliousness of adolescence. And you. You would want her more, having learned nothing, and the next thing I know Molly would be telling me she's pregnant, and both of your lives would be ruined. It is not my intention, Jeremiah, to damage Molly's life, or yours. As a parent I realize I should try to guide her, teach her if you will, to be successful in the world. You know that I feel that responsibility fervently. I feel it toward you as well, Jeremiah. Really. You arrived at just the most opportune moment, just after I lost my beloved Robert, and you have been a great help to me. To Molly you are a sweetheart, an adolescent lover. I know time will see your romance take its course, given opportunity. If I banish you to your parents, what will be the point? They are inattentive and permissive, they will shout for a few minutes and look the other way as you flounder again, and I'll have lost a handyman. No, that's not entirely honest. I'll have lost another male presence in this old house, and Molly and I will live together in its lonely gloom, silently. You've brought life to our door, Jeremiah. I don't wish to chase it away, I enjoy watching you two young birds preparing to leave the nest."

The cigarette was only about half-consumed, but she crushed it out. She stood now, smoothed her black velvet robe over her hips. Her eyes were measuring me. It was time for her to offer her proposal, but she seemed unsure. She moved to the drapes, parted them, looked out to the street. In a breathless whisper, she announced her decision. I shivered, and I wasn't cold. "The alternative, Jeremiah, as I have indicated, is to be punished here, tonight, by me. Before you feel any relief, I want you to know that I will deal with you in a manner which will express all of my displeasure, all of my frustration, all of my feelings of betrayal. I must keep in mind that you are just a boy, that the sensations your body is producing are intoxicating. Molly is also too young to deal with her sexuality. One day, and it won't be long, maturity will allow you to make adult decisions about things like sex, and drinking, and smoking. Tonight you're simply not ready to judge those temptations responsibly. You need adult guidance, a parent's patience. Both of you! I must try to make you think, to make you wary. You have to learn to control your sexual instincts, Jeremiah. To go slowly. I won't have you experimenting with my daughter!" She slammed the heavy drapery shut, spun on her heel to confront me. Her eyes were dark slits beneath steep brows, and her nostrils seemed to engorge with each breath. "Oh, Jeremiah, do you have any idea what it was for me, to see my sweet little girl with a boy doing *that* to her?" Her voice was trembling with her pain. "Before long she'll be leaving me, going off to college, getting married, and I'll be alone. I have to prepare for that moment, dear boy. I cannot allow you to steal it away from me, to rush it. I am not able." Her voice was beginning to roar now, gathering momentum, rich with emotion. "You two know better, Jeremiah! If this is what you do when I'm in another room, what must you be doing while I'm away at work? My imagination frightens me!" She busied herself lighting another cigarette. She did not look at me when she passed sentence. "If you agree to take a lesson tonight, Jeremiah, know that it will be a hard lesson. You must offer yourself willingly, but completely. You will be punished, and the matter will be largely forgotten. No, not forgotten. I'll make such an impression on you that you'll never forget it, then we can move on. I will have to take some measures to ensure that you will behave after school when I'm away, but perhaps the best I can do about that is to put the fear of God into you. Know that this is not the easy choice, boy. That's all. Know that you will wish you had chosen to go home to your mother, but in the long run this alternative can be better for everyone because I will make it better. You've made me angry and upset tonight, of course, but tomorrow will be a new day. I would miss you very much if you were banished from this house, but know that you will pay a very dear price for my affection and caring." She paused to suck reassurance from her cigarette. I still wasn't sure what she was asking of me. The clock seemed to clatter. She stood beside her chair, her left hand rested on its back as if to steady her. Her back was to me, but she had me in her power.

"And so, my proposal is this, Jeremiah." She spoke softly, demanding my attention. "If you wish, I will forego any discussion of tonight's indiscretion, creating no problem for you at home. Instead, I will discipline you myself.

Punish you. You won't sit comfortably in school tomorrow, dear boy, and maybe not the next day. I'm not talking about a mere spanking; you'll know the full measure of my displeasure. A hardwood paddle across your bottom. Your *bare* bottom. And when you howl that you can't stand anymore, the leather belt." She seemed to swell up now, at that thought, and then she exhaled. I felt a suspicious tingling in my groin. "I'm suggesting that you take down your trousers, Jeremiah, and present your backside, accepting that you have earned a discipline and that now you must bear it. It will hurt you, but I want you to stand stock-still for as long as it takes, until I am satisfied. The next time Molly asks you to kiss her sex I want you to cower in fear. Yes, I know what happened. Molly has felt a hardwood paddle kiss her bottom tonight, and I am confident that she will hesitate and consider very carefully before she offers herself to you again. Do not take me lightly, Jeremiah. I am suggesting a hard, harsh discipline." Her voice had been low, quivering with emotion. Now it became almost a whisper. "I have experience in these matters." She bent to her ornate side table, crushed out her cigarette with a determination that signaled finality. She was a proud woman, elegant and shapely, aloof. She was, of course, my girlfriend's mother, to be respected and feared. Another generation, and more. Her English background seemed odd any time she discussed it, and I sometimes felt that their far different ways were unnecessarily restrictive. Always, it seemed, Mrs. Bivens was governed by an unyielding code of conduct, something traditional and confining, something we Americans could never abide. The perimeters of right and wrong were clearly drawn in her mind, by a stiff, formal but intangible code of conduct saturated with embroidered images of bejewelled royal propriety, despite the fact that Mrs. Bivens had become an American living in a middle-class community. She was, viewing "the colony," always slightly amused by the ludicrous spectacle of American independence. She was sceptical of rock 'n' roll, even the British bands. "The music of American commoners," she sniffed. She was appalled by cookouts and paper plates, by plastic forks, cutoff jeans, and the Corvette. "A sports car is a British endeavor," she would sniff. "The MG, or the Jaguar. But what would one expect of the Americans?"

I was only a boy seeking guidance, a youth becoming a man, and searching for structure, for boundaries. The human body is seventy percent water, the saying goes, and the description fit me. I was available as water, to take the shape of any receptacle. My parents criticized, but offered no alternatives. No guidance, no motivation. I was, but for no stated reason. I had abilities, talents, desires, but no direction. Not from home. There were no goals, no destinations, no uses for my talents. It wasn't done meanly, not physically; the cruelty was the inattention. I admired precision and desired structure. With the proceeds from my paper route, I had purchased a textbook on electricity. Sound systems, radios and microphones. I tinkered, admiring the rigid rules. "The science of physics," Molly's mother had said. I felt strangely at home within its complexities, creating paths, allowing the invisible particles of energy to flow. I purchased model kits, boats and planes and cars, and as I assembled them I investigated how things work, the vast technical trains of components contributing to the end result in an orderly sequence, the organization of pieces to make a whole. Mrs. Bivens recognized my fascination, and encouraged me. I loved baseball for some related reason I could never explain, the surrender of each individual's talents to the good of the team. *That* was what I admired, what I strived for. Belonging, the opportunity to contribute to something powerful and important and sensual, to earn respect and admiration and yes, female attention. I knew one day my life's direction would come, the ignition of my soul and intellect into an irresistible bonfire of purpose and execution, and that I would succeed at life.

But that night, alone and bewildered in the Bivens' living room, all of that confidence had evaporated from me. Suddenly I was caught in a maze, a complicated puzzle with no way out, and I was ashamed and wary. I needed help! I wanted recognition, not tongue-lashing and restriction. The answer was hardly in doubt. She had offered to include me into her family, to take me to discipline as she had taken her daughter a few minutes before. I longed to be part of a real family, longed for someone to care about me. At the same time, I was fascinated by her words. It was, somehow, a curious dare, and I wondered if this elegant woman's secret thoughts and fantasies could possibly parallel my own. I couldn't divulge my deepest, most private fantasies. The front of me spoke all too obviously about that! And, I could not be eager; this was unknown, threatening territory. I did not relish the reality of my fantasies. I recognized that I was facing a very real test, a prolonged session of carefully administered pain under the watchful eyes of one, or possibly even two women! Could I? Did I dare? After so many imaginings and masturbations, could I face real pain? I wasn't at all sure.

She smoked another cigarette, eyeing me expectantly. I shifted on my footrest perch. This couldn't be happening! I was confused, breathless, distraught. I was trembling. Should I be so desperately frightened? Was I a "chicken," utterly intimidated by a mere woman? There was a dense, intimidating atmosphere in this room, something dark and unknown looming up like a summer storm. Trapped by an accumulation of bizarre events I could not mention to anyone, there seemed to be no alternative, no escape. Punishment? My insides trembled, I thought I might throw up, but there was something else, an undercurrent of sexual excitement. Could I absorb the hurt and somehow, by not letting it overwhelm me, prove myself manly to Molly and her mother? Should I attempt it, and might that focus help me to succeed? Thoughts seemed to collide and clatter in my head. I didn't feel brave, exactly, but I couldn't escape the reality of being trapped. Helpless! What to do? Tears threatened to engulf my eyes, there was a deep sexual tension brewing, percolating from my head to my loins. I didn't dare speak, afraid I was overlooking some key to escape the whole mess. I was a passenger on a boat at the crest of Niagara Falls, caught in rushing waters that could only sweep me to disaster! Inevitable doom. How would I do against the hurt? The dilemma was primitive, and steeped in the rich essences of my adolescent sexuality. I sensed an opportunity to put my masculinity on display, but the boy in me cowered. I wasn't at all sure how a woman judged masculinity! I suspected that the older, experienced lady awaiting my answer would have vastly different expectations from my teenage lover's, but I wasn't confident that I really understood either of them, or any woman. I only knew that in facing this I must maintain dignity and absorb the punishment, whatever form it might take, without whimpering. This was the essence of the male persona. Yes! With that simple realization came confidence. This is what I must do. Still, I was not eager.

I sucked in a deep breath, but quietly. "I'm sorry, Mrs. Bivens. I guess I let you down. Molly is a very special, wonderful girl, and I was, well... investigating. I mean, the guys have talked about it at lunch... I mean, not about Molly, you know, but... One of the advantages of doing it that way is that she can't get pregnant, and so I wasn't threatening her future..." It wasn't coming out the way I intended. Mrs. Bivens' eyes focused on me and melted my reasoning, dissolved my confidence. "But I know it was out of line," I stammered, "and that I shouldn't have. I... well, ma'am, I really do appreciate it if you don't have to tell my mother, because I really love Molly and I couldn't stand it if we weren't allowed to see each other. I mean, well, I really thank you for giving me this choice. I understand that, well... umm, that it won't be easy, but I want to, umm... try to...you know, be... punished. By you, you know. Tonight." I felt like a little kid, like a fool. I looked for her reaction, but she was only staring at her cigarette. Had she heard me? Should I repeat myself, but louder?

She whispered, her eyes downcast. "Jeremiah, this is very unusual, and I don't want you to talk about tonight with anyone. Ever. Is that understood? This has to be our secret. You're like our family, and families have secrets that stay inside their houses. Promise me you'll keep this private, just in this house."

"I feel like part of your family, Mrs. Bivens. Thank you. I promise." My chest thundered with fear.

She drew deeply from her cigarette, holding the porcelain ashtray in her left palm. She crushed the fire to death, busy now, brimming over with impatience. Looking up at me, her eyes were almost too intense. Fear began to churn inside me, dissolving my confidence.

"There's no turning back from this moment, Jeremiah. If you follow me, it's your decision. You cannot change your mind later."

"I understand."

She climbed out of her favorite chair and came close to me, and grasped my left wrist in her fingers. I got to my feet, my heart thudding. "You're a fine young man," she said softly. "Be brave, and it will be over soon. I won't injure you. Naughty boys are spanked, Jeremiah. It's that easy. Focus your thoughts and you'll be fine." I was shivering.

She took me to the cellar, into the secret room beyond the furnace. Molly screamed when we entered, utterly horrified. She had been standing in the corner, stark naked below the waist, her backside a steaming red thatch of swollen welts. Warned to be quiet, she stood in the dark corner and whimpered pitifully, pleading that I not be shown this aspect of the family.

I was ordered to undress to my underpants. Molly begged as I complied, then turned away to stare into the concrete corner and weep. My underpants were bulging obscenely as I was positioned before a straight-back chair, facing away from Molly. "I'm going to punish you on the bare bottom, Jeremiah," Mrs. Bivens said softly. "Push your underpants down to your ankles, please."

It was a small, dark chilly room, dimly lit with candles. I was electric with the combination of fear and anticipation. My erection was immense, bobbing with a will of its own in the cool air. She showed me how to place my palms flat upon the chair's seat, and ordered me to spread my feet. She stepped behind me, and I heard Molly pleading. Pleading for me. I became very aware of the chill. Molly sobbed, wailing in her great distress. Her mother stepped in front of me. She had removed the robe, and was dressed in a black bra and a black girdle with the stockings attached to garters at the bottom. My erection trembled. She was holding a wooden paddle.

Mrs. Bivens reached out and gently touched my cheek. Our eyes met in the dim light, and she was very solemn. "Jeremiah, you must promise me that what happens here tonight will be our secret, something you share with Molly and myself and no one else."

"Yes, ma'am." I was trembling again.

"I have stood where you're standing, Jeremiah." Her voice was just a whisper, and emotion seemed to be gripping her throat. Her eyes were ablaze with something scary and exciting. "Robert used to punish me here, sometimes." She struggled to control herself. "It was a loving thing, something special we shared. I..." She choked, cleared her voice. "Sometimes, Jeremiah, I punished him. He stood exactly as you're standing now. He was very strong." Her fingertips caressed my cheek. "Later, you'll feel his belt," she croaked, fighting her emotions. Then she shivered, and took her fingers away. She seemed to take a deep breath and swell with authority. "We'll talk more later, about this. First, Jeremiah, I am going to punish you for taking sexual liberties with my daughter. You are to hold position, offer yourself to correction without avoidance, and I expect you to be perfectly quiet. Is that clear?"

"Yes, ma'am." I was afraid I might cry.

"Do you think ill of me, Jeremiah?" She moved behind me.

"Oh, no Ma'am."

"Molly, if you like you may turn around and watch." I wasn't sure if she had turned or not. The hardwood paddle whirred through the air and smacked across my backside like a lightning bolt. Again! Again! It really hurt!

She worked me hard that evening. I tried to overcome the humiliation and pain, but she was determined to break me. I cried, I begged, but still she spanked me, and the flat wood cracked as it exploded against my pulsing burnt bottoms to paint me, as it were, with a thick coat of raw, red discomfort.

Perhaps this evening was the culmination of a lifelong desire. Perhaps it was the thrill of being seen naked before two beautiful women, or the intensity of the whole scene. As the paddle smacked hard and hot against my flesh, I felt the familiar adolescent excitement building in my loins and then suddenly, spontaneously, my body betrayed me and I humiliated myself, discharging great molten globs of my most private, intimate syrup out onto the cold cement floor for all to see! I erupted into an enormous, splashing, powerful orgasm! Mrs. Bivens hesitated while I shuddered in the throes of spontaneous ecstasy. When it was over I felt her fingertips on my buttock. Her voice was hoarse. "Since you enjoyed the paddle, Jeremiah, let's see how you like the leather strap."

I recognized the differences immediately. The belt wrapped over and into every curve of my body, fitting itself to my contours, a terrible liquid flame that sought out every sensitive nerve ending! The pain was altogether different, more cutting, certainly cumulative, far worse than I had ever expected. I stood, legs apart and up on the balls of my feet, presenting my sizzling rump to her as if it were a swollen, scarlet, pulsating gift! I writhed, desperate to avoid any additional hurt. She paused, touched me, and whispered a few words of encouragement. I struggled to present myself, to see it through. The belt flailed again, smacking hot across me. I searched for resolve, for courage. The belt took me again, and again, slashing bittersweet, flaming kisses all across my tender, quivering ass. Molly's mom saw me writhing again, and she paused, and put her hand under me in front, right over my scrotum, and urged me back into position. I was hollow inside, really straining, suffering. In some crazy way, I wanted to impress her, and Molly too, and so I managed to get up again onto the balls of my feet, and to jut my tormented buttocks defiantly. She went slower now, carefully filling in the pale swatches, working me. She saw my inner struggles, and respected them, allowing me time after each stroke to compose myself, to gather up the spilled bits of my commitment and to rise up off my heels and offer myself again. She whispered praises now, and encouragements, and I glimpsed her lovely hair dangling loose and wet, the perspiration on her chest above the exciting black brassiere, and I saw the girdle, and the silver garter tabs tugging the dark stocking bands in such contrast to her milky white thighs. I saw her fist gripping the black leather belt, the menace in its strength, and I felt my utter vulnerability, but at the same time I knew my secrets were safe here, and valued, and that this was only the first time, and that I needed desperately to experience all of this! I knew, as the leather crashed against me again, that I was going to further embarrass myself, and I closed my eyes and strained back to invite the awful kisses, and then another sweet orgasm discharged out of me and the punishment stopped, and Mrs. Bivens wrapped her arms around my torso and cried. Clearly, she was thrilled. "Oh, magnificent!" she exclaimed. "It's in you, Jeremiah! I sensed it was, that you are one of us! That's wonderful, so wonderful!" The first discharge had been physically and emotionally devastating, the second deeper and more meaningful, almost a religious experience. But, when the wonderful surges were over and I wanted to relax into a sweet, rewarded state of lethargy, Mrs. Bivens insisted upon finishing.

I was sobbing, utterly miserable. At last she paused. "Have you learned your lesson, Jeremiah?"

"Yes, Ma'am!" I was not exaggerating.

"Yes," she said thoughtfully, "I believe you have. Pull up your under-pants, then, and go to the laundry room. Get a bucket of soap and water, and a rag. Then come right back here and clean up your mess." I knew exactly what she meant.

When it was over she watched us dress, Molly and I both. We avoided looking at each other. The three of us went upstairs and had a long, emotional conversation. Molly had had suspicions of her parents' strange hobby, but it had never been discussed before. She had been taken to the dark room in the cellar, had been made to lower her panties and feel the paddle's sting across her bottom. She felt intuitively that the secret locked room had been important to her parents, but she hadn't realized why before tonight. I thought my reaction had helped her to be accepting of it. Molly admired that I had been brave and strong, but she couldn't understand how I had become sexually stimulated by the pain, and I was unable to explain. There would be more discussions in the future. Mrs. Bivens had unleashed something powerful and romantic into the big old house, and it would run its course. As a male, I would not be privy to all of their conspiring. Most of the surface hurt was gone before I went home that evening, although I sat carefully for a few days to avoid the deeper soreness that had soaked through my youthful buttocks. Molly had begun to giggle about my wounded bottom, and to tease me about additional punish-ments I could expect if I did not please her. And I, despite the hurt, felt immense pride and satisfaction.

19

Like a prisoner
I'm trying to get something out
That's locked inside.
She thinks I go to the dominatrix
To have things added.
To acquire
Stripes, the hot rash upon my flesh.
No, I go because only
The dominatrix knows
How to open the cell door
Behind which my soul
Is held prisoner.
That's the relief I crave
And it's not
Only sexual.
It's only necessary.

by the author
composed during a sex addiction 12-step meeting, 1992

It was late afternoon, and I was traveling a state highway across the mountains of western North Carolina. My career had accelerated, I was a factory representative now, with increased responsibilities and a business card that elicited reactions of admiration. I was on the road, away from home more than ever before, traveling lonely roads to lonelier hotel rooms, replaying tired cassette tapes, creating marketing strategies and sexual fantasies in parallel strains punctuated by Interstate highway intersections. Sharon was home with our child, tired but joyfully domestic. We had taken a huge chance, having another child after the first had died. Our pain and guilt were still intense, and there were nightmares rooted in fear. It was clear that we needed to move beyond tragedy, to try again and pin our hopes on a new little child. We were young, too young to wallow in sadness or despair.

Sure enough, our second child was an antidote, a bright and happy little girl with dimples and blue eyes under a tangle of blonde curls. Then, as if our luck had changed completely, a job opportunity appeared.

I had never heard of a dominatrix. Which is to say, I was familiar with the species but not the appellation. Cruising across North Carolina on my way to an appointment I stopped at a roadside adult book store and bought a magazine. I rarely go to those places, but I was alone, and sometimes I think these moments are preordained and cosmic, that we are required by some God or life-force to deviate a moment and be introduced to new choices relevant to our lives, exposed to new thoughts or knowledge because a master plan dictates that we must fulfill some necessary role. The magazine introduced me to the realm of dominant women, all pictured in their black leather costumes, with addresses and phone numbers. I would be going to California in about three weeks. I called, nervously, spoke with the Mistress for a few minutes, and made an appointment. That night I began to anticipate and sweat.

The tempest was unleashed. Over the next twelve years I would do fifty-six sessions with forty-two dominatrices. Some were wonderful moments, and some were disgusting. Sometimes the lady understood my need, listened to my desires, and made them real. Other times they ridiculed me, or offered a mild, emotionless parody of my requests that was demeaning by nature of its insincerity.

Mistress Gretchen was a slender blonde Germanic woman, wonderfully attractive with just a hint of an accent to accompany her exotic persona. Her studio occupied the upper floors of her immense Victorian mansion on Main Street in a little New Jersey town just across the river from Philadelphia. Clients were instructed to park along a shady side street, and come to the rear entrance. Inside, the Mistress led you through the kitchen to the formal dining room, where you offered her tribute in a plain white envelope and then undressed completely, folding your clothes neatly and placing them on one of the heavy wooden chairs at the table. Standing naked, feet apart and hands crossed in the small of your back, you explained your fantasy to the attentive, leather-clad dominatrix. Her eyes seemed to measure you, and then she pronounced sentence. Only then did she take you upstairs to your fate.

I liked Mistress Gretchen, and did a number of sessions with her. She was a stern, demanding woman, but incredibly well-equipped and inventive. After hearing my fate, I would kneel and kiss the toes of her high-heeled boots. Then it was up the stairs, and briskly, the Mistress following closely behind. I always found this a most humiliating exercise, my sex bobbing wildly as the

Mistress studied the movements, and perhaps the musculature or anatomical highlights of my naked backside.

The first room on the left at the top of the stairs was a TV room, but without a television. This was a frilly feminine bedroom with a daybed and an elaborate dresser, and a closet full of outfits for her transvestite clients. Mistress Gretchen knew my history, and she always laid out glorious outfits for me. Once I was dressed as a schoolgirl, with a short dark blue uniform skirt and a starched white blouse, knee socks and patent leather shoes. She wore a severe dark blue suit that time and played the schoolteacher, and took me upstairs to her third floor studio for a terrible scholastic caning. Before all the imaginary children in the classroom, I was summoned to the teacher's desk and reprimanded for inattention and sloppy work. There was a tall wooden stool near the blackboard, and I was brought to stand before it, my back to the class. Mistress bent me over the stool, my wrists and ankles fastened to its four stout legs, and then she very ceremoniously lifted up my skirt and petticoat and took down my frilly panties. My classmates snickered, but they grew silent as she measured the thin rattan cane across my seat.

"You'll count each stroke aloud and thank me clearly," the Mistress said. "Failure to do so will result in the stroke being repeated, with two punishment strokes added at the end. The same for fidgeting or avoidance. Two dozen on the bare, Sir. I'll begin when you request them."

I was quivering now, feeling uncomfortable in the schoolgirl's costume, the padded cups of my bra crushed tight to the seat of the wooden stool. I was, of course, sweating profusely, except for my exposed bottom and thighs which were cool and feeling very vulnerable. Leather restraints buckled around my wrists and ankles were fastened securely, there was no escape. The Mistress cut the air with her instrument as if to remind me of what I must do, and the whirr of the slender switch made me shiver.

"I'm sorry for my misbehavior, Mistress," I said. "Please correct me, and teach me a lesson." The cane sung through the air, and the pain exploded in a fiery stripe full across the broadest portion of my behind! The first strokes are always hellish, far beyond one's ability to anticipate or imagine. Jumping into a refreshing pool or stream for a swim on a hot summer day yields a similar shock, and then body and mind come to grips with the exciting sensations, and one becomes acclimated. As the first cuts seared my flesh, I always wished I weren't here, that I could be anywhere else. But this was necessary, my lot in life, and I richly deserved it. A talented dominatrix would take me beyond the pain to a spiritual paradise in my mind, and Mistress Gretchen was very, very good.

Mistress Gretchen had an elaborate studio under the high, steep gables of her converted attic. I especially remember her whipping trestle, an enormous piece of European furniture that positioned the victim ideally for flagellation. Fully adjustable, the dark wooden device resembled an oversize vaulting horse, but the padded top angled sharply downward to stretch and tighten the gluteals and maximize their sensitivity. The restraints were awesome, rich oiled black leather with gleaming silver buckles. During one session she fastened me up there in my panties, and then cut them off me with a straight razor! I was completely ready when she took up the whip.

Still, my most memorable session at Mistress Gretchen's hands actually happened miles away from her. I had a weekend business engagement in Atlantic City, and called for an appointment to do a session as I passed through on Friday afternoon. She never told me she had other plans. I arrived at her studio, undressed in her dining room, and offered my envelope. The Mistress positioned me and then dialed the phone, and I, standing nude with my hands clasped in the small of my back and my legs widely spread, could only listen. What I heard shocked me.

"Hello, may I speak to the manager please? Oh, hello. My name is Mistress Gretchen, I am a professional dominatrix from Philadelphia, and I have a client who is in need of your services. He's a young gentleman, a successful businessman, but with a tendency to be mischievous or naughty. I have another obligation, I cannot accompany him, but I'd like to send him to you tomorrow, to have him fitted for a panty girdle. Yes. Yes, that's right. I'd like you to help him choose the garment, something very restrictive and tight, I want him to be quite uncomfortable when he's wearing it. Yes, to punish him if he misbehaves. Yes. Yes, of course. I would prefer black if you have something. Yes. And he is to be seen, to show himself off to you and your staff. Yes, customers if you wish. I want him to feel completely humiliated. Yes. Yes. And I'll call you tomorrow afternoon, and I want you to be completely honest about his behavior. That's right. Yes. If he does not comport himself as a perfect gentleman while undergoing this test, well, he won't sit down for a few days, I'll promise you that! I think he'll be on his best behavior. He's been personally trained by me, and he won't disappoint me, I'm sure. What time would be convenient? Eleven o'clock? Does that fit with your schedule, Jeremiah? Okay, very well then. Eleven o'clock. And he is to wear his new garment away, and to carry his male underpants in his hand without a bag, is that clear? And what time shall I call tomorrow? Two o'clock? Yes. Oh, yes! All right, then. Thank you very much. Thank you."

Mistress Gretchen hung up, ignored me, and jotted a note on a piece of paper. Only then did she tell me that we couldn't do a session just at that moment. Instead, she was sending me to a corset shop in Atlantic City, just a few blocks from my hotel/casino. She showed me the bold display advertisement in the yellow pages, and smiled. "You won't disappoint me, will you, Jeremiah?" She had seen the shop during a recent visit, and a lady entering accompanied by a man. She handed back the tribute envelope. "You'll need this tomorrow. Get dressed now, I have a date tonight. Enjoy yourself tomorrow. And Jeremiah..."

"Yes, Mistress?" I was hopping on one foot, tugging on a sock.

"I *will* call and inquire about your behavior. If you don't honor me, your next session will be most memorable!"

I did not disappoint Mistress Gretchen!

There were so many memorable sessions, so many exciting, intense experiences. At that time there was a club in L.A. called The Chateau, a fully equipped establishment just off La Cienega near Wilshire. Basically, The Chateau was a nondescript two-story home in a quiet, upscale residential neighborhood. The manager was an affable, balding gentleman who called himself Sir James, and who claimed to have been trained at the famous Roissy chateau made notable in *The Story of O*. I enjoyed a number of visits to The Chateau, and experienced a number of new sensations within its chambers.

The Medieval Room was a dark, foreboding chamber downstairs, just off the lobby. Within the space of a small bedroom I experienced the rack, the pillory, and the suspension hoist (on different occasions). After a wicked flogging I was fastened naked on the rack and stretched tight as a bowstring. The agony is acute, making breathing difficult, and my suffering was exacerbated by the Mistress combing my pubic hair with a steel horse brush! I achieved a rare spontaneous orgasm on the rack, but unfortunately it erupted as Mistress was attaching clamps to my distended nipples and it splashed onto her expensive leathers, so my punishment was drawn out to terrible extremes.

There was another room at The Chateau, across the hall from Victorian. I don't recall the name of that room, I only visited it once. It was a special evening, the twentieth anniversary of my first S&M punishment, and I had requested a frightful ordeal to mark the occasion. I had been undressed downstairs in the Medieval room, and kept crouched in a tiny cage for a long and agonizing while until my ceremony was to begin. I was blindfolded, and my hands were fastened behind me so I could not touch myself. Of course, with so many of my senses incapacitated my hearing had become acute, and they tormented me by coming into the room a number of times "to check on me." My fate was irreversible, and I was frightened, but I was also becoming eager to get it over with. Finally, after an eternity, I was released from the cage, collared and leashed with my hands still fastened behind me, and led through the lobby, up the stairs and across the main lounge to the assigned chamber where the horse waited. Everyone knew the ordeal I faced, and I heard hushed comments as I shuffled blindly with my tumescent genitals bobbing. I endeavored to move past the unseen audience with great dignity and pride reflecting my courage and the many years of prior training. I don't think they were impressed.

The horse is a frightful machine, an actual medieval torture device. Made of smooth, polished wood, it is simply a wedge or upside-down V. The victim sits upon the sharp edge, and when the supports are removed from under his feet gravity creates acute discomfort. The hurt soon becomes so terrible that the miscreant struggles to escape, but any movement only serves to increase the suffering. The horse is awful for a man, and it must be positively fiendish for a lady. I was broken by the horse, reduced to a pitiful, sobbing wretch within minutes.

Sadly, The Chateau began to deteriorate. There began to be questionable people hanging around, sloppy people, biker types. Once a clean and quiet place, The Chateau became noisy, tawdry and threatening. I saw in a magazine that The Chateau had moved, then moved again. Finally, shortly after the release of the book *Whips And Kisses*, the autobiography of Mistress Jacqueline, The Chateau was raided by police. I have never met Mistress Jacqueline and have never done a session with her. She is obviously well-funded, with extensive advertising, phone sex lines, and a popular computer website. The good Mistress is, I suppose, somewhat of a Hollywood celebrity, but her book did irreparable harm to the S&M community. Based largely upon her experiences as a dominatrix at The Chateau, an obviously insecure Mistress Jacqueline describes a nightmare lifestyle of promiscuity, drinking, and drugging. The book was released at the time my wife was struggling to understand S&M, and she saw Mistress Jacqueline on a TV talk show and was appalled. As a dominatrix, Mistress Jacqueline may be effective, although I certainly wouldn't want to place myself into her care when she is stoned, drunk, or otherwise out of her mind. How sad that she found it necessary to degrade the entire S&M scene to feed her irrational lust for attention! How sad that most of the books about S&M are focused upon the stereotypically wacko, self-destructive minority of players who sacrifice themselves and the Scene community in ever more sensational exposés that ignore 95% of the fetish community. What novice in his right mind would engage a dominatrix who is an admitted cocaine addict?

Other sessions are memorable. After The Chateau faded from prominence in Los Angeles, a wonderfully homey establishment known as Lady Laura's became popular. I had written a long and very detailed letter explaining my desires, but the staff at Lady Laura's exceeded my wildest expectations.

I had asked to be pilloried in feminine shame clothing, viewed by the girls while I waited as if in the village square, then ultimately whipped for all the townspeople to see. When I called to make the appointment, I was ordered to bring a complete set of womanly underclothes, including panties and bra, pantyhose, and a half slip. Lady Laura's featured a large staff of competent, enthusiastic dominatrices, and also a few submissives. When I arrived the atmosphere around the reception desk and waiting area was joyous and fun, with the various ladies and their clients arriving or departing. The ladies were gathered at the desk, obviously planning their sessions, and generally giggling merrily like coeds in a college dorm. It was always a clean, neat and elegant environment, carefully maintained under the watchful eye of Mistress Laura herself.

My business plans and flight arrival conspired to make a Sunday afternoon session best for this visit. I had made arrangements to do a one-hour session beginning at three, and I arrived precisely on time. The receptionist referred to a handwritten note, explained that I would be serving Mistress Elizabeth today, but she wasn't available just now. Mistress Rachel would show me to a room where I could change into the clothing I would wear to punishment. The Mistress took me to a punishment chamber and made herself comfortable as she watched me change. Finally, I was able to finish dressing.

Mistress put my clothes into my bag and led me back to the reception desk. Mistress Elizabeth had arrived, but was changing into her leathers. I was taken to the comfortable waiting lounge where two young men were reading magazines. "This is Jeremiah," Mistress Rachel announced. "He's waiting for his assigned Mistress. Jeremiah is facing a very strenuous ordeal this afternoon." She positioned me in the corner, on full display to the other men, and then I felt her fingers at the back of my knees, lifting my slip to expose my pantied behind. She tugged my hands to the small of my back so that I would hold the slip up, and so that my bottom was clearly displayed. "We don't deal in sex here," Mistress announced, and I could feel their eyes crawling over my back. "This gentleman likes to be put into a very pretty pair of panties, but if he becomes sexually aroused and oozes his slime all over the front of them, he'll be punished until the heat coming off his ass will seem like a radiator in this room!" I felt her finger low on my backside, tracing the outline of the crescent crotch panel. "He's been here before, fellas, and we know how he acts. We'll be watching for any sign of wetness, and if it's there he's facing a very strenuous punishment for his lack of control. Your underpants will be checked, too, gentlemen, and any sign of arousal will be dealt with severely, I assure you. Mistress Elizabeth will be along for you soon, Sir. Please maintain your position until ordered to do otherwise." She touched my bottom lightly, and left the room.

"I'm in trouble," one of the men whispered, and they both laughed nervously. I stood quietly. My organ wanted to inflate again, but it was held captive by the taut panties. I struggled to seize control of myself, to sink into the protective mental cocoon I would soon need.

Mistress Elizabeth took me to an elaborate chamber with a worn, realistic pillory at its center. The pillory is a familiar colonial device, often mistakenly referred to as "the stocks." The pillory is a shoulder-height wooden panel hinged at the center, with cutouts for the head and wrists. The victim is locked into its embrace, back bent, to wait helplessly until someone deigns to release him, or her. I stood before the pillory while Mistress adjusted the lighting and laid out a group of flagellatory implements on a nearby table.

"Do you have plans this evening, Jeremiah?" she asked.

"I'm staying at a hotel, Mistress," I answered humbly. "I'll have dinner and go to bed."

"You'll be confined for two hours, then bared to receive two dozen strokes."

"Permission to speak, Mistress?"

"Granted."

"I've only paid for one hour, Mistress. I cannot afford any more."

"You paid for a session, Sir, and you'll have one. We all enjoyed your letter. There will be no extra charge." She had lifted the upper portion of the pillory. "Take your place." The yoke was lowered, and I was imprisoned. Mistress came around to face me, a beautiful dark-haired woman in her forties, with sparkling eyes and breasts that threatened to spill out of her black leather corset. "Your safe word is 'parachute'. Your slave name is Juliette. Remember both words if you know what's good for you. While in my care, you are to be a young lady, is that understood? I'll expect you to comport yourself in a ladylike manner at all times. You're to be on public display, the other ladies will be encouraged to visit you and witness your shame. I'll expect you to be respectful of them."

They came in clusters, two or three at a time, to tease or mock me. They ruffled my humiliating clothes, slipped their fingers into my bra to pinch or twist my breasts until I squealed in pain, lifted my slip and tucked it into my waistband so that my shameful panties were clearly on exhibit. "A lady's panties should be dry and exquisitely clean, Juliette," they chided, examining the front of me roughly, snapping my bra strap or stroking the backs of my thighs as they laughed at my predicament.

"Yes, Mistress," I whispered, blushing furiously.

My back ached, and the backs of my thighs were aflame. My mouth was dry, I was afraid I might have to go to the bathroom soon, and I had been alone for a long while. There was no way to tell time, no indication how much longer I must stand here on display awaiting the whipping that was surely approaching. I could feel the presence of the instruments on the table near my left hip. The clatter of boot heels seized my attention. The ladies went to my rear, I could not see them, but I felt their fingers as they described my shame.

"Juliette, this is Monica." They dragged a woman before me, an attractive thirty-something brunette with frightened, pleading eyes. She was collared and leashed, her hands fastened behind her, and her ample breasts wore gleaming metal nipple clamps. A simple white nylon panty was her only garment. I did not recognize the spokeswoman, but she explained that Monica was a submissive, and that she would be sympathetic to my situation. The poor slave was positioned directly in front of me, and she kept her head lowered. One of the other Mistresses knelt and reached out to Monica, and tugged her panties down! The woman howled pathetically and tried to squirm away, only to be soundly spanked. It all happened in an instant, but on the gusset of her panty I saw a rumpled pad liberally stained with her menstrual flow. She stood quietly now, crimson with shame, crying dejectedly.

Her hands were released, and Monica rushed to tug her panties up into place. Now the Mistresses brought her close to me, face to face just inches away. "Watch him, Monica. Watch his face as the whip lands upon his bottom. Watch his face contort, and how he tries to hide the suffering from you." I felt their hands at my panty. They banged my knees together and tugged my satin panties down, and I could feel the cool air soaking all across my bottom, and then the whip hissed through the air and slashed full across my seat! I yelped, writhed, and the poor woman's face responded with horror and shock. She wailed now, but stared at me, and as the next stroke landed, and the next, she became very upset and disturbed. "No," she moaned, "Oh, please, no." I suffered, my back bent low, my thighs aching, and the whip slicing into my backside. I was not ready, and the woman's horrified look undermined me. I tried to hold in the hurt, gritting my teeth against it, but I failed. I allowed a groan to escape, deep and guttural from my gut, and then I cried, and her eyes added to my anguish. The whip was etching my flesh with strands of liquid flame, and I had begun to howl and scream, mindless in my agony. I thought Monica might faint!

It ended, finally, and they made her kneel and put my panties up over my steaming ass, and then they took her away. I was alone again in the quiet room, still fastened, hurting all the more. I was beginning to need to use a bathroom. The passage of time was mercilessly slow.

"Are you cramping, Juliette?" a gentle voice asked. I hadn't heard anyone come in. I said I wasn't, although my back was breaking. Suddenly a group of fingers locked around my testicles, squeezing brutally! I writhed, groaning, but I could not escape. "How 'bout now?" the voice asked, and there was a chorus of cruel laughter. My shame and humiliation were desperate, and my eyes grew damp with tears. I cried out, begged for mercy. To my great amazement, I heard her lifting the pillory's yoke and releasing me!

My panties had been tugged up into some semblance of their proper place, but they were twisted and uncomfortable, and my back and thighs were cramped solid. I could hardly back away from the device, shuffling slowly, wracked with stiffness and pain. Mistress Elizabeth eased me back gently but inexorably. My hands were numb, and my back was locked into the agonizing stooped position. Mistress was stern and businesslike, fastening a collar and leash around my neck, and restraining my hands behind me. Then she tugged the leash, and led me stumbling out into the hallway, and to another room. I saw Monica stretched between two posts, her wrists and ankles fastened, her back and shoulders a mass of scarlet welts and traces from her shoulders to her knees. She wore her panties, but the waist had been lowered. The garment was nothing but a narrow strip of wrinkled material at the very lowest portion of her loins, and her heavy, shuddering buttocks had been severely disciplined. The poor lady's head hung forward on her chest, and she was sobbing. Mistress Elizabeth took up a slender switch and whipped Monica harshly about three strokes, and the woman's shrieks became a crescendo. As she quieted, I was led around to face her.

Monica was dazed, her hair tousled and sweaty, and drool hung in a string from her mouth to a heaving breast. "You have company, Monica," the Mistress said softly, pushing a damp clot of hair off the poor woman's forehead. "Juliette has come to watch you suffer." Her eyes seemed to plead with me, and she hung limply from her wrists. Mistress positioned me, then went behind and took up the switch again. I heard it whistle and I cringed, but then the face before me wrinkled and exploded screaming, shaking, distorted. Another cut slapped home, and the face distorted again into a totally different crazed contortion, something surrealistic and plastic shaped by the pain. Monica's eyes were dazed. She was lifeless, hanging, absorbing the pain, writhing in response until her fatigue weighed her, then starting the dance again with another impact of the lash. She was someplace beyond frenzy, but as I watched she seemed to take it all in stride, to adapt to it. I saw her body regain its strength, saw her stand taller, eyes closed. Her lips had become a seam, sealed tight against her screams. The whip whistled, but Monica defied it. She rose up onto her toes and threw back her bottom with utter disdain, offering her flesh.

"Transcendence." Mistress whispered the word, but I heard it plainly. I was watching a masochist enter into her kingdom of ecstasy, and it was a magical transformation. The broken, pathetic woman had become beautiful, serene and collected. The whip hummed and snicked against her flesh. The corner of her mouth twitched as if to signal her acceptance of the pain, but it was a most cursory grimace. She swayed slightly, her body relaxed and accepting, available. I was spellbound, a religious pilgrim at the altar, mystified.

Monica began to pee, the fragrant liquid pouring forth and making a puddle on the dark wood floor. The woman stood still now, relieving herself, taking her pleasure from out of the sea of pain, and I could smell her urine clearly. Mistress whipped her with renewed ferocity. "Stop it, Monica! Stop it, now!" Those words seemed to interrupt the poor penitent's reverie, and she opened her eyes. At about the moment when she realized what was happening and began to wail miserably, a stinging smack on her glowing bottom quieted her abruptly. She wept and whimpered as I took a deep breath. Mistress came for me, led me away.

I was fastened back into my restraints and returned to my own chamber to face the pillory again. Mistress Elizabeth closed the door. "Everything off below the waist, Juliette. I promised you twenty-four strokes, and Mistress Rachel has recommended ten more for soiling your panties. I always administer punishment in doses of a dozen, I'm afraid, and so it will be thirty-six." She raised the yoke of the pillory again. "You know the position by now, Juliette." I moved forward at a shuffle. Mistress grabbed a handful of my hair and hauled me toward the pillory, and I felt the wooden yoke close over my wrists and neck. Monica's plight was forgotten. I know my poor penis drooled abundantly, but my attention was seized by the first cut of the whip across my behind. She was very good, Mistress Elizabeth. She made me cry before the second dozen was complete. She whispered. "Transcendence, Juliette."

20

In speaking to you of his submissive desires or fantasies, he is
baring his soul. Please treat this like the precious gift it is... –
Claudia Varrin, THE ART OF SENSUAL FEMALE
DOMINANCE, A Birch Lane Press Book, 1998

I don't believe you can standardize fantasy. Fantasy is unique. I
have thumbed through books of fantasies, looking for my own, and
I cannot find them... When you exit the S&M studio and go out
into the blinding sunlight, having seen what you have seen, you are
more alone than ever. That's the terrible secret O knew. – Erica
Jong, FEAR OF FIFTY, HarperCollins Publishers, 1994

She had seen to everything, she assured me. I had just checked into my
Los Angeles hotel and, following instructions explicitly, I called Mistress Mary
at precisely seven o'clock in the evening.

"This will be very special," she told me, "and totally unlike anything
you've done before. An extreme test, but I believe that you can do it. I would
never suggest this to any of my other clients. Besides, I owe a favor to an old
friend. Will you trust me, Jeremiah, and obey me without hesitation? I promise
no harm will come to you."

Fear seemed to cast a prickly rash over my arms and neck. This was most
unusual. She suggested we meet at a parking lot. "We won't be going to your
studio?" I asked.

"No, dear. You're going on a little field trip." She laughed. "We have an
appointment, so be punctual. And Jeremiah...," she paused, "*do* make me
proud tomorrow. I've told my friends all about you. Don't disappoint me. I'm
trusting you." The line clicked dead. I hung up the phone and began the
infernal anticipating.

We met in the parking lot of a large restaurant. She was standing near
the valet's desk, absolutely stunning in a flowing dress of rich dark blue satin.
She wore high-heeled boots laced to just below her knees, and had a small

leather purse over her shoulder. In her left hand she held a little riding crop, and in her right, a paper sack. Her mane of tawny blonde locks was tousled and sexy, and she looked like a Hollywood starlet playing a dominatrix. Mistress slipped merrily into the passenger seat of my rented car and gave me directions. She was playing a role, but not for a movie.

Our destination was a medical office building in a carefully landscaped, upscale residential neighborhood. It was early evening, and the parking lot was crowded. I found a spot and maneuvered the car into it, moved the shifter to "park" and looked to Mistress for guidance. She was searching in the paper sack, busily arranging something. "Jeremiah, are you wearing clean panties?" Her voice had a steely, no nonsense ring to it.

"Yes, Mistress." I was apprehensive, on guard.

"Good. And are you oozing onto them as you usually do?" She was stern and direct this evening.

I blushed. "I don't think so, Mistress."

She sat back on the seat, checked her wristwatch, drew a deep breath and turned toward me. She seemed expectant, almost frightened. I wished I could take her hand. "Jeremiah," she said softly, "you have a doctor's appointment this evening." She seemed to expect more reaction than I was able to offer. "You'll be seeing Doctor Linda Stevenson, my personal friend and my gynecologist. You'll be having a complete feminine exam, Jeremiah, including a pelvic. This is a very real doctor's office, and the procedure will be as realistic as the staff can make it. You're going to be treated as a young teenage girl, including a very explicit young lady's introduction to menstruation." The paper sack rattled loudly, commanding attention in the confines of the car. "You will carry this, Jeremiah." There was no question in her voice, it was simply an announcement of fact. She withdrew a clear plastic bag from the paper one, a bold transparent pouch of feminine napkins, pads, and tampons. She offered it to me, and I felt my cheeks and ears turning crimson.

"Time after time I've warned you about the discharge in your panties," she smiled. "As a submissive serving his Mistress, I would expect you to treat the panties I prescribe with the same respect as any other of my instruments, but you can't seem to control yourself, can you? So, tonight you will learn all about caring for your panties on those difficult days. You will learn to be a young woman tonight, Jeremiah. To the doctor, the nurses, the other patients you will encounter. You will carry your pouch proudly and not try to hide it or obscure it from view in any way. You will do exactly as you are told, and you will perform in a manner which honors your Mistress. Again, Linda is a personal friend. Can you do those things without embarrassing me, Jeremiah?"

I swallowed hard, just imagining. Her head turned to me and her eyes searched mine. She was grinning wickedly, obviously enjoying my distress, and she was absolutely lovely! "Yes, Mistress." She breathed deep, expanding her bosom and then exhaled hard as if she had completed a great test. I could see that she was proud of herself, and I wanted to make her proud of me as well.

"Linda and I have a bet," she whispered. "She doesn't believe I can train a man to do this. Certainly not to do it with dignity and grace. I've chosen you above all my others, Jeremiah, because I believe you will obey and not embarrass me. If you disappoint me and ever dare to come back for another session with me, God help you! If you perform to my expectations, however, there will be more than enough pleasure to balance your discomforts." She stretched her left arm, glanced at the tiny gold watch that had slipped out of her sleeve. "It's getting near time, sweetheart. Are you ready to do this for me?"

I was distraught, ashamed to say anything. My mouth was so dry my tongue was adhered to the roof. "You know I won't embarrass you, Mistress." I swallowed hard. She was gathering her things, reaching for the door handle. "Mistress..."

"Yes, Jeremiah?" Her eyebrows arched, her hair tumbling off her shoulder.

"May I make one request, Mistress?"

"Go ahead."

"You know that I will do anything you ask, Mistress. Thank you for choosing me. I assume that this is important to you, and so I ask that you make it clear to everyone we meet that I did not request this. Please explain my motivation, Mistress. Explain for me, for both of us. Make it clear that I accept shame and humiliation out of devotion to you, that my actions are an expression of respect and admiration for yourself and, ultimately, all women. Doing these things is, well..., an offering I place at your feet, Mistress. I would not do this if not for you."

"Rest assured." She winked, then reached across the car and squeezed my hand, grinning broadly. She was ravishing, easily as lovely as any movie star in the city, and I would not disappoint her. We both knew it. Her eyes wrenched at my heart and soul. "I believe in you, Jeremiah. Remember that. Now, we have to go!" She popped the door latch.

It was a fairly typical medical office, a wooden door off the quiet carpeted hallway, plastic plaques listing all the doctors' names. Obstetrics and gynecology. The scent of alcohol was inescapable, but faint. I clutched my shameful package of feminine items, Mistress paused with her hand on the door knob. "Okay?" she asked. I nodded, and she winked. She opened the door and we entered into a very small, cramped waiting room. Three women watched us as we crossed to the receptionist's window. I was being examined, and I felt the heat of a scarlet blush spreading up over my neck and face.

The receptionist was in crisp, starched whites. She greeted Mistress by name, her face dissolving into an enormous smile as her eyes came to me. I shriveled. "This is Jeremiah," Mistress announced to the room. "He has an appointment with Doctor Stevenson at seven-thirty." The waiting room was small, and I knew that the three ladies had heard every word.

The receptionist checked her chart. "Yes, here it is, with Doctor Stevenson." She bent closer to the appointment register. "For an exam?" I cringed, wanting to disappear.

"Yes," Mistress said precisely. The room was still, expectant. "A young lady's physical, with a pelvic." I felt prickles everywhere, needles and pins at my temples! I was afraid I might fall down.

"Yes, I see it here. Will this be his first pelvic?"

Mistress turned to me. "You've never had a pelvic exam before, have you Jeremiah? Answer the lady."

"No, ma'am." The blood rushing to my head made it feel like it might burst.

"And I have him scheduled for an introduction to menstruation as well," the woman announced. "Normally I would ask if the patient has begun her periods yet..." I was feeling lightheaded and hot.

"Just a little discharge sometimes." There was a twitter of suppressed laughter behind me. "He's kept in panties, and sometimes he becomes aroused and makes them damp. Doctor Stevenson's going to teach him about wearing pads to protect them." Mistress touched my elbow, gave it a little squeeze.

The receptionist was very professional, but also hugely entertained by my situation. She leaned out over her counter to get a closer look at my embarrassing pouch of womanly items and her face was stretched by a playful, mocking smile. "And he's brought his own things! Very well, it will just be a few minutes. You can have a seat and I'll call you." There was a rustling as the ladies returned to their magazines.

She went to one of the grey fabric and wood chairs and settled herself. I was standing, on display with my package of shame. Mistress crossed her legs, dangled one foot about a foot off the floor. "Honor me, Jeremiah." I went to my knees, kissed the toe of the proffered boot. I felt her lean forward, and some-thing touched my cheek. It was the riding crop. "How are you doing?" she asked. Her voice was barely a whisper, intended only for me. The other women squirmed and shifted.

"I'm okay, Mistress." I felt claustrophobic, panicky.

"You're doing very nicely, Jeremiah. You may get up, go to the table and choose a very feminine magazine to read, then make yourself comfortable right here." She patted the chair to her left. "You keep your package on display, though. These ladies all recognize what you're experiencing. They've been there." The tongue of the crop touched my cheek. "Okay." She nodded. I rose, the blood pounding in my temples, the hot blush flooding my cheeks.

I sat alongside Mistress thumbing through a magazine. A voice, thick with a Latino accent, broke the oppressive silence in the tiny room. "Is he your husband?"

"No, I am his dominatrix. I'm training him to be more understanding and sensitive to women during their periods." Silence slammed over the room like an electrical charge. I waited, desperately apprehensive, trembling and shamed. I flipped pages in the magazine, turned to a full-page advertisement for maxi-pads. Mistress leaned close, pointed with her finger. At that moment the door to the examining rooms opened, a nurse stepped halfway into the waiting room and summoned one of the other ladies. I shifted in the chair, desperate to get on with it.

The door opened again. "Jeremiah?"

I closed my magazine, rose and put it back where I had found it. I felt everyone's eyes studying me, studying the transparent package of humiliating articles I carried. I moved toward the inner offices, shaky and unsure, but then the Mistress appeared alongside me. I felt a moment's relief and then POP! the crop hissed through the air and bit my bottom, and I jerked in surprise at the hurt! I almost stumbled past the nurse, I was ungainly and terribly disoriented, and then she shut the door and led down a bright hallway to an examining room. "Everything off but your underpants," the nurse ordered, holding out a folded rectangle of soft white cloth decorated with small, faded blue flowers. "Put this on, dear, and I'll be right back." Her tone was not playful, and her eyes seemed to mock me without pity.

Mistress sat down on a plastic and chrome chair along the far wall, studying me with some amusement. I sucked in a deep breath and began to disrobe. I had chosen my panties carefully in an upscale department store's "Intimate Apparel" salon, simple pink Vanity Fair briefs, size 5. They offered some support for my male organs but were sheer, almost transparent. Mistress smiled admiringly as I lowered my trousers.

The gown was feminine and completely open in the back. When I was dressed in it the Mistress summoned me. She was searching her bag. "Raise your gown, Jeremiah." I did, and she fitted chrome alligator clips to my nipples, wicked little devices with serrated teeth that bit painfully into my sensitive buds. "Honor Me," she whispered, and the nurse returned to find me kneeling at my dominatrix's feet, lips pressed reverently to the toe of her boot.

"Jeremiah, my name is Eleanor, and I am the nurse assigned to you this evening. We're going to start with a few vital signs. If I may, Mistress?"

"Of course, Eleanor. Rise, Jeremiah. Do as the lady asks." My panties and the nipple clips were obvious under the ridiculous gown. She led me to the scale where she recorded my height, then adjusted the sliding brass weights until the arms balanced and she could record my weight. She sat me on a corner of the examining table and checked my blood pressure and my pulse. Now she took out a thermometer. "Are you going to take his temperature?" Mistress asked.

"Yes."

Mistress searched her bag again. "I would prefer that you use a rectal thermometer," she said, holding out a small black plastic device that resembled a fountain pen. I felt the scarlet blush returning, flushing my ears and face. "He's learning to accept anal penetration. Touch your toes, Jeremiah," the Mistress ordered, "and hold position." The nurse had taken a tube of lubricant from the cabinet, and I heard her snapping latex gloves onto her hands. "Panties down, Jeremiah, and return to position. Don't let them touch the floor." There was a split-second hiss and the crop exploded against my left thigh. I shrugged the panties to my knees, then resumed my position. "Good boy," Mistress whispered, patting my flank. She returned to her seat. I felt the nurse's fingers adjusting the gown, then at my rear. She opened me, greased me, and then I felt the slender instrument penetrate my most private place.

"Three minutes," the nurse announced. Blood was rushing to my head again.

"Don't let it fall out," my dominatrix warned. I was straining, feeling the clips on my nipples and the tension beginning to cramp the muscles along the backs of my thighs and calves. I felt the two women studying me. I was still bent to the task of warming the thermometer when the door opened. "Hello, Linda!" Mistress rose, and there was an embrace.

"So, this is the famous Jeremiah! He's very good, isn't he?"

"Very good. Say hello to the doctor, Jeremiah."

"Hello, Doctor." I could see only her feet and ankles, sensible nursing shoes and white hose. I caught a faint hint of her perfume, or maybe it was Eleanor's.

"The ladies in the waiting room were certainly excited by your visit, Jeremiah," the doctor offered, folding back my gown and wiggling the thermometer inside me. "My receptionist wants to know why you do this?"

"Because my Mistress requested that I do it, Doctor."

"And if your Mistress asked you to jump off the proverbial bridge, Jeremiah, would you?" She was obviously trying to sound like a scolding mother, and amused with herself. She turned the thermometer, her free hand on my rump.

"Mistress would never put me into a situation that might cause me harm, Doctor."

"A splendid answer! The thermometer should be warmed by now, Eleanor. Mistress, I'll be back in a few minutes. Eleanor will take care of him." The door opened, and as she left the room the Doctor encountered someone else, another patient, and there was a brief conversation. The door was wide open and I was on display! Was it intentional? Had the other woman seen me, seen the nurse removing the thermometer from my rectum? I went to a deeper shade of scarlet. Eleanor wiped around my anus, then draped the ridiculous gown over my backside. I held position until Mistress gave me permission to rise.

"He really is very good!" Eleanor seemed to be warming to her task.

"Panties up, Jeremiah." the Mistress commanded, then, "Yes, I'm very proud of him. Thank you, Eleanor."

There were other tests. She examined my ears and nose, and as she listened to my chest she moved the stethoscope and knocked one of the clips off my right nipple. The blood rushed in, and I grimaced at the pain. "I'm so sorry!" Eleanor exclaimed, obviously flustered, and it seemed that she hurried through her remaining observations. I asked permission, retrieved the errant clip, and Mistress carefully refitted it. "Do those hurt?" Eleanor asked.

"You may answer, Jeremiah."

"Yes, ma'am, they do."

She was finishing up, making notes on my chart, cleaning and putting away her equipment. She had swabbed the thermometer with alcohol before returning it to Mistress Mary, and the pungent-sweet odor made me feel slightly woozy. "Okay!" Eleanor said, "All done. The doctor will be with you in a few minutes."

We were alone. "Submit position, Jeremiah." Mistress knew that I would obey. I knelt before her, my knees spread wide to offer my genitals clearly, back bolt upright, eyes lowered, palms resting upraised on my thighs. She moved from her chair, leaned forward and kissed my cheek! "You're really special!" she whispered, and then she placed the clear plastic pouch upon my left palm. "I'm very proud of you, Jeremiah!" She sat back on her chair. I waited, listening to her breathing, shivering with anticipation. Her words had comforted me. I would see it through!

I was allowed to stand when the doctor entered. She was a petite middle-aged brunette with a wide, sexy mouth and metal-rim glasses which could not obscure her gentle dark blue eyes. Eyes that seemed to be having fun with my predicament. She was demure in a beige denim skirt and a print blouse under her white lab coat, and of course she wore a stethoscope around her neck. The doctor was surprisingly professional, as if she did this type of thing every day although she frequently complimented Mistress as we progressed through her routine. The nurse, Eleanor, was a larger woman, and although her busy manner offered no real clue, I thought she might be the kinkier of the two. She had obviously considered this appointment carefully, and her every movement was somehow sure to maximize my humiliation. She was younger, a buxom redhead with a smattering of freckles on her nose and cheeks. She wore a crisp white pantsuit and when she bent I could see her underpants clearly outlined across her plump behind. Eleanor, I thought, was an exciting woman under a thick coating of professional white paint. She smiled at my ordeal and played her role relentlessly but with innate kindness, as if she were actually helping a frightened teenage girl. Her eyes belied the raw, prurient fun she was having at my expense!

They had me stand in the hot, confined room. Mistress was seated, and Doctor Stevenson perched herself up on the examining table. Her tiny bottom elicited all manner of crackles as it landed upon the white paper stretched there. Eleanor hovered near the door.

I was sweating, the hot blush soaking all under my skin. The doctor said, "Turn toward me, darling." I complied. She was a kind woman, I thought, but excited by this special occasion. Her nostrils flared. "Why is he here, Mistress?"

"I've been finding some discharge on his panties, Doctor. I think he may be beginning to menstruate. I'd like you to check him, and help him to understand what's happening to his body."

The doctor's eyes seemed to mock me. "Lift the gown, Jeremiah, so I can see you." I raised the front of the embarrassing little cover, felt it open across my lower back. I knew that I was almost fully erect, and that the front of my sheer panties must be soaked. She lowered her eyes, saw my predicament, and smiled. "Yes, it's rather profuse, isn't it? His panties are a mess. I'm glad you brought him, Mistress. Are you familiar with menstruation, Jeremiah?"

"Somewhat, Doctor."

"That's nice, dear. Jeremiah, there comes a time in every girl's life when she becomes a young woman..." Eleanor brought out a well-worn, spiral-bound cardboard picture book and for about ten minutes the two women gave me their standard young lady's introduction to the menstrual cycle. I chafed, standing nearly nude, my cheeks aflame. In some strange way this was all very stimulating, but I tried to resist becoming aroused.

Finally, the nurse closed the book. "Do you have any questions, dear?" the Doctor asked. "No? Jeremiah, your Mistress has noticed some discharge on your panties and I think it's time for us to take a look at the private parts of you to see if you're ready to begin wearing the pads, like we've just explained, to protect your underpants and your modesty." She noisily slipped down off the examining table. "Of course, we know you're not going to be comfortable when we have to touch you there, but we know that it's necessary, don't we? And Eleanor and I are just checking your development, dear. Just relax and it will all be over before you know it." My sex began to twitch!

Eleanor came closer. "I'd like you to slip out of your gown, Jeremiah. Doctor Stevenson wants to check your breast development, and your overall physical appearance."

My breasts, of course, were acutely developed by the alligator clips sawing away at my nipples. The doctor avoided them, but probed and squeezed the surrounding tissues in a crisp, businesslike manner that caused the clamps to hurt like hell. "This tenderness you're feeling is quite normal," she said, "and a sure sign of approaching menarche. Are your nipples tender, dear?" I assured her they were. "So nicely trained, Mistress. Okay, let me see them," and she removed the clips. The blood, of course, rushed in and I winced visibly at the pain. "Ahh, yes, yes," she whispered, tweaking my sore little nubs, pinching them between the edges of her nails. From the corner of my eye I saw Eleanor readying the stirrups at the end of the examining table. The two curved aluminum knee supports resembled oversized silver seashells to me, and she was spreading them far apart.

The doctor returned to my chart, and Eleanor approached me. "All right, Jeremiah, we're going to get you up onto the table so the doctor can examine your private parts. Step out of your panties, dear, and sit up here. Then I want you to swing your legs around and put them up onto these supports. These are the stirrups you've heard about, and they'll help you to be very open and exposed so the doctor can see everything she needs to see." I lowered my underpants carefully, folded them and put them with my clothes. Unrestrained, my erection came immediately to full bloom. I approached the table, lifted myself up and onto the noisy, rattling paper. Mistress was smiling, sitting forward on her chair. I wriggled myself around and lifted my legs up onto the cold metal dividers, and found that they had been spread very, very far apart. Eleanor was beside me now, touching me, urging me to scrunch lower, to spread myself even wider. She quickly made adjustments to the stirrups, and I was shamefully displayed. "Interlock your fingers behind your neck, Jeremiah, and you're not to move them under any circumstances." I complied, and Mistress came forward to attach the clamps again. My nipples were sore now, and I groaned as she screwed the clamps down hard. I had never, ever, felt so naked and exposed! My rampant sex organ bounced over my belly, and I could feel the greasy jelly coating my distended anus. Mistress stroked my upper arm, obviously admiring me as I lay helpless. She had put me into a pretty pickle! Our eyes met, and she winked and smiled at me.

Now Doctor Stevenson moved between my outsplayed thighs, and asked me to "scrunch my bottom down" toward her just a little more. "Those are the words every woman least likes to hear," Mistress said, and there was laughter. I wriggled, trying to comply, and felt myself even more blatantly exposed, my thighs stretched even farther apart! I felt the doctor's fingers now, gentle but insistent, at my scrotum, my anus, probing and investigating my organs in a most humiliating, exciting manner. I was teetering at the very precipice of orgasm, my erect cock twitching and drooling, and I think she recognized my plight. Her fingernail raked my sensitive perineum, tracing the corded central seam just behind my balls, and I squirmed at the hurt. A puddle of juices was forming on my belly. The doctor touched my inner thigh, scratched me again with her nail. I was rigid, utterly desperate!

Eleanor wheeled a table of instruments up alongside the table. The doctor was probing, truly examining me. She paused, reached to the table and took up a strange chrome device. "Do you know what this is, Jeremiah?" She held it up. It seemed like a pistol grip handle, with a strange rounded blade that was almost cigar-shaped.

"No, ma'am."

"It is called a speculum, dearest. They come in different sizes, and I've chosen a small one for you. I'm going to put this into your vagina, Jeremiah, and then I'll squeeze the handles together and the instrument will open you so I can see up inside you." She closed the handles and I saw the blades open. Surely she wasn't going to put that thing into me! She squeezed some jelly onto her fingers and began to lubricate me, especially inside! "Okay, sweetheart," she cooed, bending closer to her work. I felt the metal at my anus, then it began to slide into me. "Good girl," she said, and the instrument went deeper. "Okay, Jeremiah, I'm going to open you now."

It was not painful. I was stretched a little, and it felt very odd, but it didn't hurt. She had clamped the thing and now she was probing with a long Q-tip swab, and I thought I felt some liquid ooze dribbling down between my buttocks. She released the instrument and withdrew it, and I squirmed. My anus felt like it had been stretched and might never return to its original size. Eleanor held out a blue plastic dish and the speculum was placed inside.

"Well, Jeremiah," the doctor said, her eyes mischievous, "I'm glad you've come to see us today. You were right, Mistress. He has begun to have a discharge, and we're going to have to put you on the pads, darling." Mistress stood to see, and the doctor's rubber-clad fingers spread the puddle across my belly. One hand tweaked my anus while the other squeezed and teased my penis, and its twitchings became more intense. Eleanor, too, moved close to witness my shame, and she lifted my balls and bent to study them. Her fingers seemed to tighten, squeezing, hurting me. Just as I was about to cry out, she released me. The doctor moved back from me. "He's really flowing, Eleanor. I think it would be best if you washed him and cleaned him up a little first."

The "wash" turned out to be an enema, although they liked to call it a douche. A heavy dose of steaming hot, flower-scented suds administered with a lady's douching tip while I was still up in the stirrups. Now a new emergency gripped me! They examined me again, then finally suggested I get down. I had to wriggle and clamber to get off the stirrups, to turn and swing my legs over the side of the table, and I thought I was going to explode and shower the entire room. My insides were frothing, swollen and painful, surging hard against my sphincter seeking relief. I slid down off the table and its terrible rattling paper, but I would not be allowed to unburden myself right away. I was cramping now, shivering, frantic. "You can expect this feeling every month, Jeremiah. The water retention, the bloating, the cramps. It's awful, isn't it?"

"Yes, ma'am."

"You'll learn to function as if nothing was happening, Jeremiah. To play tennis, or run marathons. To work all day. Come on now, Eleanor has your panties. Slip them on and we'll get you onto your first pad." I was instructed, in agonizing detail, how to strip the waxed paper strip off the adhesive on the rear of the pad, and how to position the thing into the gusset of my panty, and how to smooth and settle it into place after raising my panties into place. How to position it for maximum protection, and how to carefully tuck my masculinity back between my legs so that the tip of my phallus would fall into a center groove I had fashioned into the absorbent pillow. (I had, mercifully, softened as I concentrated upon squeezing my anus against the pressure of the hot soapsuds struggling to escape.) Every detail, every nuance of the humiliating pad was explained. Each of the women found some excuse to touch me, to adjust my panties or the pad, to stroke my inner thigh or measure the swelling of my poor belly. The cramps were devastating now, I tottered from foot to foot or shivered at the force of the churning waves crashing against my bowels. They explained that they had put me on an "overnight" pad, far longer and thicker than those a lady might ordinarily use, because the overnight was better suited to my circumstances, and "man-size." I was trembling now, my teeth chattering, losing control. I thought I felt seepage into the pad and I begged Mistress for permission to speak, and then for permission to relieve myself! To my horror the nurse drew down my panty from behind me and discovered the shameful puddle on my pad!

There was a bathroom off the examining room, the door was opened now, and Eleanor led me away. It was, she assured me, impossible to control the flow. I would learn to watch my calendar and recognize the feelings and prepare by wearing the pad in anticipation. "Every young lady has had the experience," the doctor assured me, "of getting her period unexpectedly and soaking through her clothing. There is no more embarrassing experience than that!" I thought there may be one possible candidate as I stood before the toilet in panties, leaking onto a maxi-pad while three attractive women watched me struggle to avoid shitting myself! I felt sick inside. My insides were roiling, bubbling, hammering me with cramps! Finally, I was allowed to lower my panty and sit and empty, although Eleanor took the opportunity to instruct me in the proper methods of removing and rolling the soiled pad and installing a fresh one.

I emerged from the bathroom feeling shriveled and empty, my intestines shuddering and quaking. To my horror, I was made to strip and go back up onto the table, and up into the stirrups, where a second dose of the sweet-smelling douche solution was inserted into my loins. This time I was instructed in the use of the feminine sanitary napkin, the dreaded sixties icon suspended from a white elastic harness or from hooks sewn within a special sanitary panty which features the added protection of a plastic gusset. The ladies were amazed to learn that I had worn them all before, in the days before adhesive pads were invented. Mistress Mary was familiar with my adventures in service to Lady Sarah, and explained while I stood in dire distress, my belly in turbulent rebellion. The Lady Sarah, I suggested, had required me to wear a firm control panty girdle as added protection on my "heaviest" first days!

After emptying again, I was made to hold my ankles while nurse Eleanor washed my behind thoroughly before returning me to the examining room. Now I was taught to stand naked on one foot under the watchful gaze of three women while, with the other foot up on a chair, I received instruction in inserting a tampon. Three times I plunged the telescoping cardboard tubes into myself, then turned my arse to the ladies so they might examine the humiliating string dangling between my buttocks.

"Well, that about does it," Doctor Stevenson announced, peeling off her latex gloves. I was fatigued, my insides still roiling from the enemas.

"Come here, Jeremiah," Mistress Mary ordered, and I stood before her waiting to be praised. "Bring me the nipple clamps," she smiled, "and your panties, and a fresh pad." She nodded, and I hurried to obey, hopeful that my ordeal was nearing an end. "When we leave here," Mistress said, "we're going to dinner and I'm going to reward you for a wonderful performance." The ladies agreed enthusiastically, taking time from their cleanup to touch or praise me. The doctor was making notations on my chart. "But, Jeremiah," Mistress continued, "we cannot forget that you've been having a heavy discharge, so I'm going to have you wear both the tampon and your pad. A girl can't be too careful about these things."

I stood before her, my sex starting to stir again, holding out the items she had requested. She took the nipple clamps, fitted them. I groaned. "Step into your panties, Jeremiah." Her voice was firm. "Bring them to your knees." Now she took my left hand and positioned it so that my forearm was rigidly horizontal and my palm was upraised. She unwrapped the giant maxi-pad from its delicate pink plastic envelope, unfolded it with great care, pushed a depression into its center, and placed it face-up across the palm of my upraised hand.

"Turn to face the ladies, Jeremiah." I obeyed, not knowing where she was taking me. "I promised you a reward if your performance pleased me," she said. "I'm very pleased, sweetheart, and so you may masturbate. Enjoy yourself. But I want you to catch your discharge on the napkin, Jeremiah. Every drop. You'll wear it and sit on it throughout the evening." Nurse Eleanor hurried to a cabinet, removed a tube of lubricant and squeezed a liberal glob onto my right palm. "Spread your legs, Jeremiah," Mistress ordered. "A little more." I began my humiliating chore. I felt Mistress toying with the little string between my buttocks, and then the crop cracked against my bottom! I was blushing again, looking down to avoid the amused stares, and I felt the tongue of the crop gently lifting my balls.

There was a knock at the door! Doctor Stevenson answered, "Yes?"

"It's Thelma, Doctor. Everyone has gone, the door is locked and the lights are off in the waiting room. Will there be anything else?"

"Would you like to watch Jeremiah? He's performing for us."

"May I?" The door opened, and the receptionist slid in kind of sideways. I was standing fully exposed with my right hand on my throbbing erect organ and my left displaying an enormous feminine pad. Her eyes bulged and her hand flew to her mouth. "Oh, my!"

"Jeremiah is having his period, Thelma, and we have showed him how to wear the pads, napkins, and tampons. Turn around, Jeremiah, and show Thelma your tampon." I turned, blushing madly. "Bend forward, dear." Mistress reached around and found the little string and tugged it until I grimaced.

"Let's continue your chore, Jeremiah." I returned to position, eyes avoiding the three ladies who were now perched up on the examining table to watch my performance. The doctor explained what I was doing, and that the approaching orgasm would be my reward. "He's so good," she cooed. "You wouldn't believe!" I was concentrating on my task, working feverishly, and I felt the crisis nearing.

"Permission to come, Mistress?" As I had been trained.

"Delay it, Jeremiah." I paused, sweating, my knees trembling. "Good boy, Jeremiah. Permission to come onto your pad." It took only a few more strokes. I exploded profusely, almost buckling my knees. The jets were high-pressured and so extravagant I had to put the feminine pillow right up to the source if I was going to catch the entire emission. I felt blissful and serene as the final deep spasms rattled through me, and I straightened up to resume my position. Eleanor jumped down and brought a tissue for my greasy fingers, and I was ordered to fit the pad into my panties and raise them into position utilizing all the skills I had learned this evening. "He'll wear it all evening," Mistress announced, and she knelt to be sure that my limp penis would be tucked back onto the pad. I stood, scarlet, and then Mistress asked if the receptionist wanted to examine me.

Thelma was reluctant, but Mistress wanted to show me off. "Touch your toes, Jeremiah." I heard the woman come close, felt her fingertips lightly tracing the edge of my panties at the crotch, testing the pad.

"Is there any limit to what he'll endure for you?" she asked.

"I don't think so," my Mistress said proudly. "He's wonderful!" She ordered me to "submit" position alongside her and tousled my hair as she accepted their congratulations. There had, indeed, been a bet, and Doctor Stevenson left the room to fetch the payoff. She returned with a fistful of money and awarded Mistress her prize with exuberance and a long, emotional hug. The room had turned giddy and festive, filled with exclamations of wonder and praise. Finally, Mistress mentioned that we needed to go off to dinner. I was required to go around the room on my knees and honor the ladies, thanking each of them aloud before bending low to touch my lips to a snowy white shoe. I was sent to the bathroom to wash up and dress, and when I emerged I had to touch my toes while Mistress's fingers checked for my maxi-pad.

It seemed a long, long time had elapsed since we had first approached the receptionist's desk. I clutched my plastic pouch as Thelma presented Mistress a "no charge" receipt for my visit. "I'm going to have this framed," Mistress whispered. "It's a trophy, and I want to hang it in the waiting room at my studio. Guys will look at it, but they'll never comprehend what it means." As we walked to the car she held my hand and told me that I had made her very, very proud. The moon shone down through the palm trees, and I proudly basked in its glow.

21

When he touched his penis as a boy, he was risking his life, or so it felt; grown older, the man still confuses fear, pain, and anger with love and erotic desire. The prostitute knows his fantasies, but his wife is in the untenable position of naysayer, which is how life began. If only women understood the power of permission. – Nancy Friday, THE POWER OF BEAUTY, HarperCollins Publishers, 1996

I had found in the pain, even in the disgrace, a mixture of sensuality which had left me less afraid than desirous of experiencing it again from the same hand... – Jean-Jacques Rousseau, CONFESSIONS

I hurried out of the office and into the car, and plunged into the maelstrom of traffic moving toward the Lincoln Tunnel. The radio's crackling hysteria seemed to add to the frantic chemicals bubbling through me. Tension wrapped around my chest like a hard steel band; perspiration dripped coldly down the sides of my ribcage, threatened to soak my white business shirt's underarms yellow. All my life I had wrestled with my demons. Sometimes, once in a while, I would be granted an opportunity to exercise my inner strengths, to measure my character and reinforce my convictions. This evening, I would face the challenge. I was apprehensive and frightened, but also stimulated in the rich, forbidden way I knew so well.

I popped in a Billy Joel cassette and endured three stop delays in the belly of the tunnel, anxiously checking my wristwatch and the digital readout on the dash of the Taurus as if I expected them to disagree; as if one might suddenly accelerate and make me late. I mustn't be late!

The stereo changed to an older Joel hit, "The Stranger," which begins with a pensive piano introduction, then gently becomes an anxious whistled theme. I reversed the tape, listened again. We were moving now. I reversed the cassette again, the simple musical theme seizing my mind, perfectly comple-menting my inner fears.

New York City was a foreign land to me, and I prickled with tension. A few days before, on a company mission, I had ridden through her with a co-worker, and he had warned me about this neighborhood and the dangerous people who congregated here. I parked the car in a pay lot, gathered my packages and wandered off into Manhattan. There were almost ten minutes until my appointment, and I knew that to arrive early would be viewed with as much disdain as arriving late. I walked down the street a few moments, humming the Billy Joel melody, searching throughout myself for the random particles of courage and resolve which might come together and get me through the approaching ordeal. At a moment or two before six o'clock I stepped into the foyer of the apartment building, found her buzzer, and checked my watch. My heart pounded, caused tidal waves of hot blood to crash against my temples. If there was a musical note to her bell, the answering buzz was an octave higher. The elaborate wooden and beveled glass double doors clicked loudly, unlocking, and I entered.

The hall was long, marble, as resonant as a great Chinese gong. My shoes clacked down it like a horse's hoofs, unmistakable. I wanted to be discreet, unnoticed. The elevator offered some respite, then it opened onto the second floor and I stepped out, and it closed and disappeared. I was desperately alone, almost trembling in anticipation. This hallway was carpeted, and my tentative steps went unnoticed.

I had met so many dominatrices. Ultimately, most had disappointed me, but sometimes the bizarre ceremonies they conjured up would approach the exotic movies playing in my head, and during those splendid moments I was transfused with surety, and worth, and raw masculinity. Sometimes, the ladies understood my aberrant standards of measure. Very rarely, they approved. When it all came together the magical lady would reach out and, placing her fingertip gently onto one of the scale's tenuous platforms, she would confirm the validity of all my convoluted thoughts and secret, forbidden dreams. These were precious women, the ones who saw value in me, the ones who cared enough to listen, to get beyond my inept, childishly desperate pleas and recognize that all of this was vital to my existence. The grandest moments were terribly infrequent and the understanding women desperately unique, but not impossible. Beneath my polished, professional exterior like a vein of silver or gold in the dark cold depths of a mine, there lurked a sweet ore of kindness and gentility. It was available to all women, of course, but only a gifted few would dare to extract it from me. Would Mistress Beatrice be one of them? I was magnificently alive with anticipation and dread.

Only rarely did it really work, but I always expected that it would, and so I came back time after time, truly captivated by my fantasies, and I slipped each lady her tribute in a plain white envelope, and I put myself into her hands. Total strangers, hard women, dominatrices. When they were good I suffered, and I soared.

I had stepped left from the elevator but the numbers on the apartment doors were going the wrong way, so I doubled back, clutching my precious bundles. All too soon, I was at her door. Long minutes had passed since my finger had excited her buzzer. Would she think I had dawdled? Punish me?

I rapped my knuckles against her door, heard the clatter of stiletto heels approaching. The dark, flat panel banged away, the aperture filled with her. She was magnificent, a slender, towering woman with cropped platinum blond hair, broad lips, deep unfathomable eyes, and a simple dominatrix's costume consisting of a sheer white blouse, a straight black leather skirt, dark stockings and high-heeled swashbuckler boots to her knees. A beautiful, omnipotent woman. "Come in," she said hoarsely, and I, of course, complied. The door closed hard, and locks were thrown. My blood seemed to race throughout me.

She brought me into an apartment, a surprising development. She moved to my left, came to the front of me and stopped with one boot's toe slightly forward of the other. I knelt, careful of my packages, and bent far forward to kiss her toe. The leather of her boot was gleaming and fragrant, freshly polished. I heard gentle New Age music from the depths of the apartment, and smelled the sweet fragrance of a scented candle.

"What have you brought for me, Slave?" she inquired with a booming voice, and I worried that passersby in the hallway might hear.

"Flowers, Mistress. As you suggested." I had been well-trained, and so I barely lifted my lips off her boot leather to respond.

"What else?"

"Courage, Mistress, and commitment. You will enjoy working with me."

"Get up," she said, "and go into the kitchen. You'll find a vase under the sink. Arrange the flowers, and bring them to the table." I complied, and as I clipped and arranged the bouquet, she fixed refreshments. There were dirty dishes in the sink, and notes on a bulletin board. She actually lived here! She said she liked flowers, especially wildflowers in springtime. I had never visited a dominatrix in her home. They maintain professional names, and work in "dungeons" far removed from their off-duty personae. She put the flower arrangement onto the dining room table and invited me to sit down. I waited, standing, until she was seated before I complied. The dominatrix had placed two tall, frosty glasses of iced tea upon the table. Her eyes seemed to penetrate me, to suck all of my secret fantasies and behaviors out into the gentle candlelight. I felt naked, but not necessarily ashamed. She was beautiful, and a magnificent woman.

She seemed rigid and aristocratic, her leather skirt creaked as she moved but her eyes sparkled invitingly, and she offered a warm smile as she studied me. "What can I do for you, Jeremiah?" she asked.

"I'm here to be disciplined." I was, at that time, a powerful man, approaching middle age, but athletic and vital. I spoke timidly, my voice wavering with fear and anxiety.

"Why do you think you should be disciplined? Have you misbehaved?" Her voice was gentle. She didn't wait for an answer. "I enjoyed speaking with you on the telephone the other night. You said some interesting things. You have done this for a long time?" Her eyes were magic, filled with fire and joy.

"Since 1963, Mistress."

"More than a third of a century! I expect you to be very well-behaved." She sparkled. "Who started you? First trained you?"

"My girlfriend's mother, Mistress."

"You were in high school?"

"Yes, Mistress."

"Jeremiah," she whispered, not disturbing the moment, "first, you must learn my rules. You will address me as 'Mistress Beatrice'. These days any ten-dollar hooker with a black leather skirt from K-Mart calls herself 'Mistress'. I don't want you to forget my name, nor that I am completely unlike any dominatrix you have ever known before. Do you understand?"

"Yes, Mistress Beatrice." I did, and I had to admire her marketing savvy.

"Were you spanked that first time, in 1963?"

"Yes, Mistress Beatrice."

She smiled, and the room seemed warmer. She nodded to me, beautifully. "Nicely done, Jeremiah. You're paying attention. These practices must have been very intimidating for a young boy." It was a statement that asked a question, and her eyes studied me.

"I was brought up," I began, whispering to the beautiful, mysterious woman, "with the idea that because I was a boy, I wasn't supposed to show emotion. Not hurt, not frustration, not joy. Suddenly, I was given permission to feel, to cry, to love. I was willing to pay the price that was demanded, Mistress Beatrice."

"You hold everything inside, and it seems to eat away at you. But society demands that you bear the pain."

"Yes, exactly!" I had been recognized, perhaps even understood. I was elated.

"But to come here, to examine your relationship with pain, is considered sinful and perverted." Her eyes studied the depths of me.

"Perhaps," I answered, "but then those people cheat or steal, and so I don't much give a damn what they think, Mistress Beatrice." Her eyebrows arched.

"You're married?"

"Yes, Mistress Beatrice."

"Can't you be yourself at home? With your wife?"

"Not with this." I had to look away from her penetrating gaze. "My wife doesn't approve of these things."

"You've discussed it?" She spoke softly. I was transparent to her eyes; she quickly recognized my aching needs and my realities did not frighten her.

"Not in great detail. I have approached the subject, and she isn't interested."

"How have you approached the subject, Jeremiah?" She leaned forward, took her sweaty glass of iced tea and sipped from it. She was beautiful, and very elegant.

"I have asked her to read books, or passages from books. I've taken her to movies, suggested birthday spankings, or that she tie me."

"And she refused?"

"Sometimes. Sometimes she just made her lack of enthusiasm so evident that I would be discouraged for a long time. I've written her letters suggesting fun scenarios I'd like to try, but they usually create huge upsets so I try not to rock the boat. I masturbate a lot, and visit a dominatrix once in a while."

We had settled into a very comfortable, meaningful conversation. I eyed my watch, and she assured me that we had all evening. She had no other sessions scheduled, and wanted to get to know me before determining the "course of treatments" that would benefit me most. I was fascinated, as this was a radically different approach from other dominants I had visited. "I've suggested we try the mildest things," I continued. "I've pointed out books, taken her to movies with S&M scenes. She isn't interested, and she's almost hurtful in the ways she lets me know. So she doesn't cut hair and I go to a barber, she doesn't fill teeth and I go to the dentist, and..."

"And she doesn't spank a naughty man's bottom so you visit professional dominants?" Her eyes were playful, but challenging.

"Yes. But it's not that simple. She says she loves me, that she doesn't want to hurt me, but she can't understand that it's the rejection that really wounds me. I love her, she is my companion for life, so I just quietly do what I have to do. Life is all a series of images and appearances, isn't it? We rarely get to be ourselves."

"But with your wife, Jeremiah. In the bedroom. How sad." Her look told me that she pitied me.

"Mistress Beatrice, you don't know me, but I'm a man who takes his responsibilities seriously. I have a family, and a very responsible professional position. I feel enormous pressure, stresses. And I have a conscience, I'm an ethical man. I saw suffering in the war, and I read the papers. I hurt so, inside. Do you know what I mean? But I can't cry! I held my daughter's dead body in my arms, and I didn't cry! And so I sneak off to the dominatrix and surrender my body to the whip, and I purchase permission to cry." I paused. Had I overstepped my bounds?

"I understand," she whispered, and her eyes required that I believe her. "Tell me about your daughter, Jeremiah."

It was a painful memory. "She was hit by a car, on a Thursday, right in front of us. I went into work to get my check on Friday so I could pay for a coffin and a cemetery plot. The boss called me into his office and said he was sorry but we all have personal problems. If I wanted to keep my job I would report to work on Monday, as if nothing had happened, you know? That's the way a man's expected to be. Insulated from feelings, too busy and important to grieve."

"And, did you go to work on that Monday?" Her eyes seemed to study me.

"I had no choice, Mistress Beatrice."

"Every moment of life we have choices. Too often, we ignore them, or even worse, we deny them. Do you still work for the same man?"

"Oh, no! I left about a year later."

"So, you acted upon your choices. Very good. And, did you ever take time to grieve for your child?"

I shrugged.

"You were scarred by Vietnam?"

I fidgeted, wished I hadn't mentioned it. "Is it that obvious?"

She smiled, and there was kindness in her blue eyes. "Just a guess. I have to read my clients, Jeremiah. I've learned to recognize certain things. Many of my bottoms are combat veterans." Her face wrinkled, her eyebrows descending. "I should study that some day, I guess. I've always felt that it screams to be recognized, not analyzed. You need permission to feel?"

"I was too young, uhh, Mistress Beatrice. I saw things no one should ever see, and we weren't allowed to feel. Do you understand? So I came back and put on a white shirt and a tie and I built a career. I negotiate with customers, I sell, I fix things, I have a huge technical background, but still I'm not allowed to feel. Corporations don't recognize human beings, they just see potentials and dollar signs. Their computers analyze data and spit out pie charts and sales graphs and all those are supposed to be portraits of me." I paused, took a breath. Was I chattering too much? Her look encouraged me. "Like I said on the phone, Mistress Beatrice, I have a lot of experience with being disciplined. This is when I get in touch with myself, when I'm able to feel and cry. Does that make sense? Just to take a little time out and visit my heart, be required to crawl down into my core, almost like turning inside out, and find my humanity, my vulnerability. To measure my courage and endurance, my ability to absorb and go on. I can be honest under the whip. With myself, as much as anyone." I realized that my voice had become louder with the emotion, and I stopped short, ashamed.

Ashamed, and amazed. I had visited many, many dominants, but I had never been invited to discuss philosophy at a dining room table. The other women performed their feats with varying degrees of expertise and imagination, and I played the eager recipient, and then I drove away to my other life. But this lady had deftly coaxed my reality out of me, and had even cared enough to approve, and to suggest! As a trained submissive, I should keep my eyes lowered in the presence of a dominatrix, but I was fascinated by this unusually kind, perceptive woman and she smiled, and there was genuine caring in her expression. She was an incredibly attractive woman, costumed somewhat as we had discussed on the phone, as a sexy schoolmarm, and my fantasies raged at her demeanor. She reached across the dining room table and touched my hand, gripped it and squeezed. "I'll demand that you be honest here, okay? It's an absolute requirement. You need to move beyond some of this, Jeremiah. Examine it, then understand it, experience it at its most vivid, and grow out of it. You can emerge a stronger, more confident person. Do you sense where I'm heading? I think you realize that you have potential, and that this repression is a barrier to your full achievement of life."

Once again I was aware of subtle New Age music from the living room. I was a guest in this beautiful woman's home! It was a quiet, elegant place, a sanctuary, and I felt very, very fortunate to be here. "Don't get me wrong, Mistress Beatrice. By all the usual measures I'm successful. I have a good job, a terrific family."

"And what gives you joy, Jeremiah? Where is the great joy in your life?"

Her words clattered against me with a hard, metallic ring. I could not conceive of joy. I sat quietly at the table and pondered the question. I had never thought about it! I could not answer, could not even imagine joy. "I don't know." I slumped, profoundly saddened by this realization.

She smiled, tipped her head slightly. "I graduated from high school in 1967, and went to college," she whispered. "It was a very vivid time. Our generation has seen a lot of history on the six o'clock news. As a professional psychologist, I can assure you that many of our peers are struggling more than you. Vietnam scarred our generation, Jeremiah. The assassinations, Watergate. We are all cynics, all disappointed that the America our high school teachers described was exposed as a lie."

I was overjoyed to hear these words from her. Operation Desert Storm was in the news every evening, and the Reagan-Bush years had transformed America and the world. We had become a debtor nation, and alarmingly militant. "As I have tried to rationalize and understand Vietnam I've considered all of that very carefully, Mistress Beatrice, and I agree with your viewpoint. Our generation has experienced incredible upset and change. I remember when our neighbors got their first TV set, and when we got ours. I remember the first space flights, the first portable radios and the first electronic calculators. Our generation was conceived under the shadows of Hiroshima and Nagasaki, Auschwitz and Bergen-Belsen. Nothing has been the same since the day JFK was assassinated in Dallas, and then a few weeks later the Beatles were on the Ed Sullivan Show. We've experienced the sexual revolution, the psychedelic era, Woodstock and the Haight-Ashbury scene, Janis Joplin and Jimi Hendrix. Richard Nixon and Ho Chi Minh, Neil Armstrong and My Lai, the civil rights movement, Martin Luther King, the 1968 Democratic convention, Contra "freedom fighters" and Beirut bombings. Institutionalized horror and death, mines in Nicaraguan harbors, and genocide in Cambodia, Bosnia, and Rwanda. Millions of lives destroyed. Still, *I'm* evil, I'm a pervert because I find pleasure in pain."

The beautiful dominatrix winked at me. "Windows and fax machines and cellular phones," she said, obviously entertained. "We were so idealistic in 1968, and we've had to cope with massive doses of reality. Corporate greed, pollution, misinformation campaigns, blatant corruption. Yes, it has been a vivid time to be alive. Stress is so much a part of our everyday lives. Anxiety and fears threaten to drown us. But the sixties were also good years. I remember going to Yankee stadium and seeing Mickey Mantle, Yogi Berra, and Whitey Ford all in a single afternoon."

"You're a baseball fan?" I was amazed.

"I've been a Yankees fan since I was a little girl. I love baseball!"

"I have to admit, Mistress Beatrice, coming from the Washington, D.C. area, I'm an Orioles fan. Your Yankees were terrific in the early sixties, but by '69 and '70 the Orioles were on top."

"I'll try to forget that remark before I whip you." She smiled, and it was a playful, kindly smile. Her eyes twinkled. "I seem to recall that the Orioles lost the World Series in 1969. Something about the 'miracle' Mets."

"Okay, I give. Getting back to the stress we've undergone in the second half of this century, I've always been impressed that words like 'stress' and 'depression' never occurred in the early times. I think of the ancient civilizations, the black plague, the crusades, our American pioneers going across the continent in covered wagons surrounded by hostile Indians, and there is no reference to stress! But we have computers and central air conditioners and electric dish washers, and Prozac! Today depression is the fashionable malady. What does that say about our lifestyle, our civilization?" We were survivors, veterans of the great conflicts, and communicating. She was not a Mistress, she was a kindred spirit, and we shared experiences and feelings for a long while. She had been sexually molested by an uncle. I had seen a Vietnamese peasant murdered. She had her Doctorate degree, and she did not believe most of what our politicians told us. I sold Japanese and European sound equipment to Americans despite the trade imbalances. She had never been married. I could not tell my wife my desires. I paid professional women to whip me, because there is no hypocrisy or "spin management" when the whip cuts across your ass.

We talked for a long while, sharing, delighted. "It's getting late," she whispered. "I believe I can help you, Jeremiah." She stood, majestic and lovely. "Go into my living room," she ordered, and I remembered why I was here. I rose and shuffled into the next room. "Look to your right, above the sofa."

Utterly compliant, I obeyed. There were three huge documents in opulent frames. Officious certificates, college and university diplomas. They were protected by sheets of glass, and the names were taped over, but I saw that the dominatrix had been awarded a bachelor's, a masters, and a Ph.D., all in psychology. "I was Director of Human Resources for a prestigious Wall Street investment firm." Her voice came from the dining area. "One afternoon I went to lunch and decided to be honest with myself, to become a professional dominant. I called from a pay phone and told them I wouldn't be back, and then walked into a leather shop in the Village and bought a few things, and I've never looked back. Have you ever hurt anyone with your S&M play, Jeremiah?"

"No, Mistress." I was gazing at her living room, mesmerized by its elegant Oriental motif.

"Mistress Beatrice!"

"I'm sorry. Mistress Beatrice. No, I've never hurt anyone." We had returned to the S&M arena. I felt the anticipation prickle under my collar and in my belly.

"Neither have I, Jeremiah. The other night you told me that you visited dominant women because the experience of erotic submission enhanced your life. I accepted your request on the merits of that statement alone! You have obviously studied this subject in some detail, and I agree with your conclusions. My clients come to me because I empower them. My sessions are good for them! I choose my customers very carefully, Jeremiah. I don't want to associate with losers or the self-destructive. You bring your strength, your power and confidence, and you lay them at my feet. I accept your gifts, and my years of study will allow me to stir your essence, to stimulate you physically and mentally. You will accomplish here, Jeremiah, and gain enlightenment and confidence. I ask only that you surrender, that you trust me and believe in me. I will not injure you, but the road to satisfaction will require focus and perseverance." She went to the closet by the front door, opened it and withdrew a small black leather riding crop, then closed the door softly and strode into the room to join me. "Do you dare, Jeremiah?" I fell to my knees and kissed the toes of her boots.

"I need to cry, Mistress Beatrice!" There were tears in my eyes, and I couldn't understand why.

I knelt before her, a receptacle. "How many dominatrices have you seen, Jeremiah?"

She was incredibly on-target! "Funny that you would ask that, Mistress. I just made a list a few nights ago. Exactly forty-one. You are the forty-second, Mistress Beatrice."

"And how many sessions have you done?"

I lifted my lips from her fragrant boot leather. "Fifty-five, Mistress Beatrice."

She sipped from her iced tea, but I could feel her eyes searing my back. "So you've seen some mistresses more than once?" She paused, as if choosing her words with care. "What draws you back for a second or third session, Jeremiah? What works for you, and what doesn't?"

A fair question. "It's difficult to explain, Mistress Beatrice. Some sessions are demeaning, and you feel dirty or ashamed when you leave. Sadly, they're the norm. But once in a while it's like the direct opposite. Once in a while you find a lady who knows what this activity promises, who understands what she's about, and why you're there, and what she can make of you. I mean, it's as if I am a mass of raw material, and something magical and mysterious happens. She opens doors and allows me to peer down into myself, into the depths of my very soul. I know that probably sounds corny, but when it's right it's incredible! I like to feel that I'm being schooled, that I'm being trained in a very special, secret curriculum developed by women throughout the ages, and entrusted to only a very few chosen men. Men who have proven their worth by undergoing a series of difficult, painful tests. I suppose a good Mistress brings a sense of purpose to the session, and a taste of mysticism. She gives me permission to show her my essence, my masculinity, my courage and heart. I like to feel that my suffering is appreciated, and when I meet the harshest obstacles, I like a Mistress who will encourage me and help me to overcome myself. I enjoy sincerity, Mistress. Oh, Mistress Beatrice, I'm sorry!"

Her voice from above encouraged me. "You're learning, naughty boy. I, too, appreciate sincerity. Please, continue."

"Am I making myself clear, Mistress Beatrice? The best Mistresses require me to challenge my own limits, and they accompany me. I can't really explain it, but I come away knowing myself, and appreciating myself, and proud of what I've just done. It's as if I gain insights into my capabilities, my strengths. My endurance, to borrow a word you used a few minutes ago. The best doms seem to sense that I have promise in my heart, and they work to draw it out, and encourage me. They don't laugh at me or call me a pervert; they are in this work because they believe in it, and in their ability to help their clients. I come away satisfied, not so much sexually, but satisfied with myself. More confident. Does any of this make sense? It is very personal and private, and difficult to describe."

"You've had a professional dominant laugh at you and call you a pervert, Jeremiah?"

"Yes, Mistress Beatrice. It's not at all unusual."

"I'm sorry," she said. "I'm very sorry that you had that experience. It won't be repeated here. I believe you have a right to your thoughts, Jeremiah, and to express them." We connected. I was still kneeling at her toes. She bent, grabbed a handful of my hair in her long, beautiful fingers and dragged me up to my knees. I could smell the leather of her skirt, and her perfume, and I was wonderfully alive, expectant. "Your thoughts make perfect sense to me, Jeremiah," she whispered. "And, you express them nicely. Please continue."

I chose my words carefully. It was as if I were in church, and my words must be an offering. "Mistress Beatrice," I began, my mouth dry and barren, "I've always felt that S&M holds promise, that it can somehow liberate me, unlock my life and make it better by making me a better person. Isn't that crazy? The entire civilized world recognizes that S&M is evil, and I dare to question. I've examined the subject in depth, and I accept the danger incumbent in every session that maybe tonight, maybe in the next moment I will be consumed by the great evil that everyone else recognizes. The devil will show himself, and destroy me. That's the sweet tension in this activity, isn't it, Mistress? The danger that is always lurking, far more terrifying than the physical. Will I be consumed by evil? Will my life be destroyed? Will the demon show itself tonight? Mistress Beatrice, I've surrendered my dignity and my flesh to a lot of dominatrices over the years. Name it, I've done it. I've been stretched on a medieval rack, I've been in the tightest and most incredible bondages, I've been whipped and flogged with just about every instrument imaginable, humiliated, exhibited in frilly feminine underthings, enemaed, my balls hung with weights, just the most incredible tests, and still I believe that one moment I'll find my enlightenment. You know, like a spiritual thing, almost Buddhist. At the best moments, trained by the best and most sincere Mistresses, I've had small flickers of insight, quick glimpses of the sacred lamp. I honestly expect that one day I'll be invited into the temple and the whole truth will be made known to me. Am I crazy?"

"Crazy? You're human! You feel. You investigate your world, your body, your life! You resist the pressures to feel ashamed of your thoughts and vulnerabilities. No, sweet Jeremiah. I think you are a wise and gifted man, and I'm very glad you've come to me."

There was a long pause. I knelt at her feet, anticipating. She did not stir. Was she waiting for me to say more? Should I? I held position for a long while. "Permission to speak, Mistress Beatrice?" She had opened a door, and I was eager to be understood. Desperately eager.

"Permission."

"Please know that what I'm describing is very real to me, Mistress Beatrice, but most mistresses don't even know that it exists. Yes, I've had dominants take my money and then laugh at me and ridicule me to my face, Mistress. Sessions that left me feeling ashamed or dirty. I mean, there's a difference, I think, between being shamed, and being ashamed. I have dignity. I'm a very successful person. When I yield to a beautiful woman, it's a precious offering I place at her feet. Myself, my heart, my body! That's no small thing, for a man to strip naked and offer his ass to the whip. It's not play! Nothing to be laughed at. And the woman who takes your money and ridicules you is a mugger, both emotionally and physically. She's robbing you, just as surely as if she has a gun. So many times, I've left sessions just feeling disappointed and frustrated." I had been getting excited, and now I quieted, and knelt humbly before this tall, magnificent woman.

She was serene, wonderfully confident. She caressed my cheek with the tongue of her crop. "Do you think you'll be disappointed and frustrated tonight, Jeremiah?"

"No, Mistress Beatrice."

"Perhaps all of your successes and accomplishments are superficial, just plastic imitations of the accomplishments that really matter? I would like to train you, Jeremiah. I can take you to those exotic, spiritual places that are hiding within you, and show you the most miraculous sights. But then I can lead you back from those places and train you, I can help you to examine yourself, and teach you to carry those insights forward into a new life. Today's lifestyle smothers humanity, Jeremiah, especially for a man. Roles are changing, technology is more important than humanity. So many of my clients feel like you. Portions of your heart have gotten flabby and weak, poisoned by the environment we live in. We need to exercise your heart, get it back in shape. That's what's bothering you. You're at mid-life, you have a number of crises nipping at your heels, and you're looking for the strength, the reinforcement, to go forward into the fray. You doubt yourself. Corporate life is designed to destroy confidence, to make an employee dependent and fearful. To supplant the spiritual, and ultimately the self. You are in touch with your inner self, Jeremiah, with your heart, and so I can help you to communicate, to explore and examine your potentials and possibilities. The secrets are all inside you, but you have to learn to access them. I can lead you to them. If the army trained you, I can train you. I'll make you tougher than they did, and better. You won't do damage, you'll learn to find strength in surrender. That's all I ask, Jeremiah. Surrender. It sounds easy, but it is very, very difficult for a man to accomplish.

Acceptance. Obedience. Respect, both for yourself and for others. Do you dare?"

She put a finger under my chin and lifted so that I looked up at her. "Do you dare, Jeremiah?"

Mistress Beatrice commanded the room. She was tall, over six feet in her black seamed stockings, a Scandinavian blonde with high cheekbones, lively expressive eyes as cool blue as an after-dinner mint, and a broad smile that registered her inner joy and self-confidence. Her body was svelte, youthful breasts, tiny waist, legs as long as interstate highways, a pert bottom encased in tight black leather. She wore a sheer ivory blouse that allowed filmy glimpses of her rich lace underpinnings, and I realized that my groin was raging with desire. My lips were just inches from her primitive, aromatic black leather skirt, and her outrageous knee-high black leather boots with their precarious heels. She wore clunky gold earrings, and tasteful makeup. She was not garish; her manner was relaxed and sophisticated, serenely professional.

The phone on the coffee table rang, Mistress Beatrice excused herself to answer it, and I dared to look around, to investigate. This was obviously her apartment, not a rented room equipped as a dungeon. This place was luxuriously decorated in a Chinese theme, simple bamboo shapes, giant urns, a smiling fat Buddha idol, swooping chrome modern lamps, black leather couch and matching armchair that seemed inviting and comfortable. The kitchen was tiny, with dishes drying in the wire rack, notes and coupons fastened to the refrigerator door with magnets. Up on a bookcase I saw cookbooks, psychology textbooks, Jane Austen, Charlotte Brontë, Pauline Rèage and von Sacher-Masoch. Two photos on the top shelf, standing tall in slender plexiglass frames. In the first her hair was longer, she was wearing a red blouse and smiling broadly, and she was beautiful as any movie star. In the other she was in jeans and T-shirt, romping on the grass with a Labrador retriever.

She made another appointment, set the answering machine, and returned. She stood over me, staring. I started to speak but the dominatrix hushed me, and I waited nervously, my eyes locked on her boots. She was supremely confident, lovely. I shivered, knowing that I would soon endure great discomfort in her presence.

"Rise, slave. Stand facing me, and get undressed. Be seductive, thrill me with your body. No, no, not like that! This isn't a carnival sideshow. You're a very spendidly built gentleman in an expensive business suit. Disrobe for a lady showing your elegance and restraint; give the gift of yourself. You can be far more magnificent naked than in that suit, Jeremiah. Show me the value and the beauty of you. That's it, that's it! Your suit is expensive, isn't it?"

"Yes, Mistress Beatrice."

"Very nice. I don't want you to wrinkle your clothing. Fold it carefully and lay it over the armrest of the couch, and hang your shirt from the bathroom doorknob. Very nice. Now come here and stand before me, feet apart, hands clasped behind your back. Ahh, you are beautiful, Jeremiah. Your bottom is made for the whip, my dear. I notice that your penis is oozing, Jeremiah. I know you are stimulated, but that is very disrespectful. A man in panties must control himself. Why did you wear panties to this meeting, Jeremiah?"

"In the early days, Mistress Beatrice, I was required to wear panties. I usually wear them to my sessions. The feel of them against my bottom is like a preparation, and when I undress I hope that my sincerity becomes obvious. It seems the right way to present myself to you, Mistress."

"I don't disapprove, but I don't like seeing your arousal. You're stretching the front of them obscenely, and soaking them in your disgusting male juices. Your erection has no place here. Make it shrink immediately or I'll have to waste time with that, and I would rather work with other areas first." She stretched a rubber glove over her right hand, snapping it menacingly, watching with delight as I cringed. "Turn around. Now lower your panties to your knees, but don't let them fall." Her fingers caressed my buttocks, then greased my anus and spread me and probed deeply. When she was satisfied that she knew my bowel intimately she withdrew, removed the glove noisily, and examined my scrotum with hard, vise-like fingers. She turned me, stood me upright, clamped a nipple between her knifelike nails, squeezed until tears formed in my eyes. She went to a candle, heated two straight pins until their tips were red hot, and probed the other nipple. I couldn't help it, I winced noticeably, and she seemed disappointed, so she heated the pins and tormented me again. The hurt was real, and intense. She went to the refrigerator, brought nipple clamps from the freezer, screwed them tight upon my screaming nippleflesh. The cold made the ache penetrate deep into my chest cavity. "Have you ever been caned, Jeremiah?"

"Yes, Mistress Beatrice." I was short of breath, panting.

"The cane is a very effective instrument, as you know. The British have a formal etiquette relating to its use, are you familiar?" She rose, the leathers of her clothing and the couch groaning in unison, and went to the closet near the front door. She opened the closet, bent at the waist, and extracted a three-foot rattan rod, a thin and terrifying implement.

"I am only familiar, Mistress Beatrice. I have not been formally trained. I know they value holding position, and asking permission to rise after punishment."

"Yes." She examined me, tugged at a clamp, weighed my scrotum in her palm. "Obedience is a problem for you, isn't it, dear? You're still dripping. I want you to turn to the coffee table, bend at the waist and put just your fingertips on the table surface. You are to spread your legs and bend your back, I want your sensitive bottom to be the very highest part of you. That's it, very nice, bend a little more, that's splendid. I can break you with six strokes, Jeremiah, but there would be no point. I prefer to punish you, to take you on a journey. Don't you dare to bend a finger or a knee. You'll be getting a dozen. Come on now, strain yourself for me, invite it. Up on your toes. That's it!"

The rod whistled through the air, cracked hard across my white buttocks. The hurt could not be worse if I had been struck by lightning. It seemed white hot, a searing seam of agony that sliced directly to my heart. I gasped, tears overwhelming my eyes, but I managed to hold position. I have been trained, and I feel that these moments reflect upon many previous dominatrices. Some were disappointing, but a few deserve my lifelong respect, and the best way to honor them is to perform properly under discipline. The second cut whistled and smacked home. Ten more! I sobbed like a child before it was over, but I struggled·to hold position despite the awful hurt until given permission to rise. My delicate nylon panties had not slipped below my knees.

The session lasted nearly two hours. After the cane she fitted me to a leather restraint harness, spanked my scrotum carefully with a wooden spoon, adjusted my position, then strapped my fiery backside with a Scottish tawse, a terribly effective instrument. Then it was the riding crop, which had been menacing me, just waiting, since the start. Finally I broke down and sobbed, overcome with pain and exertion and devastated with emotion. I knelt on the carpet at her feet, trembling, struggling to regain control of myself. She sat on the couch above me, and leaned forward to touch my cheek. "Get it out," she whispered. "Just let it flow." Her hands went to my testicles and alternately caressed and crushed them, and the pain consumed me but the pleasure transported me to forbidden, erotic lands only the most daring and gifted tourists ever see. I was free, even in the harsh leather restraints, and then she brought me back and made me worship her boots again, and she allowed me to orgasm. I was on hands and knees, and she reached up under me like a milk

maid until her nimble fingers created an earthquake, and she caught my
pulsing deluge in a crystal wine glass. I wept passionately, absolving my devils.
The Mistress accompanied me throughout my agonized travels, touched me
reassuringly, punished me mercilessly one moment and whispered sincere
encouragement the next. She was patient, having seen it all before. This was her
calling, her profession, and she was very, very good at what she did.

When I had come back from my desperate journeys she required me to
perform obeisances at her feet, and to take the delicate crystal goblet with its
pearlescent cargo into my hands, to offer a heartfelt toast to her beauty, abilities,
and her authority. She left me on my knees, naked and depleted, while she went
to the kitchen and refreshed our glasses of iced tea. She came back to the couch,
sat close, touched me gently, and handed one glass to me. "I have many years of
formal training in human behavior," she said, looking down on me. "I spank
the bottom, but I try to soothe the mind. You're very good, Jeremiah. Well
trained, and self-disciplined. You're searching for something spiritual, you
expect a session to illuminate it in the deeper recesses of your character. That's
very unusual, and actually quite perceptive. I suspect most men secretly want to
achieve something like that, but they haven't thought it through, and so they
get lost and never glimpse the possibilities. The mental and the physical can
each be addressed, but when you combine the two it makes for a very potent
cocktail, don't you think?" She laughed merrily as I readily agreed. I had been
on an incredible vacation, and she had been the tour guide. I was physically and
emotionally spent, but also refreshed, renewed. "You know," she continued,
"most people can't bring themselves to imagine that sadomasochism, S&M,
dominance and submission, whatever you want to call it, can be good for them.
Without that premise, of course, they do it, but they're always basically
ashamed. That's why you see it portrayed in such tawdry, disgusting ways in
the movies and books. They can't stretch themselves to imagine that this
practice embodies anything constructive. Every aspect of S&M is rooted in the
basic paradox of pleasure from pain, and without understanding and study,
and a little bit of blind faith, people fail to discover that they're stimulating areas
of the brain that are adjacent, living cells that travel in parallel like a set of
railroad tracks. Most people come to S&M looking for a rush, and nothing
more. They see the pain as an extreme stimulation, which it is, but they don't
pause to consider how they might put the sensations, and any insights gained
along the way, to use in their lives. You, Jeremiah, have dared to look beyond
the obvious, and I admire that. I have enjoyed this evening very much. You've

made me think, and forced me to be honest with myself. Thank you, my dear. I hope I'll see you again."

I showered and dressed and Mistress Beatrice saw me to the door, where I knelt and kissed her toes in heartfelt gratitude. She accepted my obeisance patiently, then sent me away down the luxurious hallway. Entering the elevator, I spontaneously burst into tears. They came in torrents, from my heart, and as I walked toward the car many people noticed. I didn't care. They couldn't imagine! I was very, very alone, but not nearly so alone as I had been a few hours before. I was wringing out stale emotions, and it was all right. I had permission! It took a few moments before I was able to regain myself and drive out into the chaotic New York City streets. The west side can be a cold, inhospitable neighborhood, but I was very comfortable in it that evening. My life had unexpectedly, unmistakably changed. I had permission to be myself!

22

"I want to adore a woman, but this I can only do when she is cruel toward me."
"But, Severin," replied Wanda, almost angrily, "do you believe me capable of maltreating a man who loves me as you do, and whom I love?"
"Why not, if I adore you the more on this account?" – Leopold von Sacher-Masoch, VENUS IN FURS, 1870

The cry was conceived in Sharon's chest, deep in the cavity, somewhere in the vicinity of the heart or the solar plexus. It grew, fueled by the crumbling of all her life's securities, it was fed by the realization of betrayal until it became something akin to an animal roar or the sounds produced by a speeding locomotive as it rushes out from a dark tunnel. A cry, a roar of indignation, a scream of acute pain; as the operatic high note shatters glass, this sound demolished every aspect of the marriage, every tenet of our family. Certainly Sharon intended it to register the pain of betrayal, to inform me, but it was unleashed, and it seized control of the atmosphere of the house, chilled the air until it was crisp and fragile, menacing.

It was a primitive wail, utter agony, and far more. The sound an Aztec maiden might have set free atop the sacred pyramid as her heart was being torn out from her bloody bosom. The raw bellow of loss filled the house, seeped under or through the hollow doors, ricocheted off the cupboard doors and television screens. It banged against the framed photographs, the proud histories of the children immortalized, the somber likenesses of relatives, and tranquil landscapes from long-ago exotic vacations. The children heard it, downstairs in the family room, and they flew to each other's arms and hugged, hoping to find comfort there. Even the dog stopped in her tracks and looked longingly at the closed bedroom door. Eerie as a fire siren, this impassioned moan signaled an end to the way things had always been.

"When?" Sharon whispered, shivering, sitting empty and miserable, unbelieving, stunned.

"Many times. Lots of times. Over the years."

"Why didn't you tell me? Why did you stay married to me, lying to me?" Her teeth were gritted, her breathing heaved with emotion.

"I didn't lie. We couldn't get into enough of a conversation to allow lies. You wouldn't discuss it, you shut the door. I love you; I didn't want to not be married to you."

Sharon's eyes blazed with hate, red and wet and squinted, but unmistakable raw hate overpowering all else, and her gaze was a weapon that wounded me, her husband of twenty-some years. "You lied, and you deceived, and you manipulated, and you dare to say you love me? You betrayed me, had sex with other women, and you expect me to believe that? You..."

"I didn't have sex with them."

"What do you call it?" Her eyes grew large, bitter, blind to any realities I might try to offer in explanation. She simply could not comprehend. "Did you have erections while they spanked you? Orgasms while they whipped you? Did you?"

"Sometimes, yes. But we didn't make love, it wasn't something grounded in affection. It was mental, Sharon. Coping. Spiritual. All of that outweighed the physical, dammit! It's just necessity, something in me that has to be. A need, a hard physical necessity that you won't ever understand, that you refused to hear or consider..."

"You never..." Her lips seemed to twist to the side, it was a venomous sneer, a hiss that would, just in its tone, cause any jury to condemn me.

"You could never hear my requests, never answer my pleas. I gave you books, asked you to read chapters, and you gave them back and sort of spit at me, 'I don't want to read that!' What was I supposed to do? I wrote letters, suggested different fantasies in writing, and we would have these explosions, huge screaming confrontations, and then we would both promise to try to create a more exciting love life and within a week everything would just slip back to the same old..."

"I've done things for you that most women would never do." A sharp, clipped, accusatory sentence.

"Yes, once. We had sixty-nine once, when you were pregnant the first time. Jesus, Sharon, if she had lived the kid would've been driving now, in college! Yes, you've done all those things. Once! And then it was as if that settled your obligation. It wasn't that you were trying to please me, you were just crossing off the various items on a list." I didn't want to be hurtful, only to explain. I spoke with a low voice, calming, trying to cast off years of burden.

Still, she sobbed disconsolately, a distraught and shattered wraithlike image of her former self. This had been building for a long time. A cancer, with the potential to destroy our marriage, our lives, and I had always kept it hidden, avoided it. About six months ago, one night in my study, she asked how I could write about sadomasochism. "I've talked to people who are into it," I'd answered, not lying, and she just turned and walked away. That's how it always happened, the dismissive shrugs, the rigid body language, the stone wall. Rejection, not adversarial, just utter disdain. Followed by loneliness, sadness, an overwhelming sense of loss and abandon. I had searched for the words that might unlock her heart, the book, or paragraph, or sentence, the movie that might create some spark of curiosity or thrill. But no, she was a good woman, a solid, conventional, beautiful, serious, hard-working mother, a loving companion, a workmate. She was the only person in the world who ever seemed to sense my worth and really believe in me. My eyes flowed over; all of that was lost.

"You've gone outside the marriage," she said bitterly, still weeping. "We'll have to have AIDS tests, tests for all the diseases."

"There's no need for tests," I replied, hurting. Her eyes were hollow with loss and pain. How would I ever explain that she was mistaken? She moaned, deep in her chest, and it was a sound I had heard before. The sound of dying. I was distraught; what had I done? In an impetuous moment I had told her the truth, and now I stood in the midst of the consequences, the shambles of our lives, and I was essentially, desperately alone. Despite the apparent stillness, the house was still reverberating from her reaction. The reverberating, I knew, would go on a long, sad time.

My outburst impacted the house and family like an earthquake. There was wreckage strewn everywhere, and beneath the heaps of visible debris the structural damage threatened to collapse the entire family unit. Once meticulously painted and cheerfully decorated, the basic relationships of everyone in the house were charred, black, powdered grotesque images of their former selves, a trembling framework, a skeleton decayed with cancer. Sharon was numb, haunted, her security shattered. The children saw her move as if her body was weighted, they saw the loss and horror and utter despair in her eyes, and they knew that the family structure, the most reliable of all certainties in their young lives, was not a certainty at all, and that soon they might have to go to their friends in school, the ones whose parents were divorced, the ones who had expressed so much pain and misery in the past, and beg for help. Had they earned compassion from these friends? They had heard the anguish but couldn't comprehend it; now they needed to scream in harmony and share, and perhaps they wouldn't be heard, and their rooms were no longer sanctuaries because the house reeked of disintegration.

Sharon rolled over and tucked the covers up under her chin as another restless night confronted the morning's light creeping around the edges of the venetian blinds, and she was not refreshed. "Are you awake?" she whispered.

"Yeah, sort of." The alarm wouldn't ring for another forty- three minutes, but urgent, explosive thoughts had infiltrated our heads, and any semblance of rest had been chased away. There was only chaos and loss in our fields of vision, and the stark, awful scenes did not disappear when our eyes closed.

"I value our family. I want to work it out if we can."

I rolled to face her, put a light kiss on her cheek and tasted the salt of tears, and her arm came over me to pull me closer. "I want that too, sweetheart."

"I'm so scared, so confused. You said you want to leave."

"I want to leave if things are going to stay the way they are. If we can change, if I can be accepted as the person I am, if I can be allowed to be vulnerable sometimes, and to express..."

"You vulnerable? You've done this! I'm the one who is vulnerable, and the children. They have to live through whatever we create for them." She began to cry again and squirmed to reach for a tissue. She'd kept a number of them under her pillow, the last few nights, to have them close at hand when she cried.

I was quick to pounce, despite her sadness. "Why do you always interrupt? The simple point is, Sharon, that I can't be the Superman you expect. I work hard every day, but we're never going to be rich. I burp, I fart, sometimes my underarms stink, my beard gets scratchy about four o'clock every afternoon, and I can't help it. I try to control those things, but sometimes they get away..."

"I never called you a Superman." Her voice was rich with mockery and hate. "Oh, no, not Superman. My expectations have been shrinking since the day we met, but I never thought you would betray me."

"Did you ever think that I might have something to say that you should hear, and perhaps you should stifle yourself and allow me to form one complete sentence before you tell me I'm wrong?"

There were a few moments of silence. We were at the brink again.

Her voice was tiny and frail, a quivering whisper into the wrinkled covers. "We're not getting closer."

I moved nearer to her, physically, and fought my arm through the tangled sheets to drape it across her, across the familiar flesh, and she wriggled closer to me, physically, her arm squeezed me, and she still fit up against me in that uncanny, totally comfortable manner that I believed in my heart to be a physical manifestation of our being right for each other. In all the universe no other body could fit so close, but she would have to hear me, to know me again, because we had lost track of each other's needs. The kids kept her busy, my job demanded hours and attention, and we had learned to find recreation apart. She was home all day, making friends in the neighborhood, and I hardly knew anyone outside my office! I was constantly traveling, I would come home with stories of restaurants and exotic cities, Chicago or Houston, but my friends were all business associates and she had no access to my fun. We would collide on weekends, at the common lure of the kids, trying to create a family cohesiveness, to watch the children develop and maybe, in my case, despite my professional workload, to influence their development in some small way. Sharon shaped them, but sometimes I needed to feel valid, too. It was different when they were little, when we could fly a kite or capture tadpoles together. My relationship with my daughters had dissolved at the onset of their puberties, and Sharon couldn't seem to hear when I mourned the loss.

"Darling," she whispered to my chest, and clung to me, and I gave her a squeeze instead of saying anything. "The other night you said the Mistress made you wear panties when you were going to go to be whipped. Her panties?"

"No." I was about to say more, but I hesitated.

"You haven't worn a woman's panties, have you? They can have bodily fluids, they can be dangerous."

"I haven't worn panties with any woman's bodily fluids." I felt exhausted and frustrated by her strange twists of thought, that she could pick up on something so silly but not question the psychological importance of her man, her husband and lover, in lingerie. Why wouldn't she ask about the significance of shame clothing, about the huge obstacles presented to a man by a delicate, frilly little nylon garment? About his achievements in overcoming those obstacles, in coming to accept this as a right and necessary part of his training, his coming to terms with his sexuality and relationships with women? Why?

Sharon pressed on. "Did you buy them?"

"Yes. Sometimes I would buy panties for you, as a gift, and another pair for myself. And sometimes the sales clerk would point out that I had two different sizes, and I would say that they were for two different people and maybe wink at her, and I think some of them understood, but that was all right, too."

"They laughed at you when you walked away."

"Maybe. But I knew the context of it all, the worth, and so I overcame that type of thinking and it didn't bother me. I laughed at them, too."

"Can you explain that to me?" There were no words that could be more shocking, nor more welcome, than those. In all the languages and dialects on Earth, from all the voices, all the individual lips and tongues, the celebrities and personalities, the famous or omniscient, the street-smart or worldly-wise, the gurus or leaders, diplomats or statesmen, experts or con men, there was nothing I would rather have heard than this, my wife, expressing interest in my sexual aberrations, asking me to explain, and not simply rejecting me out of hand. A flicker of hope!

"How about tonight? I'll be late for work." Why now? I knew she didn't appreciate the hugeness of this topic. Besides, it was almost quarter to seven, I had to drive fifty-odd miles to the office through the densest traffic in the world.

"What's more important to you?" She snuggled against me, her body warm and fragrant, comforting.

I struggled to find words, to convey the feelings that were bizarre but oh, so important. To explain my vulnerabilities and how I had learned to overcome them, and it was a massive subject, I could not do it justice just now, but I thanked her for allowing me the opportunity to share some of it. It was a rushed presentation, a glossed-over, reckless, incoherent attempt, but she listened intently and didn't find fault. Toward the end I wrapped her in my arms, she buried her head in my chest and fit her breasts and belly tight against mine, and I breathed in the familiar scent of her and took emotional refuge in the touch that had carried me through so many crises, and she told me it was okay. She didn't understand, but she would try to accept some of this if it would keep the family together, and she asked if I had any panties now, and then we finally began to stir, to prepare for work, and I was late but she sent me out to the trunk of my car to bring in the wrinkled paper bag that I kept hidden there. When I came back into the house she played the dominatrix role, in the bedroom behind a closed door, and she made me get down on my knees and kiss her toes, and then she ordered me to spread out my treasures across the bedclothes for her, to exhibit my hoard, and I was embarrassed but I complied. The delicate garments were wrinkled, some were soiled, especially with telltale stains on the front where a man's underpants would feature absorbent double layers at the fly, and I felt a heady brew of shame and excitement and blood pounding at my temples. Secrecy had lent these treasures a significance far out of proportion to their appearance, but I displayed seven delicious feminine garments to her, my Mistress, and resumed my position at her toes, and she examined each one, letting me stew in my juices. (Or, perhaps she was struggling to decide what to say?)

"They need to be laundered."

"I try to wash them out in hotel rooms, but I haven't traveled recently."

"I thought you were supposed to call me Mistress at the conclusion of each statement, as a sign of respect." She offered it as a statement, but tentatively. It was, actually, a question, and a playful swipe at me, but one that drew me closer to her.

"I'm sorry, Mistress." I knew this must be confusing to a neophyte, and very unnatural. She was doing this as an expression of love, and it was a most precious gift. Especially now!

"I'll punish you later. I don't want you to be late for work. I want you to wear the pink lace under your suit today."

"Thank you, Mistress." I kissed her toes.

"And when you go to the bathroom, take them down and be seated the way a lady would. So long as you don't jeopardize your job, you know. Listen to me! I expect my husband to wear his pink panties to work and exhibit good sense! Am I crazy or what? But I know you can do this, and I want it understood, I don't want to see any more of these disgusting stains, ever again. If you are going to wear these as a symbol of your submission, I expect you to care for them and show respect for them. Is that clear?"

"Yes, Mistress." My chest was thudding.

And then, mysteriously, her tone changed. She returned to being Sharon, the familiar woman who had been my wife for so many years. "Is that what you like?"

"Yes, Mistress." I kissed her toes again.

"I don't understand, but I'm willing to try. I want to continue our conversation later. I'm not inhuman, you know. I can have fun with this. All I ask is your solemn promise that you won't go outside the marriage again." She paused.

"If you will become my dominatrix, Mistress, and allow me to express myself, and listen to me, and try to find compromises, then I can promise that. We have to work out a lot of issues. Nothing would make me happier than to have this side of me accepted by you." I stretched to kiss her toes again but she deftly moved them away.

"I'm far from accepting it, but I'll try. For our family, to keep us together. Now stand up, and let me see how you look in pink panties."

Now my appointments call for me to come home to the dominatrix who is my wife. To my great wonder she listened, and for the most part she was receptive to some of my more bizarre fantasies. She read from my collection of books and we discussed the ideas she found there. We talked about ideas and feelings, invisible but powerful forces that invaded our heads. Before, these perceptions had been barriers. Now we dare to view them in the light of day, and we plan how to jump over them and go forward. There have been many difficult moments, but we overcome the obstacles as they occur instead of hiding from them.

At first I was too demanding, too obsessed. Free to express my basest needs, I did. Constantly, until she rebelled. Now I go gently, carefully. This must be something we do together, to enhance our relationship and express our love, as well as our sexuality. If she feels intimidated or threatened I yield, which is, after all, my chosen role. After more than twenty years, our relationship has taken on a fresh excitement! Now I can be truly intimate with someone, and she loves me even after hearing my aberrant dreams!

She announces her intentions, sometimes, so that I can stew in anticipation. I become electric as I look forward to our appointment, but more. Her preparations for a session require careful thought and imagination. I view those attentions as the most sincere statements of her love, and I try to return them to her tenfold in ways that will bring her pleasure and comfort. I am slowly learning how to avoid selfishness. Collared, a humble pleasure slave, I labor at the backrubs, or at her bath. I bring home exquisite peignoirs, French silk teddies, bouquets of roses, a bottle of the finest champagne. We indulge each other, and share our erotic experiences in a garden of companionship and trust that easily becomes a hot loving glow and has rejuvenated every romantic aspect of our relationship. This comes first, and sometimes she sees fit to step across the border into my secret places. Then, stretched across her knee or standing in the corner with my panties at my knees, or just fetching the newspaper on a rainy morning, I experience all of the old red-hot intensity, but so much more! I am loved! She wants to understand, and she tries to accept. The reality exceeds my craziest fantasies!

I haven't worn male underpants in over eight years. One day, when I had my gall bladder removed, in the hospital, but only that one day. We live in a small town; Sharon insisted on male underpants that day. With that one exception, I have worn panties, pettipants, even a girdle, every day and every night. Sometimes I suspect that she sees my panties as a kind of chastity belt, hoping that I won't take off my trousers with another woman while dressed this way. Her motives don't matter. It is my place to be obedient, and to please her.

I have an extensive collection which includes tap pants, feminine boxers, pettipants, string bikinis, hip huggers, briefs, tap pants, thongs, and pettipants in all the most delicate fabrics. I have cottons, nylon, satin, silk, lycra, and spandex, laces and ruffles, brand names like Warner's, Vanity Fair, Maidenform, Hanes Her Way, Olga, Calvin Klein, and many luxurious imported treasures. My work used to take me to Canada on occasion, and I have an exquisite collection of elegant pieces from Montreal, where I believe the most reasonably priced luxury lingerie in the world is made. I have two garments from England, a pair of cotton knickers from Marks & Spencer, and a horribly tight black control brief we refer to as "The English Vise." A day in that garment is true punishment. I am most familiar with camisole and tap pant sets, with some of my camisoles cut to resemble a masculine sleeveless undershirt. Others are blatantly feminine, and create the most unusual shadows under a white business shirt!

Mistress will sometimes lay out or specify a particular garment, always with a carefully considered reason or purpose which will serve to enhance my skills or magnify my secret sensations. Many of my panties, for instance, are printed with bold flowers or rosebuds. In the summer, I am sometimes required to wear flowered prints under white slacks or shorts, and the flowers are visible. As yet no one, neither male nor female, has ever felt obliged to make a comment, at least to me. I have been trained to fold up the lower portion of my shirt tail, inside my trousers, so that it will not obscure the distinctively feminine curved seam at the rear of the crotch panel of my panties. While TV advertisements promise the abolition of "panty lines," I must never dress to conceal the outline of my feminine underpants. I am required to launder my own lingerie, although Mistress sometimes combines them with her own. Whenever possible I take my laundry to the backyard clotheslines and display it for all the neighborhood to see.

In the office or calling upon a client, I become aware of the gentle fabrics or the distinctive cut of my underpants at least a dozen times a day. To be discovered would ruin me. My vulnerability is so real it's physical, and tangible. But the world of erotic dominance and submission isn't about cringing in the shadows. By confronting this challenge and overcoming it I have gained enormous confidence. Today I have achieved the self discipline to function competently and professionally in a masculine work environment while secretly clad in lingerie every moment of every day, enjoying my sexual fantasies as I live and succeed in "the real world." I am empowered by my submission.

I've grown to love the secret challenges, and the intimate, private moments when I escape from a high-pressure corporate meeting to lock myself into a bathroom stall and take down my trousers. Except in the most demanding of situations, when my career or reputation might be jeopardized, I lower my trousers and, with my panties stretched tight between my thighs, I place my bare bottom on the seat to urinate. This practice, at regular intervals throughout the day, allows me to physically perform a small but significant act of deference to my lover, and to privately confront my lingerie, the delicate garments she has chosen to define the bondaged status of my private parts. It's a refreshing moment, with this intimate token of my wife's love and understanding so vividly displayed, and my thoughts can take a small vacation to adore Sharon. These are special moments, meaningful little holidays from the pressures of corporate life. Indeed, there is good practical reason behind this practice, as I am always careful to dry myself and prevent any staining of my luxurious garments. A man is not usually so fastidious about this aspect of his personal hygiene, and so I am able to meet people with a bit more confidence, and to undress before my lady with one more subtle but eloquent expression of my loving subservience.

It was a hot and muggy summer afternoon. One of the ladies in Sharon's office remarked that she couldn't wait to get out of her girdle tonight, it was just torture. Sharon said she thought about that statement all the way home.

"Will you obey me, slave?" she asked.

"Of course, Mistress." We pored over the J.C. Penney catalog, and then she ordered me to strip and kneel at her feet. Making no pretense that the garment was for anyone but myself, I ordered my girdle. It arrived a few days later, a secret prison to which I had been sentenced.

We went to dinner. There is no male attire equivalent to a panty girdle, so the sensations I was experiencing went far beyond the pressures of strict elastic. The high waistband threatened to show under my white shirt. I could feel the relentless, secret discomfort of the "firm control" girdle from torso to mid-thighs, and sometimes I was sure everyone could see it outlined under my thin slacks. Surely something that *felt* so noticeable must be visible! I could hear the raspy sound of my trousers over the smooth stretch fabric with every step. The cuffs and garters were stiff fetters on my thighs. The contrast between the thick, rigid elastic on my upper thigh and the sheer, gentle caress of the stockings on my lower legs made me step lightly, almost as if in a ballet. The caress of the new garment was, in every sense of the word, inescapable.

Sharon had described what she could do with the "split crotch" feature of the girdle I was wearing. The gentle, elasticated folds over the gusset of my feminine torture chamber would provide cooling and comfort for a lady's sensitive core, but they suggested the most awful possibilities to my male genitalia. She could invade the garment, not unlike what a man would hope to do to a woman, to bring me pleasure or pain. She could take out my scrotum, put it in bondage, or affix clips or clamps to the sensitive wrinkles of my flesh. It was perfect access for leading me on a leash, or applying weights. "At our house," she confided, "the term 'well hung' may take on a very special significance if you don't behave!" The idea of her hand probing, thrusting up into the tight feminine confines of the girdle excited me and scared me at the same time.

She had thought this through, and her words were designed to intimidate me. Would my delicate Vanity Fair briefs protect the luxurious foundation garment from harm, she wondered? I would "drool," she assured me. All men do, encased in girdles. She'd been studying. The thin membrane of the panty would offer little protection, so my willpower must postpone any sexual stimulation until I was allowed to shed the garment. I was in discipline. Lapses in personal hygiene would be punished. We ordered dinner.

I feel that I don't walk naturally in my girdle. The elastic on my thighs restricts my movements, shrinks my steps. Sometimes the garment threatens to crush the breath out of me. Hard boning bites into my abdomen and ribs. My appetite is curtailed when I'm in the girdle. I have struggled with the hook-and-eye catches up the left side of my abdomen, and the zipper is simply excruciating to close. My stomach is compressed, hard and flat. So are my male organs. The girdle lifts my bottom noticeably. Does no one recognize my plight? Mistress smiles and squeezes my hand. She knows, and no one else matters.

The panty girdle is a punishment garment, and applied only when the Mistress feels its strict attentions would be beneficial. It is impossible to urinate in the male manner from within the confines of a high-waist, firm control girdle! Of course, "firm control" is a dominatrix's realm. Walking with my lovely wife and Mistress, I keep my posture rigidly upright and proud as I feel the thick elastic stretched taut across my loins. It is our secret, and my burden.

I do not need to pay my Mistress two hundred dollars an hour to be confined. I need to love her as she loves me, but that's easy. She accepts me, and I hope, in her own private way, she understands. I, of course, have come to adore her all the more.

23

And for you, my love, I would do anything
Kiss your feet and everything
Suffer your pain, but I'd ride your train...
  – Eric Burdon and the Animals,
  from the song "Anything," 1967

Individually or together, we saw a lot of different counselors and
therapists. It seemed I would always tell my story, explain, and then it got kind
of fuzzy. They didn't know how to fix me. They were always eager to submit a
bill to my insurance company for services rendered, but real advice was rare.
Some of the suggestions were pretty bizarre, but nothing worked. Then I met
Gordon. From the first moment, he was different. He offered advice based
upon prior experience with S&M couples, and he set up standards of measure
and discussed results. There was progress. By focusing on our basic relationship, the focus on S&M was diminished. For a while, at least, I would talk
about my kinks with Gordon, but not with my wife. Gordon believed that our
twenty-year marriage was testimony to a real love, but that we had allowed
ourselves to become too busy to share. We had to work on communications and
teamwork. Once we had achieved some stability, he would help me to deal with
the other issues.

"They warned me," I exploded. Who knows where the outburst came
from? I was in Gordon's dark, tranquil office on a Saturday morning, measuring my progress on the trek through hostile territory that is life, when I got
onto a silly streak. "They *told* me rock 'n' roll was evil, that it would corrupt me.
The devil's music! I didn't believe them. Look where it got me!" I swept my
arm flamboyantly around the office, and Gordon raised one eyebrow comically,
willing to be amused. He was, of course, a lifelong rock music disciple, a
veteran of San Francisco's Haight-Ashbury and the Summer of Love. We were
both children of the sixties, bewildered and abused in the nineties, still hoping
that simple respect for others might one day become popular.

"Rock music, huh? That's the problem?" Gordon smiled, expecting a joke.

"Gordon, how many of the songs we grew up with talked about men down on their knees to women? James Brown, the Righteous Brothers. Eric Clapton to his Layla; she had him on his knees, begging darling please. But it goes 'way back. 'You've Lost That Lovin' Feeling' by the Righteous Brothers has a line about going down on my knees for you, if you would only say you love me too. Then there was Nancy Sinatra, in boots that were gonna walk all over you. Can't you just picture a guy on his knees, head lowered, saying, 'Thank you, Mistress' when you hear that?"

Gordon squirmed in his chair. "Well, I really *hadn't*; not before I met you!" His eyebrows arched until there were deep creases across his forehead, and his eyes sparkled with delight. He was beginning to recognize something humorous but potentially valid in the question, and he allowed his thoughts to roam too many years of Top 40 hits. He grinned luxuriously, stroked his bushy mustache, eyes alive with the challenge. "I remember Lady Jane. 'Your servant am I, and will humbly remain."

I was excited! "Exactly! So the question begs asking, do people actually *do* those things? Do men go down on their knees to women? It seems a dramatically romantic thing in a song, but would a real man dare? What might he lose? What might the lady think? And what's the motivation? Is she in black leather, with a riding crop and high-heeled boots?"

"Interesting," Gordon grinned.

I moaned a plaintive "Giirrrrlll" and then inhaled loudly, a reference to the Beatles song. "Was she told when she was young that pain would lead to pleasure? Gordon, did you ever hear of a dominatrix in 1966? They existed! Von Sacher-Masoch's *Venus In Furs* was published in *eighteen*-seventy! S&M isn't something new. Our grandfathers looked at racy postcards of Victorian ladies spanking men. They were very popular at the turn of the century."

Gordon wrinkled up his face in mock horror and pointed his finger at me. "Not *my* grandfather!" We laughed, and he suggested "Ain't too proud to beg."

I offered "Love hurts!"

Gordon smiled broadly. "Hey, that's the seventies! How about 'Bend me, shape me, any way you want me'? Or 'My baby's got me locked up in chains.'" He glowed with delight.

"Doesn't work," I winked. "They ain't the kind that you can see."

"Then how about John Mellencamp's 'Hurts So Good'?"

"The seventies again. While we're there, Annie Lennox did a song when she was a Eurythmic, about 'some of them want to abuse you, and some of them want to be abused.' I always thought she was referring to S&M. And there were older songs, like The Dovells' hit 'You Can't Sit Down'."

He grinned, but Gordon wasn't to be outdone. "What about, 'It Keeps Right On A-Hurting'?"

I couldn't help but smile. "Elvis just wanted to be her teddy bear, remember? And how did he think it should go? I remember something like 'tie a string around my neck and lead me anywhere'! I was about eight or ten years old when I heard that, Gordon. And I didn't think you were supposed to take it literally, but somewhere in the back of my head there was an image. I think it's a tribute to a woman, to fall down onto my knees before her beauty, but I'm just a pervert. A social outcast! We were the psychedelic generation, weren't we? We see things in big, bold colors, in exaggerated expressions. We grew up in the shadow of a mushroom cloud! There are greater evils than kneeling to kiss a beautiful woman's feet! There's a great beauty within the rituals of S&M, Gordon. People are upset at the image of a woman in black leather boots, but they don't have any trouble accepting that the Pope is more effective in a tall, pointed hat!"

"I think you enjoy being the rebel."

"I enjoy being free. There are lots of easier ways to be a nonconformist! You can't imagine the anguish and paranoia this obsession has caused me over the years. How I've studied S&M, and all its aspects, and analyzed myself. It's a tiny piece of a complex jigsaw puzzle, Gordon. A choice, what makes you comfortable. What kind of music you like, the style of clothes you wear, whether you vote Republican or Democrat, the living room furniture you choose, a sports car or a station wagon. Personal taste, a sense of order and what's applicable to your immediate circumstances. I express my adoration and respect for the opposite sex this way. Some guys slap their women around. Who's right and who's wrong?"

"Do you still want to be whipped?"

"Sure, it's more of a question every day. I'm middle-age now, I can feel and see the changes in my body. Can I still do it? But it's more an intellectual thing, Gordon. And spiritual. There's a core of stubbornness deep inside me, a kernel of something sacred I feel is my essence, my soul. It isn't easy to access, but if I do the rewards are intense and beautiful beyond anything else I've experienced in this life. I long to go back there, to visit myself, if you will. To assure myself that it's still there. I'm seeing the decline of my life. My children are growing, beginning to leave the nest. My best friend has terminal cancer. My career is nearly lifeless, I'm nearing fifty and no one wants to pay my price any more. I've sent dozens of resumés, my accomplishments are greater than ten years ago, but I don't get replies. I see all of America in decline, financially and morally bankrupt, becoming a cruel, dangerous environment. Everything we tried to bring about in the sixties has failed, crushed under the imperious boots of capitalism and militarism and greed. So many opportunities have evaporated."

"Should you have told Sharon about your obsession sooner?"

I paused. "No. She wasn't ready for it. I might have lost her. She's the love of my life, Gordon. I've paid a great price to be with her, but in the end it's all worthwhile. I play my games, entertain my fantasies, perform my own little rituals and tell myself I'm obeying a Mistress, and you know what? I am! In truth, by complying with her wishes and not seeing a professional dominatrix, I'm performing as a true submissive. She doesn't see fit to punish me as physically as other women have punished me before. Sometimes I ache for the old days, for the hard punishments. I'm somewhat emasculated without them, searching for something to give the same intensity or sense of accomplishment. But I accepted the assignment and I strive to perform according to the high standards I learned the hard way, and truthfully, I love Sharon more than ever. Accepting that, abandoning my own desires for her, obeying her, I'm pushing myself to a new, intense, more meaningful level of submission and commitment than I've ever attempted before. It spills over to everything, all of life. Every-thing has changed. It's like I'm looking through a pair of colored glasses."

Gordon hesitated, weighing his question before uttering it. I sensed that we had arrived at one of those moments when he would measure our overall progress. "You've told me that acceptance is the very essence of your obsession. It's the quality of your personal life that I've tried to help. Your life with your family. Your sex life, both within and without the S&M activities. I think you've accomplished a great deal there, and you should give yourself credit. Are you too much of a masochist to give yourself credit?"

I sat quietly for a few moments, reviewing my life. I sipped from the ubiquitous styrofoam cup of coffee, tipped the rim toward Gordon in salute and acknowledgment, and I smiled. "You're right on target, of course. I would say we've accomplished a lot, Sharon and myself, as a marriage, as lovers. As parents, and companions. And yes, it all stems from acceptance, the acceptance that I love this person, and she loves me, and we have a family who are counting on us. Gordon, I can go home tonight and get on my knees, naked, and kiss her feet! I can wear pink panties, and sometimes she puts me over her knee and spanks me. The things I dreamed and fantasized have come true! I still fantasize, and I probably always will, but my reality is so much more than I ever hoped it would be. I'm blessed. But, still, I know there's more, and I had it and lost it. I need to recover it. Is that masochism, or just human nature? Can you honestly tell me that it's wrong?"

Gordon smiled, his elbows on the arms of the chair, his fingertips touching, and he considered them thoughtfully. "And Sharon accepts that those things are part of you. She accepts your oddities, your kinks and your love, in whatever form it takes."

"Not whatever form, but she has accepted a great deal. She doesn't understand, but she accepts me."

"She respects you enough to step far out of character and try to satisfy your desires."

"Yes, she loves me, and I think she understands that I love her. That I always have. The past is past, we can't change it. We're focusing on the future. I've not served any other woman but my wife in more than seven years! And it's okay, you know? I've been granted the sensory discipline of confinement in panties for all that time, Gordon! Sure, to her it probably means something different. If she sees them as a kind of chastity belt, God bless her, she wants to keep me. I've had some terribly difficult experiences trying to maintain the panty discipline over those years. It's not easy to see a doctor, or to try on clothes, or to take time to lower my trousers and take down my panties every time I need to pee. That's exactly the point, isn't it? To do those things and rejoice in the experience, the common everyday experience, and not be bothered by them, all in the spirit of love, celebrating my relationship with the most wonderful, beautiful, exquisite woman in the world, secure in the knowledge that she accepts me and loves me and that she's sincerely trying to address my needs. It's, well, it's a culmination of sorts. Sure, I always want more. That's the human condition, isn't it? We're never really satisfied, we strive for more. Man has walked upon the moon, Gordon, and I've been whipped by my lover! I've been allowed to kiss her toes, she's put me into both bondage and lingerie, and she has released me from both, and made love to me. The point is, she exerts herself to express her love for me, to please me. She has struggled to reconcile all of this, to be a mommy and a lover, a respectable middle-class suburban housewife and a dominatrix. Her husband comes home from the office and changes into his jeans and T-shirt, and she catches a glimpse of pink satin or lace panties. Moments later he's frolicking with the children, tuning up the car or mowing the lawn. An hour from now he'll be crouched at her feet, kissing her toes and begging her to torture him! There is no way this could be an easy transition for her, but she has done it. And yes, it has happened because we truly love each other. Above all else!

"And my goals have changed, Gordon. I want to please her, more than ever before. Sexually, and in every way. That's real growth on my part! I've learned that S&M itself isn't the end-all; I've learned to offer it as an expression of my love, as foreplay, and to care more about her joy and satisfaction than my own. I regret that it took so long to arrive at this place, but it was a treacherous, winding road. I'm here, and sometimes she dresses as a dominatrix, and sometimes she works me, and it's beyond anything I ever hoped would come true. Other times I work myself, I put my *mind* into discipline and strive to be her pleasure slave, and the motivation is honestly love, and the love I extend to her is returned to me tenfold.

"I've been trained, Gordon. Beautiful, powerful women have tried to show me the secrets of satisfying their sex. I've suffered to learn these truths, to understand, and to put my selfish desires aside so that I can truly give myself to my lover. I've come to a point where I can focus my skills, my entire being, on providing for my family. Providing material things, but more important, providing love and stability and guidance for my children. Oh, I still make mistakes, but I couldn't have gotten here without the insights into myself that I gained from S&M. I've conquered myself, to some extent. I exist for Sharon, to show her my love, to amaze her with all the joy I can bring to her! Can you imagine, after all these years, the enlightenment in that simple statement? Now I need to grow my skills, and perfect them. Maybe, as I dazzle and amaze her and earn back her confidence, she'll love me enough to punish me for it. I'm literally trying to be good enough to deserve a spanking, and if that seems paradoxical, well, all of S&M is based upon the paradox of pleasure from pain, isn't it? The ultimate paradox, and yet it works. For some people. For me. After all these years! Communication, isn't that the key to most of the world's problems? If I please her, she punishes me. It's an odd faith, but it gives me hope and satisfaction, and it's all that matters."

I am very busy, very stressed. E-mails and voice mails, faxes, monthly and quarterly reports. Always, the sales charts. Sales are increasing but gross profits are lagging. My phone rings constantly. I deal in smoke and mirrors commodities, psychological warfare, retail marketing strategies, packaging, motivation. I organize offices, businesses, departments. I change people's thinking. The ubiquitous mountain of month-end computer reports clutter my office. They don't reflect my reality. The accumulated paper threatens to overwhelm my desk, the credenza, the bookcase in the corner.

It is a Wednesday, late afternoon, and it's snowing outside, the first real snow of the winter. The phone interrupts my thinking once again.

"Hello."

"Have you seen the snow?" It is my wife.

"Yes. Where are you?"

"I'm home. I left work early. It's a wet snow, heavy and slippery. The damp makes it seem colder than it really is. Do you have your coat?"

"It's in the car."

"Will you be coming home soon?" Her voice has a familiar lilt.

"Pretty soon. What do you have in mind?"

"I want you to come in and go straight to the bedroom. Lay out the implements on the bed, then get undressed. Everything off but your collar and your panties, and then you are to stand in the corner and wait for me. Anticipate, Darling. I'm going to warm your bottom."

"Have I misbehaved?"

"I don't know. Have you? I think you deserve a spanking." Her tone is playful. My pants are tightening.

"I won't argue. I should be home in an hour."

"Turn off the car radio on the way home. Just sit in the quiet and think about your discipline. About why you deserve it, and how uncomfortable you're going to be tomorrow."

My secretary brings a handful of papers into my office and drops them onto my desk with a loud PLOP sound. She stands in front of my desk, obviously wanting to talk with me. "I've got to go," I tell my wife. "I'll be home as soon as I can get there, I promise. Thank you, Mistress." My secretary smiles. Does she recognize the term?

postscript

If you live with a man you must conquer him every day; otherwise
he will go to another.
    – Brigitte Bardot

There is so much I should tell you! There were months of agony when
our marriage teetered at the precipice, when the house was electric with tension
and we were all afraid to speak lest we might ignite the final catastrophe. There
were tender moments. The lingerie counter at J.C. Penney where she bought
me a pair of pink lace panties the very first time. She blushed, and I suppose I
beamed with delight. After I had my gall bladder removed a very imperious
nurse was barking out instructions before I could be released from the hospital.
"Monitor his temperature often," she said, and Mistress replied, "He'll like
that. I'll use the rectal thermometer." I'll never forget a snowy night in Red
Bank when we ducked into a store to ask directions and discovered that it was a
fetish and S&M shop. We had one of her co-workers along, and we strained to
keep straight faces as the poor woman's eyes registered her shock. We had
never been there before, but it was too bizarre. Later, we roared... and shared a
rollicking, very special and loving moment.

   Like all marriages, I suppose, our relationship has seen precarious highs
and depressing, devastating lows. Mostly, we live somewhere in the middle, in
a perennial middle-American rut. We watch a little TV, mow the lawn and wash
the dishes. I have not worn male underpants in more than eight years, ever,
under any circumstances. She punishes me sometimes, usually with the
hairbrush against my bare bottom, across her knee. There is also a black leather
spanking strap from Canada, and an exquisite German crop. She stands me in
the corner, or at the armoire, to contemplate my sins. I have a rigid firm control
panty girdle that she prescribes for minor infractions, to remind me that she is
in firm control at all times. For an active businessman in the 21st century,
confinement in a high-waist, long-leg girdle is a terrible imposition. I know
why women refer to their girdles as "torture." In it, along with the crushing
restriction, I am absolutely obligated to sit to pee, every time. It is so oppressive, so inescapable, but I have never had the slightest indication that my

business colleagues suspected anything unusual. The panty girdle under a man's business attire is a subtle but very effective discipline!

I wish we could do more. Early on, as we were coming to grips with this thing, I went too far and too hard. She is wary, and very careful. She will not "beat" me, although she can be very effective with the spanking instrument or the crop. My birthday spankings are given in increments now, a most troubling indication of advancing age! She will not wax me, or put anything larger than a thermometer into my rectum. I ache for the rigorous sessions, and I masturbate often.

This story does not begin to describe the awful struggles as we rebuilt our marriage. She still believes that I betrayed her, and she insists that she would never have married me had she known of my interest in S&M. I have no doubt that she's telling the truth, and to me that is exactly the point! Because I loved her, I had to hide this from her. It was only when our love began to dim that I dared to expose my great secret, and it was done in an accusing, hurtful manner. I had become infatuated with Mistress Beatrice, who insisted that the truth would improve my marriage. I was confused, desperate for the acceptance the dominatrix offered. I blurted out the truth in the midst of a passionate fight, and in that moment everything changed.

Still, we do truly love each other. This tale should be one of the world's great love stories, but it would be too thick and cumbersome. I have learned to accept many things, and I now believe that acceptance is the essence of S&M. Yes, I have my obsessions and fantasies, my uncontrollable desires and my burning, desperate urges. Sometimes, in a lonely hotel room far away from home, I weep. I am a prisoner, and the reality of that fact is overpowering. She knows my perversion, and loves me in spite of it. She strictly controls my access, but she does not destroy my hopes. She is still learning to wield her power, to coax me into vacuuming by putting me into a French maid's dress, for instance, or encouraging me to clean the toilets clad only in a flowery, ultra-feminine apron. She sees my arousal, and protects my beautiful panties with a Kotex! I do guy things and she spanks my bare bottom. It is as it should be.

Yes, I want more, but this is an honest relationship. I am not, by nature of my announced status, empowered to inflict my desires upon her. Many S&M couples grapple with this dilemma, but I must accept my fate. She is Mistress; her desires are paramount. I wait, chafing, wishing. Sometimes I am rewarded, and more often I am punished. It is an odd reality, not unlike the reversed reality of a mirror image. If I am good, and faithful, and honest, and sincere, I may be spanked or whipped, kissed, caressed, or allowed to worship my beautiful lady's toes. She does not always understand, and she often ignores. I can only wait, contemplate, and hope. She gives, and she withholds. I accept her reticence, her fears, and her punishments. It is only right. I love her. I strive to please her, to show her my love. Gordon says we have the most real S&M relationship he has ever seen! It is more than I ever dreamed possible. I love her, and she loves and accepts me! I am whole now, naked, in chains, anticipating. At last.

IF YOU LIKED *THE 43RD MISTRESS,*
YOU MIGHT ENJOY:

FICTION FROM GRASS STAIN PRESS

The 43rd Mistress: A Sensual Odyssey
Grant Antrews $11.95

Haughty Spirit
Sharon Green $11.95

Justice and Other Short Erotic Tales
Tammy Jo Eckhart $11.95

Murder At Roissy
John Warren $11.95

GENERAL SEXUALITY

Big Big Love: A Sourcebook on Sex for People of Size and Those Who Love Them
Hanne Blank $15.95

The Ethical Slut: A Guide to Infinite Sexual Possibilities
Dossie Easton & Catherine A. Liszt $15.95

A Hand in the Bush: The Fine Art of Vaginal Fisting
Deborah Addington $11.95

Health Care Without Shame: A Handbook for the Sexually Diverse and Their Caregivers
Charles Moser, Ph.D., M.D. $15.95

Sex Toy Tricks: More than 125 Ways to Accessorize Good Sex
Jay Wiseman $11.95

The Strap-On Book
A.H. Dion, illustrated by Donna Barr $11.95

Supermarket Tricks: More than 125 Ways to Improvise Good Sex
Jay Wiseman $11.95

Tricks: More than 125 Ways to Make Good Sex Better
Jay Wiseman $11.95

Tricks 2: Another 125 Ways to Make Good Sex Better
Jay Wiseman $11.95

BDSM & KINK

The Bottoming Book: Or, How To Get Terrible Things Done To You By Wonderful People
Dossie Easton & Catherine A. Liszt, ill. Fish $11.95

Bottom Lines: Poems of Warmth & Impact
H. Andrew Swinburne, ill. Donna Barr $9.95

The Compleat Spanker
Lady Green $11.95

Jay Wiseman's Erotic Bondage Handbook
Jay Wiseman $15.95

Juice: Electricity for Pleasure and Pain
"Uncle Abdul" $11.95

KinkyCrafts: 99 Do-It-Yourself S/M Toys
Lady Green with Jaymes Easton $15.95

The Loving Dominant
John Warren $15.95

Miss Abernathy's Concise Slave Training Manual
Christina Abernathy $11.95

The Mistress Manual: A Good Girl's Guide to Female Dominance
Mistress Lorelei $15.95

The Sexually Dominant Woman: A Workbook for Nervous Beginners
Lady Green $11.95

The Topping Book: Or, Getting Good At Being Bad
Dossie Easton & Catherine A. Liszt, ill. Fish $11.95

Training With Miss Abernathy: A Workbook for Erotic Slaves and Their Owners
Christina Abernathy $11.95

Please include $3 for first book and $1 for each additional book with your order to cover shipping and handling costs. VISA/MC accepted. Order from:

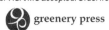 greenery press

1447 Park Avenue Emeryville CA 94608
toll-free: 888/944-4434 fax: 510/652-1674 www.greenerypress.com